MORAY
DEATH IN

CW00548917

KATHERINE DALTON RENOIR ('Moray Dalton') was born in Hammersmith, London in 1881, the only child of a Canadian father and English mother.

The author wrote two well-received early novels, *Olive in Italy* (1909), and *The Sword of Love* (1920). However, her career in crime fiction did not begin until 1924, after which Moray Dalton published twenty-nine mysteries, the last in 1951. The majority of these feature her recurring sleuths, Scotland Yard inspector Hugh Collier and private inquiry agent Hermann Glide.

Moray Dalton married Louis Jean Renoir in 1921, and the couple had a son a year later. The author lived on the south coast of England for the majority of her life following the marriage. She died in Worthing, West Sussex, in 1963.

MORAY DALTON MYSTERIES
Available from Dean Street Press

One by One They Disappeared

The Night of Fear

The Body in the Road

Death in the Cup

The Strange Case of Harriet Hall

The Belfry Murder

The Belgrave Manor Crime

The Case of Alan Copeland

The Art School Murders

The Condamine Case

The Mystery of the Kneeling Woman

Death in the Dark

Death in the Forest

The Murder of Eve

Death at the Villa

MORAY DALTON

DEATH IN THE DARK

With an introduction by Curtis Evans

DEAN STREET PRESS

Published by Dean Street Press 2023

Copyright © 1938 Moray Dalton

Introduction Copyright © 2023 Curtis Evans

First published in 1938 by Sampson Low

Cover by DSP

ISBN 978 1 915393 84 5

www.deanstreetpress.co.uk

THE WAY OF THE WICKED

MORAY DALTON'S *DEATH IN THE DARK* (1938)

The way of the wicked is as darkness; they know not at
what they stumble. (PROVERBS 4:19)

READERS who have followed Moray Dalton's Inspector Hugh
Collier's investigative saga up to this point will have noted the
passionate concern of Hugh Collier, the author's surrogate, with
achieving justice for the pale and downtrodden, the weak and
the weary (to borrow from the lyrics to Pink Floyd's 1987 anthem
of empathy, "On the Turning Away"). A favored plot device of
the author is to have some innocent ground under the heels of
wicked schemers, set up for a murder s/he did not commit, swiftly
tried and convicted and sentenced to death (in that bygone era
of righteous certitude). All seems lost, until Hugh Collier comes
on the scene and with his unfailing empathy, doggedness and
discernment finds the true path which others missed and sends
the malefactors stumbling over their own schemes to their own
well-merited dooms.

This formula unfurls at full force in *Death in the Dark*, Moray
Dalton's seventh Hugh Collier mystery. David Merle, a young
circus acrobat, ingenuously falls into the pit dug for him by schemers and is arrested and convicted of the murder in London of
wealthy circus-loving eccentric Joshua Fallowes. Only his sister,
Judy Merle, another circus acrobat (with their brother and his
wife composing the Flying Merles), and his aunt really believe
in him, although kindly Ben Levy, stage manager at the Palace
where the Merles had been performing until David's arrest for
the murder, stands by Judy, with whom he is rather smitten.
Things looks dark for David until Judy gets a note, addressed
from The Haven, Myrtle Road, Quinton Park, N., from a certain
thirteen-year-old boy named Toby, who is none other than our
Toby Fleming from *The Mystery of the Kneeling Woman*, now

Hugh Collier's stepson after Hugh's marriage to Toby's mother Sandra. Toby, who saw the Flying Merles perform and was rather smitten with Judy ("I caught the rose you threw," he divulges in the note. "It fell to pieces, but I've got the stalk."), reveals that he has managed to discover some points of interest concerning the case. This information sends Judy off to Somerset (a favored Dalton stomping ground) to Sard Manor, a run-down country mansion complete with a privately-run zoo, where in the guise of a housemaid she intrepidly does some investigating of her own. What that daring young veteran of the flying trapeze finds there might save David, if she only lives to tell about it! Fortunately Judy has a loyal friend in Toby, who comes equipped with a heroic Scotland Yard stepfather.

Moray Dalton's exceptional sympathy—by Golden Age mystery standards--with many of the "others" in British mystery—the working class, Jews, blacks, unpopular nationalities of the moment—is strongly apparent in *Death in the Dark*. At one point in the novel David's and Judy's hairdresser aunt—nicknamed Auntie Apples on account of her having sent comestibles and other treats during the Great War, in "stubborn disregard of the obloquy attaching to the wives of enemy aliens," to her interned German husband Sturmer (who nevertheless died from influenza in an internment camp)—observes the admittedly unprepossessing Ben Levy's interest in her niece, notes his "nice manners" and thinks to herself: "There's something about Jews. . . . They're civilized. And they say they make very good husbands." Perhaps such sentiments will strike some today as patronizing, but we must recall that just three years before the publication of Dalton's novel, the German Reichstag passed the Nuremberg Laws, which among other things prohibited marriage and sexual relationships between Jews and those of "German blood." To embrace Christian-Jewish intermarriage was no small thing not only in the Golden Age detective novel, but in the world at large.

Setting politics aside, the zoo at Sard Hall plays rather an interesting and unique role at the denouement of *Death in the Dark*, one that as far as I know is original for its time. Sard Hall might remind readers today of the great country estate of Longleat with its vaunted Safari Park, which inspired Peter Dickinson's 1969 CWA Gold Dagger winning detective novel *A Pride of Heroes*; yet a more pertinent contemporary example from the author's day is the Chester Zoo, developed by George Mottershead beginning in 1931 around the country house Oakfield Manor at Upton-by-Chester. The story of Mottershead's founding of the zoo was dramatized in 2014 in a six-part BBC television series. No murders were involved to my knowledge!

Curtis Evans

CHAPTER I
THE TRAP

DAVID had scribbled a note to his wife while the Flying Merles were waiting for their call. "Take care of yourself, old girl, and don't worry about money. I've had a stroke of luck and will be able to send you enough for everything next week." He stuck on the stamp and slipped the envelope into a pocket of his shabby brown overcoat just before he ran on to the stage.

The Merles's act on the flying trapeze was a family affair. The real work was done by Reuben and David and their sister Judith. Reuben's wife, Lil, a platinum blonde, had been assisting a conjurer when Reuben met her. Her job now was to stand at the foot of the ladder, smiling at the audience and passing up the paper rings and the coloured balls and finally the sack in which David made his much advertised leap blindfold into space. Her smile had been more than usually perfunctory to-night for the audience was scanty and unenthusiastic. She grumbled to Judith, whose dressing-room she shared with the Sisters Dainty and the wife of the saxophone player. They had the grimy little room to themselves, for their fellow artistes had preceded them.

"A bum place this. What a life! Hi, that's my lipstick!"

"Sorry!" Judith had wiped the paint off her face in a hurry and was scrambling into her clothes while Lil, still half naked, was examining her own reflection in the mirror.

"I need some exercise," she explained; "a brisk walk, and I forgot to ask David to wait for me."

"Walking? A night like this? You're balmy!"

Judith glanced down at her sister-in-law's opulent white shoulders.

"Can't afford to get fat in our profession."

She dragged her beret over her tangled brown curls, picked up her bag, and hurried off. But she was too late to catch David. The stage door keeper told her he had passed out some minutes earlier. It was a horrible night, icy cold and clammy with fog drifting into the lower part of the town from the river. Judith shivered, wishing she could afford a thicker coat, and decided to go straight back to their lodgings, fill her hot water bottle, and read the book she had got from the twopenny library in bed. It seemed the most sensible thing to do, but she was oddly depressed; David might, she thought, have waited for her. They had always been pals, but of course he thought more of his wife now. Daisy was expecting a baby and had gone home to her mother for the time being. Later, when she recalled that evening, it sickened her to realise how different everything might have been if David had not been so anxious to get across the square before the pillar box was cleared to post his nightly letter to his wife. He had been just in time on Monday and on Tuesday. On Wednesday he had been detained for a minute and the postman had been away on his bicycle. Daisy must not be disappointed twice. And so, on this Thursday night he had slipped out as quickly as he could. The letter was safely posted and he was turning away when a man's voice bade him good evening.

The owner of the voice was an elderly man with a grey beard, very much muffled up in a big overcoat with an astrakhan collar.

"One of the Flying Merles, I think?" he said as he fell into step with the young acrobat. "A very good turn. I wonder if you would care to come along to my place for a bit of supper?"

David normally would have declined such an invitation from a complete stranger, but, as it happened, he had heard something of his would-be host only the previous week from a ventriloquist who had been in the same bill as the Merles at the Brighton Hippodrome.

"If you're going to Holton look out for an old chap who goes regularly to the Palace Monday evenings and sometimes again if there's a turn he fancies. He might ask you home to supper. He's eccentric but harmless. No funny business. And you'll get a good blow out and a first class cigar. He's bats. No servants living in though he's got a big house and plenty of money. I was there once. The grub's good, believe me."

"You'll come?" The old man laid a gloved hand on David's threadbare coat-sleeve. His voice was curiously uncertain, with an underlying note of urgency that was not altogether reassuring.

For an instant David wavered. He had meant to accept this invitation if the chance came his way. Even if this queer old gentleman was not as harmless as the ventriloquist had pronounced him, he had every confidence in his ability to take care of himself. On the other hand there was something about his ill-concealed eagerness which had a chilling effect on his interlocutor.

"Thanks, very much," said David, after that momentary hesitation, but he was glad when the gloved hand dropped from his arm.

"Splendid. This way, this way, my dear lad. My name—perhaps you have heard it—is Joshua Fallowes. But we won't talk, eh, till we get inside. This raw night air—it affects my lungs."

It was certainly not a night to linger out of doors. The streets were deserted, the street lamps shone dimly through the fog which seemed to be getting thicker. Mr. Fallowes led the way uphill out of the shopping centre into a quiet residential district where the roads were lined with trees and the houses were detached and screened from one another and from passers-by by dense shrubberies. A gate swung to behind them and they passed up a winding gravel drive.

"Here we are!" The old man bent, fumbling clumsily with his gloved hands for the keyhole.

A glimmer of light showed through the fanlight over the door, but the rest of the house seemed to be in darkness. Mr. Fallowes paused when they had crossed the threshold, and he had closed the door after them, and appeared to be listening. A grandfather clock at the foot of the stairs ticked steadily, but there was no other sound.

"This way," he said fussily. "I won't ask you to take off your overcoat. I've no fire in the dining-room, and it's cold." He led the way into a room on the right of the front door and switched on the shaded lamp hanging over the table. "Sit down and help yourself."

David was young and healthy, and for some time past he had been trying to cut down his expenses, saving all he could to send to Daisy. Moreover landladies who let rooms to theatricals on a second rate circuit are seldom good cooks. He forgot his instinctive distrust of his host as he saw the cold roast chicken, the galantine, the meat patties and the apricot tart, and only remembered that it was weeks since he had eaten a really appetising meal.

"Do you really mean that? Thanks awfully."

Mr. Fallowes took the chair at the other end of the table and looked on benevolently.

"Can't I cut some for you, sir? Aren't you eating anything?"

"No. Not to-night. I have to be careful of my digestion."

Urged on by his host David had two helpings of chicken and salad.

"Might I have some water to drink, sir? Maybe I can fetch some. There isn't any on the table."

Mr. Fallowes' swathed and mummy-like figure was shaken with good humoured laughter. "Water? Oh, dear me, that would be very dull. You'll find a bottle of claret on the sideboard. Fill your glass. It won't hurt you. Plenty of cups there, eh?"

The big mahogany sideboard was laden with silver. David was impressed by the glittering mass of metal.

"Did you win all these, sir?"

"Some of them. The rest is family stuff. Which of those would you say was the heaviest? Pick them up and weigh them in your hands. That big fellow with the scroll handles. Lighter than you thought, eh? Well, come back and finish your supper."

David obeyed. His boyish face was rather flushed. He was unused to wine, and it had been a large glass. He cut himself a generous slice of fruit tart, but the edge of his hunger was blunted and he began to look about him as he ate.

He saw a typical Victorian dining-room, grown a trifle dingy and threadbare with the passing of the years, with its framed engravings after Landseer on the walls, and its funereal mantel-piece of black marble supporting a pair of bronze gladiators. A dreadful room, as he felt instinctively, implying as it did the arrested mental development of its occupant, who, in sixty years, had not attempted to make any change in it.

"You've finished? You'll find cigarettes in a box on the side-board. Now suppose you tell me all about yourself, eh? The story of your life."

David smiled. "That would be a poor return for your hospitality."

He fancied he had seen Mr. Fallowes glance at the clock.

"I don't want to bore you, sir—outstay my welcome. Perhaps I ought to be getting along."

"No, no. I've been looking forward to a chat. You must not go yet," said Mr. Fallowes firmly. "Gratify an old man's curiosity. You're English, aren't you? I thought so. How old are you?"

"Twenty-two. Reuben is a year older, and Judy—that's my sister—is nineteen."

Once started David was not unwilling to talk about himself. He felt good after a hearty meal and the wine had loosened his tongue. His parents had been acrobats. They had been killed in a railway accident over in the States, and the three children had been brought up by their aunt. "She's a wardrobe dealer. You know, an old clothes woman. She went in for that after her husband died. She had a shed behind her shop fitted up for us to practise in and she put us through it. She did her best for us. No lovey dovey stuff, and if we tried to dodge the work she'd give us what for. But it was the best way. I can see that now."

David was not a skilled narrator and he was getting very sleepy. He was inclined to wander from the point and to repeat himself, but his audience of one was not disposed to be critical. Perhaps actually he was not listening very closely. His eyes, bright and restless behind the tinted glasses, glanced now and again to the clock. Presently he leaned forward, stopping David in the middle of a sentence.

"I have to thank you, my dear boy, for humouring a lonely old man, but I must not keep you out too long. I wonder if you would do me a favour before you go. It's nothing very difficult. The window in my bedroom upstairs has got stuck and I haven't the necessary strength to force it up. Would you do it for me? It won't take a minute. Thank you so much."

"I'll be pleased to—" said David, but the old gentleman had checked himself and turned back to take something, a bulky envelope, from a drawer of the old-fashioned bureau standing between the sideboard and the fireplace.

"Just one moment," he said cheerfully, "I was nearly forgetting. Don't open this until you get back. Just a few little booklets. A little good advice. You may find them helpful. Young men have many temptations. Read them over at your leisure." He thrust the envelope into David's rather reluctant hand. David remembered now that his acquaintance had said something, grinning, about a parcel of tracts, the pill in Mr. Fallowes' jam. Well, why not? The poor old chap meant well, and he was not obliged to read them. He accepted the proffered literature with a mumbled "Thank you, sir," pushed the envelope into one of his overcoat pockets, and forgot it.

"And now for this tiresome window of mine." Mr. Fallowes led the way through the cold, dimly lit hall and up the stairs to the first floor landing, opened the door that faced them and stood aside to allow David to pass in before him. The room was pitch dark and David waited for the light to be turned on.

"Just a moment," said Mr. Fallowes fussily. The switch clicked but the light remained off. "Dear me, how tiresome. It must have fused. There's another point by the window. You might try that if you can find it. But that will have gone too, probably. Wait here. I'll fetch a candle. Just try the other switch. I shan't be long."

David moved forward doubtfully, feeling his way among large pieces of furniture. He noticed a close, faint, and definitely unpleasant smell. He ran his hands up and down the wall by the curtained window but failed to find a switch. No use. He would have to wait for the return of his eccentric host with a candle. He was taking his time, but perhaps he had had to go down to the basement kitchen, and if all the lights in the house had fused he would have to grope his way. David waited with an undefined sense of uneasiness. There was something wrong about this house, with its cold, gloomy rooms and its silence broken only by the ticking of clocks. His eyes were growing more accustomed to the darkness. He could just distinguish the chest of drawers on his right, between him and the door, which Mr. Fallowes had closed after him when he bustled out, and on the left the nacreous gleam of the looking glass in the wardrobe door. The bed faced the window, and occupied the centre of the room, and he was standing at its foot. There was, he thought, something dark thrown across the bed. He wondered what it could be. It was strange. He could not have said why he felt that dark patch, which was probably only a trick of shadow, was the focal centre of all the queerness that had troubled him from the first. Undefined and horrid doubts assailed him, combined with a feeling that he was not alone in the room. Suppose that while Mr. Fallowes was out of the house a burglar had got in and was now hiding in the wardrobe? He cast an anxious glance in that direction and fancied that he heard a faint creak. He tried to pull himself together. Darn it, he was not a child to be frightened of the dark. He moved towards the side of the bed and slipped and nearly fell on what seemed to be a wet patch on the linoleum. There was a rug, but it had been rucked up. Was that a bundle of clothing half on and half off the bed? He felt it, and started back with a stifled cry as his fingers came in contact with something clammy and cold.

"What the hell! Let me get out of this."

He rushed to the door and turned the handle. He pushed and pulled, but the door did not open. Locked. He was locked in.

He swung round to face the room again, leaning back weakly against the panels. The shock had been severe. He was drenched with sweat and trembling like a leaf. This was like a nightmare.

It didn't make sense. He breathed deeply, struggling to regain his self-control. Perhaps the thing on the bed was not what he thought it was. But why didn't Mr. Fallowes come back, and why had he locked the door? There might be an explanation for that. It might have occurred to the old gentleman that he was leaving a perfect stranger to roam as he pleased during his absence downstairs. Yes, but he was the devil of a long time finding that candle, and his manner had been strange all the evening. He asked questions and did not listen to the answers, and, David remembered now, he had a trick of jerking his head round to look over his shoulder that was not very reassuring.

Mad. One never knew what mad people were going to do.

"You've got to get out of this, son, and the sooner the better," said David to himself, and was oddly comforted by the familiar sound of his own voice. But the thing on the bed? Oughtn't he to make sure first that it really was a dead body? Even as he felt in his pockets for a box of matches he remembered that he had used the last to light the cigarette he had smoked after supper and left the empty box on the dining-room table. He would not be able to see, and his flesh shrank from the thought of approaching the bed again, but he forced himself to bend over it and fumble gingerly over the black, inert mass sprawling across it. This time his finger tips, warned of what they might expect, flashed a more detailed message to his brain. The feel of rough tweed, of buttons, starched linen, hair, and the chilly, rubbery texture of dead flesh—and something sticky and wettish.

David swallowed hard and backed away. He knew enough now, and too much. He went to the window, drew the curtains and lifted the lower half of the sash window, noting as he did so that it went up quite easily. He leaned over the sill, peering down into a dense mass of laurel that grew close up to the house. If he slipped during his descent the shrubs would break his fall. There was a rainwater pipe coming down from the roof. He could slide down that, but to reach it he would have to jump to the window-sill of the adjoining room. Not many men would have cared to attempt it, but to the young acrobat it seemed easy enough even in the dim light afforded by the street lamp farther down the road. He climbed out of the window. Lucky, he thought, that he was wearing rubber-soled shoes, a pair of old plimsolls, to save his only other pair. He measured the distance with his eye and with that sixth sense developed by the exercise of his profession, and jumped. His hands gripped the pipe as his feet touched the sill. A minute more and he was thrusting his way through the dripping laurels. He looked up and down the tree-shadowed road before he climbed the wall, and saw nobody. He was free. He had escaped from that sinister house and its secrets. Thank the Lord, he thought. And now he was tired. He could sleep, even on that lumpy mattress at his lodgings he could sleep the clock round. He walked away quickly, without one backward glance, going down the hill towards the lower town and the river, his slight figure passing into the light under the street lamp, vanishing into darkness to emerge again, though only for an instant. Meanwhile, in the house he had left the open window admitted the rain that had begun to fall until it formed a little pool on the sill and ran down to join another and darker pool on the floor.

Chapter II
"THE TRUTH CAN'T HURT—"

Mrs. Burt had one permanent lodger, the second violin in the Palace Theatre of Varieties, the others rarely staying more than a week. They waited on themselves, boiling kettles and frying their bloaters for breakfast on the gas rings in their rooms. They came and went as they pleased. The door was on the latch until midnight, and after that they had to use their keys. They were all, of course, late risers, and it was getting on for ten o'clock when the sizzle and the smell of sausages sticking to the pan and the ponderous tread of Mrs. Burt moving about the basement heralded a renewal of life and activity. Judy Merle, however, was awake, and was making herself some tea. She had finished her novel before she put out her light, listening all the while to hear David come in. He was still out when she fell asleep. It was very unlike him to go on the razzle, but the poor boy was worried to death over Daisy and her coming trouble. Though Judy was prepared to scold she would have defended him strenuously from any outside criticism.

He and she had the two attic bedrooms at the top of the house so she had no fear of meeting any of their fellow lodgers, but she slipped on a faded blue kimono over her pyjamas and ran a comb through her curls before she filled the two cups and carried them across the landing.

There was no answer to her perfunctory knock. David was still sleeping heavily, burrowing down into his pillow. His clothes lay in a heap on the floor. Judy set the cups down on the chest of drawers where Daisy, simpering in a silver frame, reigned among scattered studs, shaving tackle and crumpled ties, and turned to the window. The fog had cleared, but it was still raining and she looked out on a dreary expanse of wet grey slate and smoke blackened chimney pots. From the street below came the melancholy cry of a dealer in small coal.

Judy would never have won a prize in a beauty competition, but her small, resolute face had the piquancy and charm of youth, and her fine, smooth skin had not yet been spoiled by cheap cosmetics, while her body, trained to the last ounce by the exigencies of her profession, moved with the grace and effortless ease that had become second nature. So far in their nomad life she had escaped emotional entanglements. She was fond of Reuben, though secretly she despised him for being so easily caught by Lil's tawdry allure, but David she adored. Her feeling for him was quasi-maternal, he was such a boy still, so ingenuous and so helpless in some matters. Fortunately his young wife, Daisy, was as clinging and useless as she was affectionate and quite willing that Judy should mother them both.

Judy turned back from the window. "Wake up lazybones. Your tea'll be cold."

David mumbled something and pulled the blanket over his head defensively. Judy laughed and moved forward, and as she did so happened to glance down at the shoes that lay where he had kicked them off. She caught her breath and stood very still for a moment, staring with a kind of fascination at the brownish red smears on the dingy white canvas. So like dried blood. But he couldn't—Had he been mixed up with a street accident or something? Was he hurt? She went over to him quickly.

"David!"

He woke with a long sigh. "Oh, Judy, old girl . . ."

"Drink your tea first," she ordered.

He sat up obediently and took the cup from her, but before he could lift it to his lips the door opened and two men came in. The first was a middle-aged man, tall and broad shouldered, with a hard, red face and steely eyes, the other was much younger. They both wore navy serge suits and tweed overcoats and carried bowler hats.

"David Merle?"

David drank his tea, noting gratefully that it was hot and sweet, and set down the empty cup very carefully on the floor.

"That's me."

"And is this your wife?"

"No. My sister, Judith. Who are you, and what do you want?"

"Just a matter in which we think you may be able to help us. Perhaps you'd better go back to your own room, Miss Merle."

"No hurry," said Judith easily, and sat down on the foot of the bed. As she felt for her cigarette case in the pocket of her kimono she contrived to edge one of the stained canvas shoes farther under the bed. Of course there wasn't anything—there couldn't be—but those brownish smears had given her a fright, and she did not like the big man. He had, she felt, the makings of a bully. If he couldn't get on without treading on you—well, that was just too bad.

She lit a cigarette and passed her case to her brother.

"Very well," said the big man sourly. His sharp eyes roved about the dingy little room. "You came home late last night, didn't you? The landlady tells me she heard you come in, and it was past one."

"Was it? Very likely. I'd been for a long walk."

"Not very nice weather for walking. Which way did you go?"

"Round and about. I don't really know. I'm a stranger here, and it was dark."

"What's it all about anyhow?" asked Judith, trying to keep her voice steady.

The big man ignored her. "Were you alone?"

"Yes."

"You must have been wet through. I'd like to have a look at the shoes you were wearing. You have nothing to fear, Merle, if you're telling me the truth. This is just a routine matter. I am Detective-Inspector Lott, attached to the Holton Division. A murder was committed last night and we are combing the district to find the man who did it."

David said nothing. He had turned very white. Judith, restraining an impulse to thrust herself between him and the Inspector, said, "If it was a fight in a public-house my brother wouldn't know. He doesn't drink. His head won't stand it. I—"

She broke off as Lott bent with an alertness surprising in so big a man and brought out one of the canvas shoes she had been trying to screen from observation. His face, hard enough before, seemed to turn to granite.

"You were wearing these? They are still damp."

David licked his lips. "Yes."

"How do you account for these stains?"

"Stains? I don't know what you mean."

"Look at them."

David glanced at the shoe held out for his inspection and averted his face. "I don't know," he muttered. "It was dark. I suppose I trod in something."

Lott cleared his throat. "Very well," he said, "you'd better get dressed now. You'll have to come along to the station with us. You'll have time there to consider your position. Meanwhile it is my duty to warn you that anything you say may be used in evidence against you. Will you leave us please, Miss Merle. We shall remain with your brother while he gets ready."

"But it's—it's ridiculous," cried Judith. "He couldn't—he's not that sort."

"Watkins," said Lott, "go down and get a taxi. Look sharp. We don't want a crowd to collect. And as for you, Miss—" He gripped Judith's arm and pushed her out on to the landing.

"Can I come to the station with him?"

"Not with him. But there's nothing to stop you from calling round presently. If you want to help him you can pack what he'll need. Night clothes and a brush and comb."

He was speaking more kindly now. "You mustn't think we enjoy upsetting people," he said. "He may be back in an hour or two none the worse. If he's innocent he's nothing to fear."

She gulped down her tears. "Well, he is. Of course he is."

She was slower than she meant to be over her dressing because her hands were shaking but she was listening all the time.

She would hear them when they came out of David's room. But when she went out on the landing his door stood open. They were gone, and the landlady was coming up the stairs, breathing stertorously and hauling herself up by the rail.

"Oh, you're there, Miss Merle. Nice goings on, I don't think. Plain clothes police nosing about my place."

"I'm sorry," said Judith. "It's all a mistake."

"I hope so, I'm sure," said Mrs. Burt, sniffing as her little eyes darted here and there. The bed had been stripped, the drawers pulled out. "A nice old mess they've made."

"I'll straighten it up presently," Judith promised. "I've got to see Reuben."

She ran down to the next floor. There was a buzz of conversation below where the other lodgers were discussing the event. Reuben had been out for a paper. He glanced up as his sister came in.

"What the hell has David been doing? Has he told you?" His voice was sharp with anxiety. Lil, still in her pink satin wrapper, lolled in a creaking wicker chair. She was polishing her nails.

"Not a thing. What does the paper say?"

"It's the local rag. They've brought out a special edition."

She read the short paragraph under stop press over his shoulder.

Mrs. Rodd, working housekeeper to Mr. Fallowes, of Laurel Lodge, Park Avenue, going to call her employer at 7 o'clock this morning found him lying fully dressed on his bed. There were severe head injuries and he had obviously been dead for some hours. The police were notified, and an intensive search is being made for the assailant. Robbery was the apparent motive of the crime. An early arrest is expected. Mr. Fallowes, who was something of a recluse and had no servants living in, was a generous subscriber to local charitable funds and was much respected.

"Well, the police have made a bloomer to start with," said Reuben angrily.

"Oh yeah,' said Lil.

Judith looked round at her sister-in-law. "That's a nice thing to say."

"Well, you don't expect me to be thrilled at being mixed up in a thing like this. He wasn't home until past one last night. It's one hell of a mess. If they hold him what's going to happen to our turn? He's let us all down, and you expect me to get all mushy about him. But we all know how you are about your precious David. I may have my faults, but I'm not soppy."

"Soppy!" Judith exploded. "You're hard as nails."

"Shut your mouth," said Reuben harshly. "Lil's upset and you can't blame her. The question is what are we to do?"

"I'm going to the police station. It's all a mistake. It must be."

"Yes. I suppose that's the best thing. So long, Lil."

"She's right about the act," he said when they were out of the house. "We can't carry on without him."

"We won't have to," said Judy between her teeth. "Those two busies that took him away were bone-heads. They'll get told off by the Superintendent. You'll see. All the same"—she swallowed hard and ended on a lower and more uncertain note—"He's in a mess. Reuben, we've got to stand by him."

"Of course," said Reuben. He was all right, she thought, when Lil was not there. "But has he—told you anything?"

"No. There wasn't time before those men came."

It was still raining. They were jostled by the crowd of shoppers on the narrow, wet pavements of the High Street. The sham Palladian façade of the Corn Exchange loomed out of the mist. The police station was in a quiet street just behind it.

They passed through swing doors into a paved hall and were stopped at once by a tall young constable who asked them what their business was.

Her brothers had always left Judy to do the talking. She answered now in a voice that she tried to keep steady. "We want to see David Merle. He was brought here about half an hour ago."

"I see. Will you wait here, please." He indicated a bench at the foot of the stairs and left them to speak to three older men who were standing round a dusty fire at the far end of the hall and talking together in undertones. A fifth man sat at a desk writing in a book and breaking off at intervals to answer the telephone.

One of the older men came to speak to the Merles. They both stood up as he approached, and Judy moistened her lips.

"You have come to give information?"

"No, sir, I mean"—her voice sounded brittle in that cold, unwelcoming air—"David Merle is our brother. You can't keep him here. He hasn't done anything."

"You are performing together this week at the Palace?"

"Yes."

"A good show. I was there on Tuesday evening, the first house."

The tall young constable came back to them. "The Superintendent will see you. Come this way."

They followed him down a gloomy passage into a room where a florid-faced man with a deceptively light and pleasant manner stood with his back to the fire and facing the door by which they entered. Another man sitting on his left, wrote industriously in a notebook.

"Come in, come in, both of you. You are members of the Flying Merles troupe? David Merle is your brother? I see. Well, I'm very glad you came round because you may be able to help us. Now, as regards last night. Ladies first. Can you tell us, Miss Merle, what you did from the moment you left the stage at the conclusion of your act?"

She eyed him warily. She was not deceived by the superficial friendliness of his manner, but surely the truth could do no harm.

"I dressed in a hurry because I wanted to ask David to go for a walk with me, but I was just too late. The doorkeeper told me he had gone. It was a beastly night anyway, so I just went back to our lodgings and went to bed and read a book until I felt sleepy.

"I see. Did you hear your brother come in?"

"No."

"Is he in the habit of taking long walks after the show?"

"Sometimes he does."

"He walks for hours in a downpour of rain? He came home last night drenched to the skin."

"He's worried about his wife. She's staying with her mother. She isn't strong and she's going to have a baby."

"An expensive business. You were with him when the police called at your lodgings this morning. Had he told you anything about last night?"

"No."

"Did you notice his shoes?"

The hard blue eyes seemed to be boring into her head. She forced herself to meet them without flinching.

"No."

"Lying won't help him, Miss Merle."

"I'm not lying."

"Very well. We'll leave it at that. You, Merle. What did you do last night? You shared a dressing room with your brother?"

"Yes. He dressed quickly and got away before I did. He'd written to his wife and wanted to catch the last post. My wife and I and Alec Fearn had a drink together in the saloon bar of the Crown, and then she and I went home. It was a foul night. We had a spot of supper in the fish bar in the High Street on the way. We were in bed by eleven."

"Did you see anything more of your brother?"

"No."

"Did you hear him come in?"

Reuben hesitated. "Yes, I did. It was late. I'd been up to his room, and he wasn't there. I was a bit worried—"

"Why?"

"It was a hell of a night for him to be out in."

"But you heard him come back at last. Did you notice the time?"

"I didn't—but my wife struck a match. She said it was past one."

"He's in financial difficulties, isn't he?"

"I wouldn't call it that. His wife's mother keeps on at him to send more than he can."

Judith bit her lip. Reuben shouldn't have said that. It was true, but it might give the police a false impression. She had a horrible feeling that from all these seemingly harmless questions and answers a net was being woven.

"Can he come back with us now?" she asked.

"No, Miss Merle."

"Is he under arrest?"

"No. He has not been charged—yet. He is being detained pending certain enquiries."

"What about our act to-night?"

"You'll have to carry on without him."

"You're barking up the wrong tree, Superintendent."

He said nothing. Reuben touched her arm. "Come along, Judy. It's no use. And we'll have to see the manager."

"All right. I'm coming. David ought to have a lawyer to look after his interests. Can you tell us of one, sir? An honest one?"

"You might try Mr. Peel. His office is in Church Row. Just a minute before you go. Just the usual routine. Reading over and signing your statements."

"Can we see David—just for a minute?" she asked wistfully.

"I am afraid not at present."

"A fat lot of use we've been to him so far," growled Reuben when they were outside. He glanced back at the dingy façade of the police station with loathing. "Catch me going in there again of my own accord. They take and squeeze you like a sponge. We were fools to go, Judy. Oh, I'm not blaming you," he added, quickly, "you meant well."

"The truth can't hurt anyone," she said rather faintly.

He did not speak for a minute. Then he said without looking at her. "Not if he's innocent."

CHAPTER III
"ANYTHING YOU MAY SAY—"

THE assistant manager of the Palace shepherded the Merles into the cubby hole he used as an office and shut the door.

"Now, what's all this?" he said reproachfully. "I've been rung up by the police about you. They wouldn't say much beyond telling me they're holding David. Have I got to go round and bail him out? What's the trouble anyway?"

Judy watched his thick, spatulate fingers, heavily ringed, picking a cigarette from his case. As managers go he wasn't a bad sort. "There was a murder in the town last night. They—they think David was mixed up in it."

"Good God!" He made no attempt to conceal his dismay. "I've been reading about that in the *Gazette*. Old Mr. Fallowes. One of our regular patrons. Always came Monday night. He sometimes asked one or two of the performers to supper with him after the show." He sat down heavily at his littered desk. "That's torn it. They wouldn't hear of bail, and it wouldn't be any use if they did. I can't put your turn on while a charge like that is hanging over him."

"I could take David's place in the blindfold leap," said Judy, anxiously.

"You don't understand. Our audiences wouldn't stand for it. They'd tear the place to pieces. I'm sorry, my dear. It's hard on you, but you've got to face facts. I'll see you get your week's salary all right. In fact I'll write you a cheque here and now so that you won't have to come round here again."

"Don't worry," flashed Judy, "we don't come where we're not wanted. I thought in England a man was innocent until his guilt was proved."

"That's the theory," said the assistant manager, "but it works out differently in practice. I've warned you for your own sakes. His pals will stand by him, no doubt. But I've got to think of our public." He wrote the cheque and blotted it. "And now, if you'll excuse me—"

They took the hint and passed out of the stuffiness of the office into the chill of the vestibule. The cleaners were at work in the auditorium. They could hear the clash of zinc pails and the whining of a vacuum cleaner.

"The lawyer next," said Judy briskly.

Reuben said nothing. Judy in the midst of her overwhelming anxiety over David was able to feel sorry for him. He would have to deal with Lil presently, and her nagging tongue and her maddening assumption of being always in the right.

The office of Peel and Arrowsmith was on the ground floor of a Victorian mansion that had been converted to business purposes, and Mr. Peel's private room had the airy spaciousness of another age. Mr. Peel, a middle-aged man with a quiet, dry manner, invited his listeners to sit down, and waited for them to state their business.

Meanwhile the police had failed to induce David to make any statement. He had been locked in a cell and left there for an hour where his slightest movement could be observed by watchful eyes.

The Superintendent's light, friendly voice resumed. "You've had time to think things over, Merle. We're going to give you another chance. How did you spend your time last night between the hours of 8.55, when the doorkeeper at the Palace saw you leave, and round about one when you were heard to come in to your lodgings?"

"I just walked about. I don't know where exactly. It was dark and I didn't notice."

"You walked without stopping for four hours?"

David licked his lips. He had to stick to that. They wouldn't believe him if he told the truth.

"I sat down for a bit on a bench and smoked a couple of gaspers."

"Oh, you sat down and smoked. You didn't tell us that before. If we could find the bench it might help you. What brand do you smoke?"

"Pride of the Regiment."

"Can you describe this bench? Were there trees? Was it down by the river?"

David was not naturally inventive. He looked more and more harassed.

"It was under a tree."

Superintendent Fry eyed him for a moment reflectively. Then he said in a somewhat harder tone. "You have not been searched. You were under observation while you were in that cell, but though you believed yourself to be alone you made no attempt to get rid or conceal anything. I take it that you have nothing in your pockets that you would mind our seeing?"

"Nothing whatever."

"Very well. Turn out the contents here on this desk. Harris, stand by to make a list."

David produced a handkerchief, a penknife and a piece of string, a fountain pen and three shillings and elevenpence halfpenny in mixed silver and copper, and a little bundle of letters scrawled on cheap notepaper and held together by a rubber band. He flushed a little as he laid that down.

"From my wife—" And then they all saw the change in his face as he slipped his hand into his left hand coat pocket. For an instant they imagined that the bulge there was made by a pistol.

"Look out!" barked the Superintendent, but Lott, the plain clothes man who had fetched David from his lodgings, had already gripped his wrist.

"What's this?"

He laid a bulky manila envelope on the desk. David started at it with a sinking heart. For the first time since it had been pressed into his hand he recalled the parcel of tracts presented to him by his eccentric host. He had thrust them into his coat pocket and forgotten them. Fool. But the shock of discovering the body on the bed had driven everything else out of his mind.

The Superintendent was slitting the flap of the envelope. He drew out a thick wad of one pound notes.

Nobody spoke for a minute, then David said in a high voice, "But that wasn't—" and stopped himself.

The Superintendent looked at him woodenly. So young, he was thinking. A pity.

"All right," he said. "I charge you, David Merle, with the murder of Joshua Fallowes. Take him away."

"Can—can I have a lawyer?"

"Yes. Your brother and sister were here just now. They are seeing about that. He'll be along soon, I daresay. See that he has some dinner, Harris."

He was taken back to his cell. Soon afterwards a young policeman brought him a plate of roast beef with potatoes and cabbage on a tray.

"Would you like a glass of beer with it? You can have that if you like?"

"If it's not too much trouble."

After he had finished the same young constable fetched away the tray and gave him a cigarette.

When he had smoked it he sat on the end of the bench that would be his bed when the time came for him to sleep, with his elbows on his knees and his face in his hands, and tried to think. Mr. Fallowes had given him a bundle of tracts, stuff about hell fire and casting your burden on the Lord. How could tracts turn into pound notes? If he had thrown the envelope away in the shrubbery, if he had got rid of his bloodstained shoes he would have been safe enough. As it was he was in a hell of a mess. What about the act? How would Reuben and Judy manage without him? And Daisy? Would that mother of hers have the sense to keep her in ignorance? Would he be allowed to write to her? He looked up as the door opened. Not a policeman this time.

"My name is Peel. I am a lawyer. Your brother and sister have asked me to look after your interests, that is, if you are willing, of course.

"Thank you, sir. I'd be glad. But—I haven't any money."

"Don't worry about that." Mr. Peel cleared his throat. Quite a nice, well-mannered lad, he thought unhappily, and so young. A mere boy. He sat down beside his client.

"Now we have to face the facts, eh? You will be brought before the Bench to-morrow morning and charged with the murder of Mr. Fallowes. You will plead not guilty and reserve your defence. The police are bound to produce their evidence and we shall see what we are up against."

"Why did they pick on me, sir? Can you tell me that?"

"Mr. Fallowes is known to have made a practice of inviting artistes performing at the local music hall to visit him after the show. I understand that he was on the stage himself for a while as a young man. The police, very naturally, thought it possible that the crime had been committed by a comparative stranger who had obtained access to the house. Everybody performing at the Palace this week has been questioned, and I gather that you are the one who has been unable to produce one or more witnesses to prove an alibi." He hesitated. "You were walking about—alone?"

"Yes. I was worrying. I've been worried about Daisy—that's my wife. She needs more care than she's getting. That old mother of hers is as mean as dirt. She ought to have milk foods and all that. The old woman keeps on nagging me to send more." The lawyer looked at him gravely. "Yes. But I'd keep that to myself if I were you. I mean, don't make a point of the fact that you've been badly in want of money."

"There's the motive," he thought. "He's obviously madly in love with his wife."

"The less you say the better until we know exactly what they've got against you. Remember, not guilty, and you reserve your defence. But I shall represent you, and afterwards we'll talk things over again."

"Thank you, sir." David held out his hand, but Mr. Peel did not appear to see it. Afterwards, as he recalled the hurt look on the boy's face, he wished he had been less fastidious.

The small, dark room in the old Town Hall where the Petty Sessions were held was crowded to the doors when the case was opened the following morning, and there were representatives of several London papers at the press table. The inquest had been opened half an hour previously and adjourned indefinitely in view of the police proceedings. Mr. Savory appeared for the Crown and outlined the case for the prosecution.

"The facts, your Worships, are as follows. Mr. Fallowes, a gentleman of considerable means, well known and esteemed for his benefactions to this town, was one of those people who do not care to have servants living under his roof. A Mrs. Rodd, whom we shall call in due course, did what cooking and cleaning was required. She had a key to the front door and let herself in usually about seven in the morning, leaving at three or as soon as she had cleared away her employer's mid-day meal, and laid a cold supper in the dining-room. He never took tea. She knew that he occasionally entertained a visitor to supper and, by his wish, the table was always set for two. Yesterday morning she went, as usual, straight to the kitchen to put the kettle on the gas stove, and within ten minutes of her arrival she was taking her employer his early cup of tea. To her horror she found the bedroom, a front room on the first floor, in the utmost confusion, the window wide open and the blind torn down, and the body of Mr. Fallowes, fully clothed, lying across the bed. The head had been battered in apparently with a stone taken from the rockery in the front garden. There was a pool of blood on the floor, and evidently the murderer had trodden in it, for a red trail of foot-prints lead from the bed to the window by which he escaped, and there are smears of blood on the sill. Mrs. Rodd rushed out of the house to the nearest telephone and called the police. The police arrived with the minimum of delay and searched the house and the grounds. In the dining-room the remains of last night's supper showed that Mr. Fallowes had brought home a guest. A suitcase lying on the floor was filled with the silver trophies Mr. Fallowes had won in his youth. He was very proud of his array of cups, and always kept them on the sideboard. In the bedroom the safe built into the wall was open and the bunch of keys that Mr. Fallowes always carried about with him was found lying on the bed. Mr. Fallowes was in the habit of drawing twenty pounds at a time from the bank for his current expenses, all in one pound notes. We shall call the cashier of the North Central Bank, in the High Street, to prove that Mr. Fallowes drew out twenty pounds on Monday morning. He changed one of the notes immediately afterwards at the tobacconists'. A bundle of nineteen one pounds notes, quite new, were found on the accused when he was searched at the police station. There were bloodstains on a pair of canvas shoes that were under the bed at his lodgings. There is the further evidence of finger-prints. The finger-prints of the accused have been taken and are found to coincide with prints found on the dining-room furniture and on the silver packed for removal, and on the door-knob and the window frame of the bedroom in which the crime was committed."

Judy Merle was standing in the crowd at the back of the court. Her heart sank as she listened. It seemed as if even she would be forced to believe that David was guilty. And yet—no, no, it wasn't possible. She looked towards the dock where he stood and he glanced round at that moment and met her yearning gaze. He seemed to be trying to convey a message. Was it to beg of her to suspend judgment?

Inspector Lott had been called to the witness stand to describe what he had found at the Laurels, and the steps he had taken to follow up the clues left by the assailant.

"Not many men could have got out of the house by that window without a ladder, but a trained acrobat could do it easily. I knew Mr. Fallowes used to ask professionals to supper and listen to their hard luck stories. They're a decent crowd on the whole, but there are black sheep in every fold and he had been warned it was dangerous, but he only laughed. I saw and questioned everyone taking part in this week's show at the Palace. The only one whose alibi was unsatisfactory was the prisoner, and we found a pair of canvas shoes still sodden from the rain of the previous night and stained with blood, under his bed. These shoes have since been compared with the footprints on the floor of Mr. Fallowes' bedroom and they are similar in size. Merle was brought to the station. He said he had been walking at random the night before, but he made no signed statement. When he was searched an envelope containing nineteen one pounds notes was found in his coat pocket. He was then formally charged with the murder of Mr. Fallowes."

The Chairman of the Bench nodded approval. "Quick work, Inspector. One moment—" He conferred in whispers with his colleagues before turning to the clerk. "That's good enough for us. Do we have to hear any more evidence? He'll have to be committed for trial at the Assizes."

"Yes, Sir Gervase, but we should go through with some of the evidence."

Sir Gervase, who had an invitation to shoot over a neighbour's coverts, sighed impatiently. "What's the use of putting the poor devil through it twice? However—call the next witness." The police surgeon was brief and business-like. Mr. Fallowes had undoubtedly been struck down from behind. The first blow might not have been fatal, but several had been struck, and dealt with great force. The base of the skull was crushed. The injuries could have been caused by the jagged piece of Portland stone which had been found lying among the disordered bedclothes.

"At what time were you called to the Laurels?"

"It was a few minutes after eight. I had just sat down to breakfast when Inspector Lott rang me up."

"Had Mr. Fallowes been dead long?"

The witness paused a moment. "Some while. But I should not care to commit myself to a stated time. The body was quite cold. But then the night had been chilly, and the window was wide open."

Mrs. Rodd, who followed, was voluble and inclined to be tearful. The prisoner, who had seemed dazed at first, had been following the evidence carefully. He bent over the rail of the dock to speak to his solicitor.

"Mr. Peel, will you ask her if the bedroom door was locked?"

Mr. Peel rose and put the question.

Mrs. Rodd answered promptly. "Mr. Fallowes never locked his door. I just knocked and walked in as usual with the poor gentleman's early cup of tea, and when I saw the window open and the curtain all sodden with the rain that had beat in, and blood on the lino, and that dreadful sight on the bed it proper turned me over."

The bank cashier, who followed, identified the nineteen one pounds notes found in Merle's coat pocket as those he had paid out to the deceased on the morning before his death. Mr. Fallowes would never take notes that had been in circulation. He did not recognise the envelope. Mr. Fallowes had placed the notes in a leather case.

The last witness was a finger-print expert, who had brought with him enlarged proofs of photographs taken of prints made by Merle at the police station after his arrest and of prints found on the polished mahogany of the dining-room table of the Laurels and on one of the silver cups that had been packed for taking away. The prints were identical.

"That concludes the case for the prosecution. We are prepared to call other witnesses if your worships desire it."

"No, no," said Sir Gervase hastily. "What about the defence?"

Mr. Peel stood up and bowed to the Bench. "We have not had time to prepare our answer to this terrible accusation, your worships. My client pleads not guilty, and reserves his defence."

"Very well." There was another whispered consultation in which the clerk to the magistrates and the Superintendent took part before Sir Gervase resumed.

"We are agreed that the prisoner, David Merle, must be committed for trial on the charge of murder. He will be kept until the Assizes open in the prison here, where you, Mr. Peel, will be given every facility to see him. Remove the prisoner, and clear the court."

Judy hoped that David would look her way again, but just as he turned to leave the dock a stout woman shoving her back against the wall blocked her view and she was carried away by the crowd surging out of the doors into the dank gloom of the winter afternoon.

Somebody spoke to her as she was standing wearily on the kerb waiting for the traffic lights. It was Mr. Levy, the assistant manager at the Palace.

"Nothing like real life drama, eh? It gets you every time. I managed to slip in just before the end. You were there all day, I daresay?"

"Yes," she said dully, and then, "He didn't do it, Mr. Levy. It's a frame up. It must be."

He glanced down at the small, white face, drawn with anxiety and fatigue, and was moved to compassion. "You're all in, and no wonder. Reuben shouldn't have let you go there alone. Come along." They crossed the road together as the lights changed. "What you need is a cup of tea and I could do with one myself."

The tea shop was crowded, but he found a table for two in a secluded corner.

"Could you eat a poached egg on toast? Nothing since breakfast I'll bet. Right." He gave the order, and when he had struggled out of his overcoat lit a cigarette. "I'm not offering you one because you ought to eat first, see."

"You're being very kind to me, Mr. Levy, she said gratefully.

"That's nothing. You've had a raw deal."

"It doesn't matter about me. I'm thinking about David."

"I know." The little man nodded. "You're loyal. It's a nice trait. Now that sister-in-law of yours—never mind that. The question is what are you going to do?"

To please him she was trying to eat the poached egg and the toast, but they seemed to turn to sand in her mouth. She chewed on doggedly and managed to swallow a mouthful before she answered.

"Reuben and I might pull the turn together if Lil wasn't such a dud."

"You wouldn't get an engagement, not as the Flying Merles. You've had the wrong kind of publicity. Your only chance is to join up with another troupe. Reuben's thinking of that, I fancy. I had a talk with him in the bar of the Crown last night. But if I were you I'd go home to my people until this business is settled."

It was good advice and Judy knew it. Reuben and Lil did not really want her with them.

"You've got a home?" said Levy, watching her. "Auntie Apples who brought us up. She's fond of us all, though she can't stick Lil."

Levy grinned. "No use for languorous blondes? Isn't that too bad?"

"Yes, but I can't bear the idea of going so far away from—from David. Auntie lives in Cottingham."

"You wouldn't be allowed to see him if you stayed on here. You can trust Peel to do his best for him. He's a good sort, old-fashioned but reliable."

He observed her shrewdly as she refilled the cup he had pushed across the marble topped table. The Flying Merles had toured the south-west of England with a circus through July and August, but they had been out of an engagement for several weeks after that. Judy's tweed coat had been through more than one winter, her gloves had been mended, and the bravura with which she wore her beret tilted at the latest angle did not deceive the experienced eye of Ben Levy. And she wasn't even pretty by some standards. But he liked her. He liked her a thousand times better than the glamorous females who sometimes raised hell in his office. On the trapeze she was no match for him, he could only look up and gasp at the incredible nonchalant grace of her. But on earth she seemed touchingly helpless, like a swallow unable to use its long wings without the air to lift them.

"I tell you what," he said, "I'll lend you enough to pay your fare back any time you feel you want to come. You'll want to be here while the trial's on. I know that. I'll see if I can't find you a nice bed-sitting-room with a landlady who'll look after you. You wouldn't be afraid—I mean—you know I'm straight, don't you?"

He was rather like a toad, she thought—but a nice, kind toad, and he had really beautiful eyes, with long, black lashes that any girl would envy. And they liked him down at the theatre. He might be a hard taskmaster, getting the last ounce out of everybody, but he was fundamentally good-tempered, and he always tried to be just. And he did not take advantage of his position to be familiar with the girls.

And so—"Yes," she said gently. "I believe I can trust you. God knows we need a friend just now. And—I am short of money. I've got just about enough to pay up at my digs until Saturday and get a single ticket to Cottingham, but if you could lend me a pound or two I'll pay back in time."

"We'll make it five," he said briskly, and took out his notecase. "And if you give me your address I'll write and tell you how things are going on here. And now," he looked at his watch, "I must buzz off. Take care of yourself. All of the best." He signalled to the waitress to make out the bill. "You stay here a bit longer, Judy. I know what those diggings of yours are like."

He gripped her hand hard and bustled away. She watched him as he picked up his change at the pay desk, looking what he was, a sallow-faced young man of sedentary habits, and not in the least like a knight errant. All the same, she thought, he's a dear.

And then, with a pang like the stab of an exposed nerve, her mind went back to David.

CHAPTER IV
AUNTIE APPLES

THE landlady was lying in wait for Judy. "So he's to be tried at the Assizes. I daresay I'll be called as a witness then. A nice thing, I don't think." Her bulky figure in its stained overall blocked the narrow passage. "Your brother and his wife went off to London by the midday train. He left a note for you."

"Thanks. I'll be leaving myself in the morning."

"And the sooner the better. I've got to give the rooms a good clean out after this."

Judy was not altogether unprepared for Reuben's abrupt departure. It was Lil's doing, of course.

"Dear old Judy"—he wrote—"the Flying Merles are done for after this. I'll have to get bookings under another name, and the sooner I see the agents the better. Lil's prepared to stick to me, but she says three's an awkward number, and I suppose she's right. You and she have never hit it off very well. You've often said things to hurt her. She's very sensitive really." Judy, sitting on the end of her bed in her dingy attic room laughed aloud as she turned the page. "What I mean is I don't think it's any good trying to build up the act with things as they are. If I were you I'd go back to Auntie Apples. She's a good sort and I'm sure she'd be glad to have you."

There was a postscript written very hurriedly in pencil, probably, thought Judy, while Lil was not looking.

"I'm sorry about this. I've paid that old shark in the basement for your room as well as ours so don't let her try any funny business. I enclose receipt signed by her and something towards your fare to Cottingham."

The landlady's receipted bill had been folded round two half crowns. Judy s eyes filled with tears. Poor Reuben. He was putty in the scarlet-tipped predatory claws of his charmer. She boiled her kettle on the gas ring, filled her hot water bottle and took a couple of aspirin before she lay down wearily on the lumpy mattress. She was out of the house before nine the following morning, and carried her suitcase to the station cloakroom before she went round to the lawyer's office. She gave her name and was shown at once into Mr. Peel's room.

"I'm glad you've come." he said as he shook hands with her. "I had a few words with your brother before he was removed. He was very anxious to know what was being done about your act."

"The act is done for," she said bitterly. "Reuben will remain in the profession. He's been trained as an acrobat and can't do anything else. I'm going back to the aunt who brought us up."

"I am to tell him that?"

"No. Say we're quite all right, carrying on. He'd worry and blame himself, and it's not his fault. The break up was coming anyway. My sister-in-law was queering the show out of jealousy. But never mind that now. You are going to defend him, Mr. Peel?"

"Yes. We shall have to engage counsel later."

"Don't they cost a lot of money?"

He smiled slightly. "They certainly do. But I have already been approached by one of the Sunday papers. They make a very handsome offer for the exclusive rights in your brother's life story which will be written up by one of their staff. Will you undertake not to grant interviews to any Pressman unless he can show you a written authorisation from me?"

"Yes."

"Good. I shall be seeing your brother later in the day. We'll do our best for him."

"Will you want me as a witness? she asked wistfully. "They go by a person's character, don't they? David couldn't hurt anybody. He's too soft-hearted. Once when they were boys Reuben caught a sparrow in a trap and wrung its neck, and David cried and cried."

"I am afraid that would not be regarded as relevant. I don't want to distress you, Miss Merle, but I understand that you were present in the courtroom yesterday—you heard the evidence?"

"You mean that you think he did it?"

The lawyer was silent for a minute. Then he said again, "I shall do my best for him. Will you write your aunt's address on this pad? I shall keep in touch with you."

Auntie Apples owed her nickname to the fact that in 1913 she had married a German barber, the proprietor of a little hair-dressing saloon in a working class district of Cottingham. He was interned when the war broke out, and died of influenza a month before the armistice. Mrs. Sturmer, who was fond of her Hans, sent him parcels of food and cigarettes, and kept his photograph in a silver frame on her kitchen mantelpiece with a stubborn disregard of the obloquy attaching to the wives of enemy aliens. She lived that down after a while, and the dress agency which she had started in place of the hair-dressing business prospered. She bought dresses, coats, furs from ladies' maids and sometimes from the ladies themselves in the morning to sell again in the evening to shop girls and factory hands. She had a flair for clothes though she never wore anything smarter than a shapeless woollen jumper and a sagging tweed skirt herself, and soon she was picking and choosing to suit her regular customers. The blue panné velvet that had cost fifty guineas and been first worn at a Hunt Ball was the very thing for little Jessie Higgins, who earned her living as a professional dancing partner at a fourth rate night club. Auntie Apples, who knew Jessie had a child to keep, let her have the frock for fifteen shillings.

After the death of her brother and his wife in a railway accident in America their three children came to live with her. Mrs. Sturmer, who had been in the profession until her marriage, had the disused cart shed in her backyard fitted up for practice work, and every afternoon, on their return from school, the two boys and little Judy were systematically trained under her watchful eye. When Judy, the youngest, was sixteen, she obtained a week's engagement for them at the local Hippodrome. Their turn was a success and they were booked for a three months' tour. That was three years ago, and though Judy wrote regularly and they all sent their aunt presents at Christmas, they had only been down on flying visits for, at most, a couple of nights.

"She kept us for ten years," Judy said, "and slaved for us, and I believe she sometimes went short so that we should have enough. We won't sponge on her now." And so, during those weeks when they were trying vainly to get an engagement that autumn an appeal to Auntie Apples had been ruled out.

Judy arrived at dusk. There was nobody in the shop and she looked about her rather uneasily. Mrs. Sturmer had kept the cubicles of the hair-dressing saloons as fitting-rooms and along the right hand wall there were rows of hangers for her stock of second-hand coats and skirts and dresses. Judy had always been secretly a little afraid of the shop. It was like a waxwork show, she thought. A trifle eerie. But then Auntie Apples came bustling in from her cosy firelit sitting-room at the back and welcomed her with a bear's hug.

"God bless you, dearie. You're chilled to the bone after that railway journey, I know. Tea's ready. Buttered toast, and I haven't forgotten you like Gentlemen's Relish."

"Oh, Auntie!" It was a relief to be able to give way at last, and Judy's spurious brightness splintered like thin glass. "You've read—in the papers—"

"Yes. We'll talk about it presently. Not a word until you're warmed and rested."

When the meal had been cleared away and the fire made up Mrs. Sturmer, having established her niece on the sofa with a rug over her feet produced her knitting. "I'm expecting a customer at nine o'clock. My regulars come to the side door. But until then we're not likely to be disturbed. Now, Judy, I've read the reports of the police court proceedings. With the evidence they had they were bound to commit David for trial. What I want to know now is what's behind it all."

"He didn't do it," said Judy. "He couldn't."

Her aunt sighed. "When you've seen as much of life as me you'll begin to think that anyone can do anything. I don't want to believe it. David—he was always soft-hearted; unusually so for a boy of his age. But people change. He doesn't drink, does he?"

"No."

"Or bet on horses?"

"A shilling now and again, I daresay, and a ticket for the sweep. He's not a plaster saint, Auntie, but he's steady. I'm sure of that. He—he's been worried over his wife. She's delicate and she's gone home to her mother to have a baby. Her mother's very grasping. He was always having to send along postal orders. Why have boys to get goofy about girls," sighed poor Judy. "It spoils everything. Daisy's all right; but Reuben's wife is a cold-blooded, selfish little cat."

"What does Reuben think about all this?"

"It's what Lil thinks that matters," said Judy bitterly, "and her great idea is to keep out of the mess. They went off to London yesterday without even waiting to hear if David was being committed for trial. Reuben left a note for me. I could see he was ashamed of himself."

She went on to describe how the police had come for David.

"I'd just gone into his room with a cup of tea. He was asleep. He might have told me something if there had been time. There must be some explanation of it all, Auntie."

"That's what I say," Mrs. Sturmer agreed. "Something behind it all."

The shop door bell rang and she went to serve a customer.

"It's a tie being here alone," she said when she came back. "My assistant left last week to get married. I'll have to get another, but I'm a bit choosy about whom I have."

"Would I do, Auntie?"

"You?" Mrs. Sturmer looked startled. "You aren't thinking of leaving the profession, Judy? You've never had an accident. Don't say you've lost your nerve."

"No. But Reuben is going to join up with a different crowd. I wouldn't care to do that. I've always been with him and—and David. I'd like to stay with you for the time being anyway, and I'd be only too pleased to help in the shop."

"I'll be glad to have you with me, but I don't like the idea of you giving up. There wasn't a better turn of its kind on the road than the Flying Merles. The air is your element, Judy. And you invented some good fresh business. That rose you threw to the audience as you ran out—"

Judy looked pleased. "You liked that? It went down very well, especially when we were travelling with the circus this summer. There's more scope in a ring than on a stage. The audience is all round you. There was quite a scramble for it sometimes. It was just a bit of fun, and it filled in the time while Reuben was getting his breath after a bit of quick work on the trapeze. But there was a lot of trouble with Lil over that. She wanted to steal it, but as she never did anything but turn a few handsprings on the ground and lounge about at the foot of the ladder it wouldn't have gone down from her. Anyway David wouldn't stand for it. David—" her lips trembled. The mention of her brother's name brought back what she had for a moment forgotten.

"You're tired out," said her aunt. "Come along. I've got your old room ready. And to-morrow being Sunday you shall have your breakfast in bed."

Mrs. Sturmer, a wise woman, did not allow her niece much time to brood over her troubles. "You've got to learn the business if you're going to help me," she said, and Sunday afternoon was spent in the closed shop going through the stock. Every garment was priced in plain figures but on some tickets there were additional hieroglyphics. "This one means that if you think the customer really can't afford it you can take off anything up to five shillings. This means that it's not to be tried on. If I wasn't firm I'd have some of these bouncing girls from the jam factory splitting these flimsy dance frocks. The waist measurements and lengths are written down. I'll take you with me on a buying trip round about the end of next week, but we've got enough on hand at present. There's a staff dance at Grimley's next Wednesday and I expect a lot of girls will be in to-morrow and Tuesday. There won't be much left on that lot of hangers by Wednesday morning. Can you drive a car?"

Judy nodded. She had learned to handle several makes of car the previous summer when the Flying Merles were travelling with a circus. Most of the performers had their own third or fourth hand Fords or Morris or Austin cars picked up in dealers' yards.

"I've got one for my business," explained her aunt. "We can take turns to drive. My idea was to close down on Wednesday and run over to Holton and see the boy's lawyer. I'd like to hear what steps he is taking."

"Oh, thank you, Auntie!" said Judy fervently. There had been moments when she had feared Mrs. Sturmer might take the view that David's affairs were no longer her concern.

The elder woman answered gruffly. "Nothing to thank me for. Now you help me price this lot of coats."

They were about to start on Wednesday morning when a young man arrived.

"I won't keep you long," he said as he proffered a card. "I'm covering the Holton murder mystery for the *Sunday Trumpeter*."

"Mr. Peel said—"

He smiled. "That's all right. Here's Mr. Peel's card. We've got the exclusive rights. I just want any photographs you can let me have of the Flying Merles and a short account of your professional career for me to write up. We have to be careful while a case is sub judice, but we'll be safe with that."

"I wouldn't if I were you, Judy," said her aunt.

"I've got to, Auntie. Mr. Peel arranged it. Just a minute." She ran upstairs and came back with a bundle of photographs and a volume of press cuttings. "There's a lot of stuff there about our South American tour, and things like that," she said breathlessly.

"Thanks awfully. And do I tell our readers that you are convinced of your brother's innocence?"

"Of course I am. Absolutely, utterly, entirely."

Mrs. Sturmer intervened. "That's harmless so far, I suppose," she said grudgingly, "but mind you keep my niece's present address out of the paper. I don't want people coming to my place out of curiosity."

"I can promise you that, madam. It wouldn't suit our book to have other newspaper men trying to get interviews. Thank you very much, Miss Merle. Good morning."

When he had ridden away on his motor-cycle Mrs. Sturmer locked the shop door and they got into the car. "The wrong kind of publicity," she said disapprovingly as she let in the clutch. "I wonder at you, Judy."

"You don't understand, Auntie. Mr. Peel explained it to me. We've got to have money for David's defence. A paper like the *Sunday Trumpeter* will pay hundreds of pounds for the sort of articles that boy will turn out."

Mrs. Sturmer grunted. "I would have paid what's necessary. I have my savings."

"No, Auntie. David wouldn't have allowed that. You've done so much for us in the past. This way is better."

Mrs. Sturmer's reply was lost in the grinding of her brakes as she stopped for the traffic lights. Soon afterwards Judy held her breath as they avoided a lorry with an inch to spare. She could have used several adjectives to describe her aunt's driving, but dull would not have been one of them. But, owing perhaps to a special Providence, they reached Holton without being involved in an accident.

Mr. Peel had just come back to the office from his lunch when they called, and he had them shown at once into his private room. Judy introduced her aunt. Mr. Peel shook hands with them both.

"Sit down, please. I'm glad you've come. Merle has mentioned you, Mrs. Sturmer. I could see he has a great affection and respect for you."

"I brought the three of them up after their parents' death," said Mrs. Sturmer. "David was always a good boy. He couldn't have done this thing, Mr. Peel."

The lawyer looked thoughtfully at his visitor's shrewd, weather-beaten face. No nonsense about her, he thought. Reliable from the faded blue Basque beret she wore pulled over her short grey hair to the soles of her sensible brogues. Lucky that the girl had somebody like that to turn to.

He cleared his throat. "I am afraid the weight of the evidence is against us. The bloodstained shoes, the bundle of notes found in his possession, the finger-prints on the silver."

"What does David say?"

What does David say?"

"His story is that he was wandering about the streets until past one o'clock."

"You don't believe him?"

"The question is will any jury accept that?" The lawyer hesitated. "There is one possibility that would give the defence a better chance. It has occurred to me that he may have gone to the Laurels with a companion, and that he was no more than a witness of the crime."

"You mean he's shielding somebody?" said Judith, incredulously.

"It does not seem likely to you?" Mr. Peel sounded rather disappointed. He had expected them to jump at this theory. Judith shook her head. "He wouldn't do that for anyone but me or Reuben. He hadn't any friends here."

"Someone perhaps with a hold over him?"

"It sounds a bit far fetched to me," said Auntie Apples bluntly, "but, of course, there must be some explanation if we could only get at it."

"I'm afraid we shan't be able to do much for him if he sticks to his present story."

"Did you tell him that?"

"I did. He said, 'There's a kind of truth that would always sound like lies.' Then, just as I was leaving him he asked me a very strange question. He said, 'What was Mr. Fallowes like?' I knew the old man by sight so I told him. He was of medium height and build, with a pronounced stoop, but active for his age, which was round about seventy, straggling grey beard and moustache and hair worn rather long. He was eccentric, you know, in many ways, and it was said that he hated spending money at a barber's. Then his eyesight was poor, and he wore dark glasses, and in winter he swathed himself in scarves and shawls. Your brother listened closely to my description, Miss Merle, and then he said, 'And that's the one whose body was found? I can't understand it.' I said, 'Hadn't you better confide in me? But he shut up again like an oyster."

"If I could see him," said Judy, "I might be able to persuade him to speak out. I think he was going to tell me what had happened that morning if the police hadn't come."

"I was going to suggest that," said the lawyer. "I should have to be with you, and one of the warders is always present, but it's a very large room, and he is not supposed to listen."

She leaned forward eagerly. "Can we go now, at once?"

"I'll ring up the prison and find out."

He dialled a number. "Hallo! Mr. Peel speaking. Peel. Is Major Steele engaged? Oh, just a minute . . . yes . . . Merle's sister is here in my office. Can I bring her round to see him—and another relative, the aunt who brought him up. . . . Well, it might help. . . . I see. . . . Thank you."

He replaced the receiver on its stand and turned to the two women. "Permission granted for a short interview. I'll take you along now in my car."

CHAPTER V
DAISY

DAVID faced his visitors across a table. The warder who had fetched him down from his cell, after pointing out where he was to sit, had withdrawn to the farther end of the long, bare room.

"Good of you to come to see me, Auntie."

"My dear boy—we want to help you," said Mrs. Sturmer in her gruffest voice, "but we can't unless you tell us what really happened that night."

"Yes, David, do," Judy pleaded.

He avoided her eyes. "I walked about."

Judy fired up. "You—you pig-headed old silly. That's no use. Oh, I could shake you. You're lovely on the trapeze, my sweet, and your muscles are grand, but you haven't the brains of a louse. They can prove you were in that house—prove it. Get that. But you didn't kill that old man. It was some sort of frame up, wasn't it?"

He was looking at her now. "Judy, you're clever."

"Of course I'm clever. I've needed to be with a pair of bone-heads like you and Reuben. You've got into a mess and we've got to get you out, but we can't if we don't know all the facts."

"Wait a minute," he muttered.

They waited while he with his head in his hands, painfully trying to decide on his future course. Mr. Peel cleared his throat once or twice. Mrs. Sturmer twisted her wedding ring round and round. There had been Hans dying in the prison camp, and that railway accident. And now this.

Judy sat very still. Inwardly she was saying a prayer. "Please God—" She could not get any farther than that. She caught her breath as David lifted his head at last.

"All right," he said, "I'll tell you." He glanced over his shoulder. The warder, sitting on a chair by the door, was reading the *Daily Mail*. "He can't hear?"

"No, no," Mr. Peel reassured him.

"Well, then—" He passed his hand across his forehead. In the harsh white glare of the unshaded electric light his young face looked drawn and weary. Ten years older, thought Judy, in a week. "He spoke to me that night. I'd gone across the square to post my letter to Daisy. He asked me to supper. I wouldn't have gone only that ventriloquist who was at the Brighton Hippodrome had told me about him. He said he was a harmless old fellow and that the grub was jolly good, and that all he expected in return for his hospitality was that you would take the tracts he handed out when you left. You remember the chap, Judy, the Great Baroque. I wish to God he'd never said a word. Then I'd have gone straight home to our digs and I wouldn't be here. Anyhow I went along with him and he took me into the house. The supper was laid ready in the dining-room. Tinned stuff mostly, but all the best. He didn't eat anything himself. He was all wrapped up and he didn't take anything off. I didn't wonder at that for there was no fire and the place was as cold as a vault. Gloomy, too, with dark red hangings and a lot of that heavy mahogany furniture. There were silver cups and things on the sideboard, things he'd won, rowing and boxing and all that, when he was a young man, and he asked me to lift one of them to guess the weight. I said, 'I must be going.' He kept on asking questions, and he didn't listen to the answers. It seemed as if he was listening for something else. It sort of gave me the willies. Then he said something about life being difficult and a lot of temptations, pi jaw stuff, and handed me what I thought was a parcel of tracts. I thanked him, of course, and shoved it into my pocket and forgot all about it. Then he said would I do him a favour before I went. The sash window in his bedroom had got stuck and he wasn't strong enough to move it. I said I'd try, and we went upstairs. He opened a door on the first landing and told me to go in first. He was following me and he pressed the light switch. It clicked but the light didn't come on. He asked me to wait a minute while he fetched a candle and he went away quickly closing the door after him. I'm not a kid to mind being left in a strange room in the dark, but it seemed queer." He shut his eyes for a moment, and they saw beads of sweat break out on his upper lip. "I waited and listened, and I didn't hear a sound. Then, as I got used to the darkness, I could make out the shape of the wardrobe and the bed standing out from the wall. There was something black lying on the bed. It—it sort of drew me. I put out my hand and touched flesh. It was cold. I—I—that got me going. I rushed to the door and grabbed the handle. The door was locked. My one idea then was to get out of the house. I made for the window and slipped on a wet patch by the bedside. That's how I got blood on my shoes. I got out of the window easily enough and slid down the rainwater pipe to the ground. I don't know what time it was, but I walked about for some while before I went back to my digs trying to calm down and think things out. When I got in I was dead beat, and I just got out of my clothes and slept like a log, and I'd only just woke up in the morning when the police came. That's the whole truth, so help me God, but who's going to believe it?"

"I do," said Judy.

Mr. Peel had been taking notes. "This is a very strange story, Merle," he said slowly. "It covers the known facts. I mean it accounts for the traces of your presence in the house. But if we accept it the mystery is deepened. The body of Mr. Fallowes was found as you describe it lying, fully dressed, across the bed, in the front bedroom. But you say Mr. Fallowes took you upstairs and left you there, saying that he would fetch a candle, and that when he failed to return and your eyes grew used to the dark you saw the body. According to you the dead man was not Fallowes. Could you describe him?"

"No. It was dark. I—I touched him twice. His hand was cold. The second time I felt something wet and sticky. Blood."

"And the man who accosted you and brought you to the house. What was he like?"

"Middle-sized and he stooped a good bit from the shoulders. He had an untidy sort of grey beard and hair straggling down over his coat collar. He wore his hat all the time and his overcoat and muffler, and he had dark spectacles, and gloves on his hands. He had what they call a cultured voice, very precise and sort of B. B. C.ish. He seemed a bit nervy and on edge, I thought."

"Anyone could dress up to look like that," said Judy.

"Yes, yes, no doubt." Mr. Peel sounded unconvinced, "but it does not sound very likely that anyone would."

"It might be somebody in the profession who had been asked to supper some time ago. He might have thought how easy it would be to rob the house. Perhaps he didn't mean to kill the old man, but when he had he decided to impersonate him and get somebody there so that suspicion would fall on them."

"You mean that the crime had been committed when the man whom your brother supposed to be Mr. Fallowes invited him to supper?"

"Yes, of course. You heard David say the dead man's hand was cold. He must have been dead some time."

The warder, after glancing at the clock, had folded his newspaper. "Time's up, sir."

"Very well." Mr. Peel stood up. "I'll think this over, Merle, and see what can be done. You'll appreciate that this story is not likely to be accepted without corroboration. If we can find evidence of the existence of this third person, someone who saw him going to the house or coming from it. Well, try not to worry. We shall do our best."

"Thank you, sir." David looked across the table at the two women and tried to smile. "Thank you both for coming."

Mrs. Sturmer said nothing. Her face was working. She turned away abruptly.

Judy heard a voice that did not sound like her own saying, "God bless you, darling."

"Judy, I haven't had a word from Daisy. I hope they're keeping all this from her. Do you know how she is?"

She shook her head. "I wrote to Mrs. Benson, but she hasn't answered. I'll go over and see them if you like."

"I wish you would. God bless you, Judy, for sticking to me."

"God bless you."

The warder touched his arm. They went out together through another door.

Mr. Peel shepherded his charges back to his car. "Very upsetting, very upsetting. You feel it, naturally. Now we won't talk on the way if you don't mind."

The prison was a mile outside the town, past the cemetery and the gas works and just beyond the tram terminus. Judy leaned back and shut her eyes. Auntie Apples was crying, and that in itself was a portent for Mrs. Sturmer did not cry easily or often.

"I'm afraid I can't give you much more time just now," said Mr. Peel, as they followed him into his room. "I'll write and let you know how we get on." He spoke kindly, but he was obviously anxious to get rid of them.

"You do believe him, don't you, Mr. Peel?"

He hesitated, loth to give pain. "I'd like to, but—it's so very improbable. What would be the motive? Robbery? I must remind you that nothing was taken but the nineteen pound notes found in your brother's possession. I shall have enquiries made, leave no stone unturned, but—"

"I see," she said dully. He shook hands with them both. Judy took her aunt's arm and they left him shaking his head ruefully over his arrears of office work. Hard on the girl who so evidently idolised her brother, hard on the older woman who had brought him up. Disappointing. He had hoped against hope for a more convincing story.

Neither Judy nor her aunt talked much on their way home. Judy was driving, and in spite of the inclemency of the night there was a good deal of traffic on the road. When they got in Mrs. Sturmer made cocoa on the gas ring in the kitchen.

"We'll each have a hot water bottle and go straight to bed. I tell you what, Judy, taking it by and large and looking back over sixty years, love's not a thing to be missed, but I've got more comfort out of a hot water bottle." She patted the girl on the shoulder and added, with a change of tone. "Have you any plans?"

"You heard what he said about Daisy. I think I ought to go and see the poor kid. I've only met her mother once, and that was at the wedding, but I'd say she was the limit."

"You mean—low down?"

"Oh no! Quite the opposite. Very ladylike and superior. David wasn't nearly good enough. She runs a little wool shop at Ranchester, in the shadow of the cathedral. The wives of the minor canons buy their jumper wool from her. Daisy was very much under her mother's thumb."

"How did she and David meet?"

"It was the summer before last. We were with Bannerman's circus and we stayed a week at Ranchester. She went to the show with a girl friend and got a pash for David. They hung about outside the tent hoping to see him and ask for his autograph, and he fell for her directly he saw her. She's very pretty. A soft cuddly little thing, very gentle and yielding. David and she have been very happy together, but since she's been expecting a baby she's been ailing, and there isn't much comfort on the road, so it seemed best that she should go home to her mother for a while."

"How is she going to stand up to this?"

"I don't know. Let's hope she's tougher than she looks," said Judy. "Good night, Auntie." She paused at the foot of the stairs. "Thank you for everything."

The train journey to Ranchester was a tedious business, including two changes and a wait of forty minutes at a junction. Judy arrived soon after one o'clock and went into a Lyons café in the High Street for a cup of coffee and a scone before she asked her way to Friar's Row. The coming interview with Daisy's mother was sure to be unpleasant, and any offer of hospitality would be grudgingly made. In the Ladies' Room she applied more powder than usual out of sheer nervousness, and altered the rakish tilt of her beret. "She'll make me feel cheap. Oh hell!"

Friar's Passage was one of the ancient alley ways, too narrow for wheeled traffic, leading from the busy High Street to the peaceful seclusion of the Cathedral Close. Judy, walking down it, caught a glimpse of stone-paved walks and green grass and an avenue of magnificent elms leading to the west front. And then as she was beginning to look up at the names over the queer little bow-windowed shop fronts she trod on something soft, and glancing down saw that it was the broken off head of a large white chrysanthemum. She bent to pick it up, but the delicate petals were hopelessly crushed. She had reached her destination, but the shop was closed and the blinds drawn. Without giving herself time to think, she rang the side door bell. It was opened almost directly by an elderly woman whom she had never seen before, who said "You're just too late. They're gone."

Judy's heart seemed to miss a beat. She saw that the woman's eyes were red-rimmed. "Gone where?"

"To the cemetery. But perhaps you weren't going to the funeral. I see now you're not in black. If it's about wools the shop will be open as usual to-morrow."

She was closing the door when Judy exclaimed, "Oh, please— just a minute. Please tell me what's happened."

"Mrs. Benson has had the misfortune to lose her only daughter."

"Daisy!"

The woman was eyeing her curiously. "You knew her? I've not seen you here before though, have I? I've been in to oblige three days a week since Daisy was a little tot, and I thought I knew all her friends by sight."

"I am her sister-in-law."

The woman's face hardened. "One of that lot. You'd best be gone before Mrs. Benson comes back. You've brought enough disgrace on decent people as it is. Thieves and murderers—"

"I don't care what you say to me. You just don't understand. I've got to know what happened to Daisy."

"All right. You shall know then, and much good may it do you. We tried to keep the newspapers from her, but it was no use. She got that worked up thinking that good-for-nothing fellow had fallen off his trapeze and been killed that it seemed best to let her know the truth. Mrs. Benson talked to her and told her she'd always have a home here and that the best thing she could do was to forget him, but it was clear that she was still as silly as ever about him, and that very night, after crying and getting herself into a state, she was taken with her pains and had to be fetched off to the nursing home. She had a bad time and the child was born dead. She had to be told, and after that she didn't seem to try. She went off very quiet, poor dear, said the woman, blowing her nose and forgetting to be angry with Judy. "She was no more than a child herself. Nineteen. Easily frightened, easily hurt, not fit for this rough world. It's all for the best really. She couldn't have borne what she would have had to bear, being pointed out as the widow of a man that's been hanged for murder, and the baby, if it had lived, branded, as you might say, from its birth. And now"—she remembered Judy and who she was—"you be off!"

She closed the door, and this time the girl did not try to prevent her. A cold wind was blowing down the Passage bringing a few dead leaves. She noticed now that all the other shop blinds had been drawn as a mark of respect to the dead. The bruised chrysanthemum, broken off one of the wreaths as they were carried out, lay where she had dropped it. She stared at it for a moment vacantly before she turned away. In a week. Her shocked mind functioned stiffly and in jerks. A week. Less than a week. The young policeman of whom she asked the shortest way to the station looked at her sharply. "Aren't you feeling well, Miss? You look, if I may say so—"

"I'm all right."

CHAPTER VI
REX V. MERLE

Two Sundays later Mrs. Sturmer, going to the side door to take in the milk, was confronted by a rather stout and swarthy young man in the kit of a motor cyclist, who, before she could ask him what he wanted said earnestly. "I believe you are Auntie Apples. How is she?" He picked up the bottle of milk and proffered it. "This must be an honest neighbourhood if this has been here since the early morning."

"I'm not going to apologise to you for getting up late. Who are you, anyway?" Mrs. Sturmer demanded, recovering rapidly from this unexpected frontal attack.

"I'm Ben Levy." His face fell a little as hers remained blank. "Hasn't Judy mentioned me at all? I haven't been able to get over before. We've had half the staff at the Palace down with 'flu and all the odd jobs get piled on me. This is my first free day since— you know—" He did not add that he had turned down a pressing invitation from his rich Aunty Becky to go down to Brighton and lunch with her at the Metropole. "How is she?"

By now Mrs. Sturmer had placed him. "I know now." She beamed at him. "Silly of me. Judy told me how kind you were. Come in, if you don't mind the kitchen. I've got a fire there. She's been very ill, poor child. 'Flu on the top of worry and shock. But she's better. I'm getting her downstairs for an hour or two this afternoon. I can't ask you to stay now, but if you'll go off and get yourself a spot of lunch at one of the hotels and come back here between two and three I'm sure Judy will be pleased to see you. I'll have a good fire in the sitting-room and you'll stay to tea, I hope."

"Thanks, I'd like to." He set a large brown paper parcel he had been carrying under his arm down on the kitchen table. "Just a few chocs. I say, Mrs. Sturmer, do I keep off the subject of the trial or not?"

"You've met my nephew, David?"

"They were in the bill at the Palace, you know. I hadn't known them before, but I liked what I saw of them, all but"—he stopped abruptly—"I was going to say all but Reuben's wife," he added. "I get very tired of these synthetic blondes, Mrs. Sturmer, too lazy to learn their job and relying on sex appeal to put it across. Judy and her brothers are first class acrobats and in my opinion she let their show down."

"I gathered as much," said Auntie Apples grimly. "I never met the young woman and I'm not likely to now. Reuben writes that they've signed on with Lambournes troupe of flying marvels for a South American tour. They can't leave until after the trial as they are both being called as witnesses for the prosecution, but they'll be sailing as soon as they can after."

"Is Judy going too?"

"Not she. Judy's not so good at thinking of number one. She's made no plans for the future. I hope she'll live with me."

"Mrs. Sturmer"—Levy's intelligent dark eyes searched her face—"has a good man been briefed to defend him? Has he a chance?"

"We've got Sir Nigel Hood. They say he's very persuasive. Judy thinks the whole thing was a frame up."

"Merle says he was walking about the streets."

She shook her head. "No. No, he's gone back on that. He says he lied at first because he didn't think the truth would be believed. That's not going to help him to begin with. Mr. Peel engaged a private detective to make enquiries, hoping for some corroboration of his story, but that's been a washout. Well, I mustn't spend my time talking now. I've got to steam a bit of fish for my invalid's lunch."

When he had gone she went up to Judy's room, to find the girl sitting up in bed. "Who was that? I heard voices."

"An admirer of yours. Mr. Levy. He's brought an enormous box of chocolates tied with pink satin ribbon. So get up and dress. He's coming back between two and three and I promised to have you on view."

A little colour crept into Judy's white cheeks. "He's rather a dear, isn't he."

She was comfortably established by the sitting-room fire when Levy arrived, as soon as he decently could after struggling through the unattractive table d'hote lunch in the dreary dining-room of Cottingham's leading Family and Commercial Hotel. He squeezed her hand hard and made a valiant effort to conceal his dismay at the sight of her.

"Do I look awful?"

"You've been ill your aunt tells me. You'll be better soon."

"I am better. I've got to be for the trial. But I can't sleep while this is hanging over us. Did auntie tell you about Daisy—his wife?"

"No."

"I went over to Ranchester to see her. She was staying with her mother. The blinds were all drawn. The baby—they were both dead. I don't know how I got back here. I can't remember that train journey at all. It was a sort of nightmare. I've been ill since. Auntie wrote to Mr. Peel, and he had to break it to David. Mr. Peel said he took it very quietly. He doesn't speak much or look at people. Mr. Peel says his eyes seem to be fixed on something far away. He wanted to know if he's ever had fits. It seems epileptics sometimes do things and don't know they've done them." She smiled faintly. "Catching at straws, you see."

"And had he? Fits, I mean—"

"Certainly not," said Mrs. Sturmer firmly. "You may as well tell Mr. Levy what David told us, Judy." She left them together while she went to prepare the tea. Mr. Levy wasn't much to look at, but there was something likeable about him, and Mrs. Sturmer was touched by the dog-like devotion with which he sat gazing at her niece.

When she came back presently with the tea tray and a mound of buttered toast he jumped up at once to help her. Nice manners, she thought. There's something about Jews, the best of them. They're civilized. And they say they make very good husbands.

"I hope you're hungry, Mr. Levy, and going to set Judy a good example. She's got to eat to get her strength back. These are potted meat sandwiches. Oh dear—I'm sorry—I'm afraid it's chicken and ham."

Ben Levy grinned. "That's all right. I don't bother much about that sort of thing. Haven't been inside a synagogue for years. My people are my people. But I think creeds are much of a muchness, and I stay outside." He changed the subject.

"Will you be coming over to Holton with Judy while the trial's on, Mrs. Sturmer?"

"Yes."

"I'm glad," he said. "She ought not to be alone. I've found some quiet rooms, not too far from the Town Hall. I'll give you the address. She'll charge you two guineas a week for a double bedroom and a sitting-room, with attendance." He did not tell them how difficult it had been to find a landlady willing to take in any relatives of David Merle, or that the price demanded was five guineas of which he had arranged to pay three. He had been startled by the fixed determination of most of the townspeople whom he met to regard Merle's guilt as already fully proved. And yet he could hardly blame them. The evidence against Merle produced at the police court was overwhelmingly strong. He looked forward with dread to probably hostile demonstrations while the trial was on, chiefly, of course, for the effect they might have on Judy. He did not doubt her courage. One had only to look at that small resolute face to know that if that frail barque foundered it would be with flying colours. No use talking about it, he thought, and so, though he stayed some time longer, he avoided all further reference to David, and talked instead of his experiences as a stage manager with a repertory company and at the Palace. "You've got to have the patience of a Job, and the tact of—who had the most tact?" he concluded when he had made them both laugh more than once over his misadventures. "The two words I hate most in the English language are temperament and publicity. Gosh, how I hate them and all they stand for! You know how it is, Judy, in the profession. Steeped in the one and grabbing the other. I say, I haven't tired you? Got to buzz off now. God bless you."

Mrs. Sturmer went with him to the door. He took the opportunity to warn her. "There's a lot of feeling against David in Holton. You—you've got to brace yourself to face that."

She nodded. "A defenceless old man brutally murdered. If I thought David had done it—"

"Judy told me his story. Are the defence relying on that?"

"They've got to. He's not an epileptic. I wouldn't stand for that. David at Broadmoor. He would be better dead."

"If it was a frame up it was damnably clever. The man who engineered it would have had to have known old Fallowes and his habits and to have been pretty good at make up. Just imagine, Mrs. Sturmer, him playing the host at that supper table, tricking poor David into handling the silver and leaving his finger-prints, while all the while the body of his victim lay upstairs. But what was his motive? The notes were found in David's coat pocket, and nothing else was taken. Was the whole thing deliberately planned to ruin David, or was he only brought into it by chance?"

Mrs. Sturmer sighed. "As a story it isn't convincing. You don't have to tell me that. Thank you for coming and for finding those rooms for us, Mr. Levy. You've cheered us up."

The first two days of the Assizes were taken up with cases of minor importance, a charge of manslaughter arising out of a road accident, a case of arson, and two burglaries. On the morning of the third day a queue was waiting for admittance hours before the doors were opened. The court room was crowded. "To capacity, my boy," Larry, the trick cyclist told Levy when he came down to the theatre that evening. Levy's duties as assistant manager had prevented him from being present, but most of the artistes who were performing at the Palace that week had contrived to get in. The case for the Crown had been opened by Stuart Robbins. Levy, sitting in his stuffy little office, read the report of his speech in the Argus. After describing the finding of the body by the charwoman and the clues that had led to the arrest of David Merle he had outlined the theory of the prosecution.

"Mr. Fallowes, who took a benevolent interest in the theatrical profession—he was a generous subscriber to many theatrical charities—usually went to the first house at the Palace on Monday evenings, always occupying the same stall in the second row. It cannot be said that he was on familiar terms with the staff. They knew him by sight and they knew his habit of sometimes inviting one of the performers to supper at his house. I should like to say at this point that the deceased was a man of unblemished reputation. He was eccentric, something of a recluse, but as a host he was above criticism. We shall call two music-hall artistes who, at different times, accepted invitations to supper with him. Inspector Lott will tell you that on finding evidence that he had entertained a guest to supper on the night of his death he had made enquiries concerning the movements of the vaudeville performers whose names he found on that week's bill at the Palace. All were able to give a satisfactory account of themselves—with one exception. David Merle was still in bed when the police visited him at his lodgings. His brother will be called to prove that he had been out the previous night until past one o'clock. He said he had been walking about the streets. A pair of rubber-soled canvas shoes were found under his bed. They were damp and muddy and stained with blood. Later, when he had been taken to the police station pending further enquiries, a manila envelope containing a bundle of nineteen one pound notes was found in his coat pocket. Moreover, Merle's finger-prints were found on a silver cup in the dining-room and on a wineglass."

After the lunch interval the long procession of witnesses for the Crown had begun. The police evidence, the medical evidence, the evidence of the prisoner's brother, Reuben, all the more damning because it was given with such evident reluctance.

"Was he worried about money matters?

"Well, he—"

"Don't beat about the bush. Yes, or no?"

"He was a bit."

"How was that?"

"We'd been out of a shop for several weeks after the end of our tour with Weston's circus. He hadn't anything put by—and his wife was ill. But—"

"That will do, thank you, Merle. You may stand down. I call Mrs. Benson."

Daisy's mother, neat and ladylike in her new mourning, stepped into the witness box.

"Do you know the accused?"

Her eyes were like flints as she glanced towards the dock.

"Yes. He persuaded my daughter to run away with him. She was only a child. I fetched her back and they were properly married from my house. I never saw him after that. He would not have been welcome, but I was always ready to receive her whenever she cared to come."

"She has been staying with you lately?"

"She was in bad health as a result of the hardships she had been made to undergo. She was expecting a child."

"Did you write to the prisoner for money?"

"Certainly. It was his duty to maintain her."

"You were pressing him to make her a larger weekly allowance?"

"Yes. There were doctor's and chemist's bills, and I had arranged for her to go to a nursing-home. The fees there were to be eight guineas a week."

"The Flying Merles troupe were getting twenty pounds a week. Five pounds a week each, and they had to keep themselves out of that. Forgive me, Mrs. Benson, but weren't you driving him rather hard?"

"He should not have married my daughter if he could not afford to keep her. I consider him guilty of her death. She didn't survive the disgrace of his arrest."

"Please, Mrs. Benson, you must confine yourself to answering the questions that are put to you."

There had been a murmur in the Court following the witness's outburst. "It was so beastly cruel." Larry told Levy.

But the prisoner had not flinched. He hardly seemed to be listening. He had stood quietly throughout with his hands gripping the rail.

The Counsel for the Crown, a little flushed and uneasy, concluded his examination of Mrs. Benson. "Does my learned friend desire to cross-examine this witness?"

Sir Nigel Hood shook his head. "No, thank you. This lady's evidence is entirely irrelevant."

The experts followed, an authority on finger-prints and the Bertillon system from Scotland Yard, the cashier from the bank who had cashed a cheque for twenty pounds for Mr. Fallowes three days before his death. The short winter day had drawn to its close. The atmosphere of the crowded Court was stifling. The actors in the drama looked haggard and weary. There was a general sigh of relief when the judge laid down his pen.

"Is that your case, Mr. Robbins?"

"That, my Lord, is my case."

"Then we will adjourn."

The Court rose. The jury, nine men and three women, got up stiffly and filed out of their box. The packed crowd in the body of the Court was in motion, streaming out of the opened doors to find their parked cars, to catch a bus, to wait for the public-houses to open. A warder touched the prisoner on the arm. He turned obediently.

The next morning Sir Nigel Hood opened for the defence.

After reading through his brief he had shrugged his shoulders.

"What do you expect me to do?" He liked difficulties, but he felt himself faced with an impossibility. To begin with he had to make a damaging admission.

"My Lord, members of the jury, my client is, as you can see for yourselves, a very young man, little more than a boy. He found himself in a very dangerous position, with no time to think, with no one to help or advise him. He made a mistake. It was not, I hope and believe, a fatal mistake, because you who are older and wiser will understand and make allowances for the state of panic he was in when he lied to the police. He will go into the witness-box presently and tell you in his own words what happened to him on that fatal night. But first, for a reason that will presently become apparent to you, I shall call Charles Higgs. I shall not weary you with dissertations at this stage. The facts will speak for themselves. Charles Higgs."

The witness, a youngish man, stepped into the box and took the oath.

"You are a house painter employed by a local firm of decorators, Messrs. Ainsworth and Strutt?"

"That's right."

"Two years ago you had the job of painting the exterior woodwork and pipes at the Laurels, the residence of the late Mr. Fallowes?"

"Yes, sir."

"Here is an architectural drawing, done to scale, of the front of the house. Does that refresh your memory?"

"I remember the place very well, sir."

"You are an active man?"

"Have to be in my job."

"Exactly. This window, marked on the plan with a cross, is twenty feet from the ground."

"All of that, sir. It's nasty because there's one of them basement areas leading to the cellars that you'd fall into if you slipped."

"If I offered you twenty pounds to get out of the house by that window would you accept it?"

"Well, twenty quid is a nice lot of money, sir, but I'd rather not. It would mean following a ledge to the next window to reach the waste pipe from the roof, and there's a gap and nothing much to hold on to."

"Thank you. That is all I have to ask you. I shall now call my client, David Merle."

The Court was very silent as David left the dock and entered the witness-box. He looked round as he gave the Bible back to the usher and saw Judy and Mrs. Sturmer sitting beside Mr. Peel. He told the story they had already heard in almost the same words. Judy, looking from the lean, wrinkled face of the judge, listening with grave attention to poor David's stumbling narrative, to those of the jury, was trying to will them to believe. "You must. You must. He's not a liar. It's the truth."

Now and then Sir Nigel asked a question.

"This person whom you assumed to be Mr. Fallowes—how did he strike you? Had he easy pleasant manners?"

"He was—sort of effusive, praising our act and all that. But he seemed very jumpy. I've seen actors like it on a first night or when there's been trouble in front and they've got to go on."

"Was there anything strikingly odd in his appearance?"

"I thought it queer he should keep his gloves on, but the house was very cold. The dining-room fire was out. He kept his hat on too, and his overcoat and muffler. He said he felt chilly."

Later Sir Nigel put another question. "One moment, Merle. I suppose that your worst moment was when you tried the bedroom door and found that you were locked in?"

"Yes. I still dream of it at night. It was horrible."

"You realised then that you had been trapped?"

"Yes. I knew I had to get away quick. I went out of the window."

"You are an acrobat, so that would be easy?"

"Easier for me than some people, but it was risky. I took a big chance. It was very dark. I felt my way along the ledge and slid down the pipe and dropped among some bushes. If I'd slipped when I first got out on the sill I'd have broken my back on the area steps."

"You wandered about for some time before returning to your lodgings?"

"Yes. I didn't know what I ought to do. What happened in that house was like a nightmare. It didn't make sense. When I got in I was dead to the world. I slept like a log. I hadn't been awake three minutes when the police came. I knew it looked bad for me so I lied to them. I hoped—"

"About that parcel that was found in your coat pocket?"

"He gave it me. I thought it was tracts. I'd been told he always handed some out. I forgot all about them afterwards."

"One final question. Are you guilty of this crime of which you stand accused?"

"No. I am not."

Sir Nigel sat down and Mr. Robbins rose to cross-examine.

"You say that Mr. Fallowes asked you to go up to his room to open a window that had got stuck?"

"Yes."

"I put it to you that you told him a hard luck story and that he went upstairs to get some money to give you, and that you followed, and seeing the safe open, struck him down with the stone you had taken off the rockery as you came up the drive."

"No, sir. It all happened as I have said. The light wouldn't go on in the bedroom. I never saw the safe."

"So that the murder was committed before you arrived on the scene by a mysterious unknown made up to look like the victim, who has since vanished into thin air?"

"I have told you the truth."

"Why did you make a statement to the police that was false from beginning to end?"

"It wasn't. I did walk about after leaving the house."

"I will accept that, Merle. Shall we call it a rather subtle mixture of truth and falsehood. But you are on oath now, you know. Was it that you needed time to invent a story that would cover the facts that could be proved by the police?"

"I didn't tell them the truth because I was afraid they wouldn't believe it. I could see how queer it sounded."

"Where did you find the suitcase you were going to use to carry away the silver?"

"I don't know anything about that. I picked up the cup to guess the weight because he asked me to. It was all on the sideboard when we went upstairs."

Judy whispered to Mr. Peel. "Why does he keep badgering him?"

"That's his job. But don't worry. He's standing up to it very well."

And, in fact, David in the witness-box had made a good impression, and when he left it to return to the dock it seemed that the tide might be turning in his favour. Sir Nigel, in his speech for the defence, dwelt on the fact that David had risked his neck getting out by the window when if he was alone in the house as the prosecution suggested, there was nothing to prevent him from going out by the door. That the bedroom door was unlocked and the light functioning when the charwoman went up to rouse her employer the next morning did not disprove his story. The stage had been re-set after his departure. His major mistake had been that he had not gone directly to the police. The delay had given the actual criminal ample time to cover his tracks and get away.

He had been shocked, frightened out of his wits, by his discovery of the body lying on the bed in that room. That fact, combined with his youth and lack of experience accounted for his foolish conduct both before and after his arrest.

Mr. Robbins' speech for the Crown was unusually direct.

"You have heard the prisoner," he said. "I think you will agree with me that up to a point he was telling the truth, and that he only began to diverge from it when Mr. Fallowes went upstairs. You have heard his version. I suggest to you that what actually happened was substantially as follows. Mr. Fallowes, a kind-hearted and charitable old gentleman, was touched by Merle's story of his financial difficulties, the sick wife and the grasping mother-in-law—these difficulties are not denied by the other side—'Wait here a moment,' he said, and went upstairs to get some money out of his safe. But Merle did not wait, yielding to temptation he crept up after him, noiseless in his rubber-soled shoes. He may not have meant to kill him but the idea of robbery and of possible violence had presented itself some time earlier or he would not have picked up a stone from the rockery as they came up the drive. It had been easy, no doubt, to drop behind, unnoticed by his unsuspecting host—"

"No!" cried David from the dock.

The judge looked at him sternly. "Be silent. You cannot speak now."

David said no more. He stood with bowed head, gripping the rail in front of him.

Mr. Robbins resumed, ignoring the prisoner's outburst. "The blow was struck. The assailant took possession of the envelope stuffed with notes. Nineteen pounds. Not a large sum, but murders have been committed for less than that. He then went downstairs again, found a suitcase in the cupboard under the stairs and was beginning to pack the silver when something alarmed him. We shall never know exactly what it was, but it may have seemed to him that somebody was moving about on the ground floor. The cat was found the next morning shut up in the pantry. The noise made by the cat jumping down from the pantry shelf might have sufficed to startle him. He fled upstairs to lurk and listen, and perhaps heard other sounds—the cat again, but to his guilty conscience it might seem that an entry was being made somewhere below. Rather than go down again he got out by the window. That, I think, was the course of events. You may, of course, accept the prisoner's version. You may be able to believe in the existence of a mysterious killer whose motive was not robbery and who, for some unimaginable reason, instead of making his escape after committing the crime, took the fearful risk of bringing a stranger into the house, having previously made himself up to look like his victim. If it were not for the tragic issues at stake one could almost smile at what under other circumstances could only be described as tomfoolery. My Lord, members of the jury, I do not ask for a verdict in any vindictive spirit. The prisoner, as my learned friend has pointed out, is very young. But we must not allow sentiment to blind us to the fact that a harmless and kindly old man has been brutally done to death under circumstances that indicate a certain amount of deliberation, and that the law exacts a penalty for such an act."

He sat down.

The judge summed up dead against the prisoner.

"I'm relying on the women in the jury," whispered Mrs. Sturmer to her niece. "Women have more sense—"

But the jury were only absent for thirty-five minutes, and their verdict was "Guilty." Afterwards it was rumoured that two women had wanted to recommend the prisoner to mercy on account of his youth, but they had been over-ruled.

CHAPTER VII

THE BROTHERHOOD OF THE ROSE

BEN Levy had sold his motor-cycle and bought a second-hand Austin Seven and he had arranged to run Mrs. Sturmer and her niece home in it. He was standing by while Mr. Peel shook hands with them both.

"We shall appeal, of course," the lawyer said, but his tone lacked conviction, and he avoided meeting Judy's eyes.

Nobody looked her straight in the face now, she had noticed that. None of her friends, that is. The others, the complete strangers who had stood in queues in the rain and pushed and fought to get into the Town Hall, nudged each other as two burly policemen made way for her and her aunt, and stared hard. "That's his sister."

Mr. Peel was kind, and so was Ben—but they didn't really believe in David's innocence. The defence had failed utterly, and the verdict had been a foregone conclusion. She realised that now. Ben did not talk to her about the case, and she was grateful to him for that. He tucked the rug over her knees and hoped she was warm enough, and then gave all his attention to his driving until they were nearing their destination. His heart ached for her, but he said cheerfully, "Runs sweetly, doesn't she? Fourth hand as a matter of fact. She only cost me twenty-two pounds, but breeding tells, eh? May I take you a run sometimes on Sundays, Judy?"

"Thanks, I'd love to."

He glanced down at her small, set face and suppressed a sigh. He felt sure that she had not heard a word he was saying. When they arrived Mrs. Sturmer gave her the latch key. "Open the door and turn on the lights, dear." Ben had come round to help her out. "You'll take good care of her, Mrs. Sturmer," he said huskily.

"She's my niece, isn't she? You must give her time, Ben. This has been a knock-out blow for her—and for me," she added half to herself.

"I understand." He carried their suitcases into the house for them, shook hands, and went back to his car.

"Young Levy's a good sort," said Mrs. Sturmer heartily.

"Yes." Judith's lips were trembling. "Do you mind if I go to bed now, Auntie?"

"Of course not." Mrs. Sturmer offered her universal panacea. "I'll bring you up a nice hot bottle."

The *Sunday Trumpeter*, though its series of articles on the Flying Merles were written in a style that made Judy flinch more than once, had respected her wish to keep her present address a secret. To her surprise and bewilderment she had received a large number of letters, addressed to the office of the paper and sent on to her under cover of her aunt's name. She read them all; some she could not help smiling over, and some she tore up quickly and threw into the fire. There had been seven offers of marriage, but the majority were requests for her autograph. The more optimistic went farther and asked for a signed photograph "Like the one in last week's *Trumpeter*."

Auntie Apples advised her not to answer any of them, but she encouraged her to read them. Anything was better for her, she thought, than sitting brooding.

Most of them came by the last post, while they were at tea in the little firelit room behind the shop, and generally the door bell rang more than once, and Mrs. Sturmer had to jump and go to attend to a customer. It was the time when the girls going home from the factory were apt to drop in to find out if Auntie Apples had any more dance frocks in stock. It was the second evening after their return from Holton that she sold the green and silver brocade.

"It's a lovely material, and it fits you as if it had been made for you, and the lady—a lady of title, but I don't name names—only wore it the once. She spilt a little coffee on it, see. It doesn't show a bit."

"How much?"

This customer, a barmaid at the King's Head, was always flush of money.

"Three guineas," said Mrs. Sturmer firmly.

"Cripes!"

"It cost ninety."

"It's too much." But she looked longingly at her reflection in the long glass fixed to the door of the tiny fitting-room. "All right."

"I've sold the green and silver," said Mrs. Sturmer five minutes later. "This tea's gone stone cold. Never mind, I'll have a cigarette."

Judy looked up with more interest than she had shown for some time. "Have you? Splendid. Auntie, this letter—I'd like to read it to you."

"Who is it from?"

"I don't know. He signs himself C. Fleming. He seems to think I'll read it."

> "The Haven,
> "Myrtle Road,
> "Quinton Park, N.

"DEAR MISS MERLE,

"I have been wanting to write to you to say I'm quite sure your brother wasn't guilty of that murder. I think the jury were asses. There's still time to save him, and the way to do that is to find the person who really did it and get hold of some proofs. I know that isn't as easy as all that, but I've got an idea that doesn't seem to have struck the defence—anyway it didn't come out in the trial. I can't explain properly in a letter, but I think it would be worth your while to consider it. I am engaged through the week, but I get Saturday afternoon off, and I could meet you next Saturday at three in the lion house at the Zoo. If it's no good you'll be no worse off than before, but I do so want to help.

> "Yours sincerely,
> "C. FLEMING.

"P.S. Last August at Seaton I went to the circus, and I caught the rose you threw. It fell to pieces, but I've got the stalk."

"Dear me," said Auntie Apples. "He evidently fell for you, my dear. He kept the stalk." She took the letter from her niece and looked through it. "He sounds very young," she said doubtfully. "I don't think you'd be wise to take this too seriously, Judy."

"I'd like to hear what he has to say, Auntie."

"Very well, you shall. As he says himself, it can't do any harm, though I must say the lion house seems a queer place to meet in. You can run up on Saturday by the day excursion."

"I'm not being much good to you in the shop."

"Never mind that at present," said Mrs. Sturmer. She had seen that the girl would not be able to settle down to any regular work while David's fate still hung in the balance. The trial was over, but an appeal was to be lodged, and until that had been heard Judy could go on hoping.

"Don't depend too much on this man's ideas," Mrs. Sturmer warned her niece again just before she started for the station on Saturday morning.

Judy had replied to Mr. Fleming's letter agreeing to meet him at the appointed time and place. "Be on your guard with him. After all, if there is anything at the back of this case, if David fell into a trap, this may be another one."

"All the more reason why I should go. Poor David was unprepared. I'm not. But I believe the poor man's quite harmless." For the first time for days Judy's small face crinkled into a grin.

"If he'd chosen the Mappin Terraces he might have pushed me into the bear pits, but he can't do much to me in the lion house."

She reached Regent's Park a few minutes before three. It was raining and the gardens were almost empty of visitors.

The seals were splashing about happily in their pond, but the sun-loving animals had withdrawn to the shelter of their dens. In the lion house the great dun beasts behind the bars gazed past her, royally indifferent, as she walked slowly by their cages. A few people had come in for shelter from the rain, but there was nobody who looked at all like her correspondent. Judith's heart sank. Had someone played a cruel practical joke on her?

A small boy wearing a faded blue raincoat over his grey flannel suit approached her diffidently.

"I say—I think you must be—are you looking for someone?"

"Yes, I am. Have you brought a message?"

His round, freckled face was red with embarrassment.

"No. I mean—I'm C. Fleming. C for Christopher, but I'm always called Toby."

"Oh!"

She was bitterly disappointed, but she made a valiant effort to hide her feelings since he was evidently very much in earnest.

"It was kind of you to write to me," she said gently.

"I expect you thought I was grown up," he remarked. "I was jolly careful with the spelling and everything. I'm thirteen, as a matter of fact, but I'm interested in crime, and I've had a bit of experience, more than you'd think. It wasn't very nice, and I'd rather not talk about it. Mother hopes I'll forget it, but it isn't so easy to forget things to order. I'll just say this—I found a body but it ended all right for us because it led to our meeting Hugh, and now he's my stepfather, and a darned good one." He paused for breath and Judy said, "I see."

She started as the lion in the nearest cage suddenly emitted a heart-shaking roar. Toby grinned. "It's near their feeding time. I often come here Saturday afternoons, but we might find a quieter place to talk."

"The restaurant opposite the Mappin Terraces," she suggested.

Toby beamed. "Good egg." He had got over his initial shyness and was quite at his ease, and Judy, though she no longer hoped for any real help from him, was as touched and pleased by his confident friendliness as she would have been by the advances of a stray puppy.

"I wish my stepfather had been called in on this case," he said, when they had chosen their table and Judy had ordered tea. "He's a detective-inspector at Scotland Yard, in the C.I.D., and he's jolly good. Local bobbies are no use," said Toby scornfully.

Judy pricked up her ears. "Has he talked about the case to you?"

"No. He's been away in the States since the end of October doing some work for the Yard, but he'll be home any time now. This thing I want to talk to you about is my own idea—mostly, I mean, though I won't say Fatty Dyson hasn't had a hand in it. In fact," said Toby, with a burst of generosity, "he's been jolly useful."

Judy, who was one of those people who enjoy the society of small boys, smiled at him encouragingly. "And who is Fatty Dyson?"

"He's just a friend of mine, but I don't see much of him because he lives the other side of London and his people are very swanky. I told you I saw the circus at Seaton in August? Well he was at Sidmouth with his crowd, and he went to the show there, and he wrote and told me it was great, and about your act, and when you threw the rose there he caught it. Wasn't that a coincidence? So I wrote and told him I'd got one too, and we sort of formed a brotherhood of the Rose like in *Westward Ho*, but of course there were only two of us. And then, when this happened we got all het up, naturally, but it wasn't until last week, when the trial was in the papers, that I really knew what the defence was. About that mystery man—what do you think yourself, Miss Merle?"

"Call me Judy."

"Judy, then?"

"Are you asking me if I believe my brother's story?"

"Of course not," said Toby, with a vigour that warmed her heart. "We don't have to argue about that. The question is not whether, but why?" He stopped to grin. "That's rather good, isn't it? Not whether but why? Your brother was a red herring dragged across the path to take the police off the scent of the real murderer. If this had happened in a book, Judy, the real murderer would be one of those sinister Orientals come to avenge the theft of a ruby taken from the eye of the idol." He paused to help himself to another lump of sugar. "What a lark if it was that really," he said, with a slight lapse from his grown-up manner. "We ought to find out if Mr. Fallowes travelled in the East when he was a young man."

"I don't think that sort of thing happens in real life," said Judy.

"Make no mistake," said Toby largely. He was quoting his Form master, but Judy was not to know that. "Everything happens. But I've got a much better idea than that. Wills."

"Wills?" echoed Judy vaguely. "I'm afraid I don't—"

Toby took an ample mouthful of éclair. "Wait a sec," he mumbled. "The cream's running out of this."

Judy waited until the éclair had been liquidated. Toby's ideas might be absurd but his complete faith in David's innocence was very cheering, and she was quite prepared to listen to anything more he might have to say.

"This Mr. Fallowes was rich, wasn't he?"

"I suppose so."

"He certainly was. He left over ninety thousand pounds."

Judy looked curiously at her young companion. "How do you know?"

"I'd heard my stepfather say you can see wills by paying a shilling at Somerset House. I rang up Fatty Dyson and he persuaded their chauffeur to look up Mr. Fallowes'. The chauffeur collects stamps and Fatty gave him some of his good Chinese ones. That's why I say Fatty's really been a help."

Judy had turned rather white. It seemed to her that there really might be something in this. "What were the terms of the will?"

"I've got it written down," said Toby, producing a very crumpled envelope. "It all goes to his great nephew, Oliver Ramblett, but if Oliver dies before attaining his majority it is to be divided equally among his three great nieces."

"Ramblett? I know that name," she said pondering.

"That's why I asked you to meet me here, said Toby. "Remembering one thing by another. Hugh explained that to me. Association of ideas. I didn't know, but Fatty was on to it at once because he's been there, though it was ages ago. Ramblett's Wild Life Sanctuary. He says it's really a kind of private zoo, rather like the one at Maidstone, but smaller and not so well run."

Judy nodded. "I know. They bought a leopard from Weston's after it got out and killed one of the Shetland ponies. But this may not be the same family."

"It is though. The address was given in the will. My great nephew Oliver Ramblett, of Sard Manor, Somerset."

Judy was silent for a moment. Then she said,

"I don't see how this is going to help us."

"Don't you? Oliver's the chap who gains by his uncle's death. Ninety thousand pounds, though I suppose the Government grabs some of it. And Fatty says the zoo didn't look as if it was paying its way when he went there two years ago. Sort of neglected, and half the cages empty."

"I wonder how old he is. He evidently wasn't of age when the will was made, but that may have been a long time ago. Did your friend's chauffeur make a note of the date?"

"I don't think so. I haven't got it down. Enquiries ought to be made on the spot, but Fatty and I couldn't do any more. You see, we're both at school unfortunately, and I'm afraid I ought to be buzzing off pretty soon," added Toby reluctantly. "I promised mother I'd be in by five. I've got a beastly lot of prep. to do."

"Then I won't keep you," said Judy. "I'm most awfully grateful to you both for taking all this trouble for me."

"That's all right," he assured her, "but it's all going to be wasted if you don't carry on. You will, won't you?"

"I shall have to think it over."

Toby had heard this phrase from adults before, and it usually meant that nothing would be done. "Don't dilly dally," he said bluntly. "There isn't much time."

"My God!" she said violently. "You needn't remind me."

"I'm sorry," mumbled Toby, experiencing the sensations of a skater who has just heard the ice crack under him. Like most boys of his age he revelled in excitement, but strong emotion made him desperately uncomfortable. His ears began to burn, and he did not know where to look. But Judy had been quick to recover herself. She signed to the waitress to bring the bill and fumbled in her purse for twopence to put under her plate.

"I've got to go too, to catch a train," she said in her most matter of fact voice. "I've got your address. I'll write and let you know what I'm doing. And I do thank you, Toby, from the bottom of my heart. Shall I send you a signed photograph? Would you care for that?"

They walked through the Gardens together and parted at the entrance. In the train on her way home Judy thought over that odd interview. Later, in the little sitting-room behind the shop she described it to Mrs. Sturmer.

"What do you think, Auntie?"

Toby's theories were not so convincing at second hand. Mrs. Sturmer shook her head. "My dear, I warned you not to take him seriously. I felt sure he was very young. What evidence is there that this Ramblett had anything to do with his uncle's death? He gains by it certainly, but at that rate we might suspect every rich man's heirs."

Her opposition had the effect of bringing Judy down on her young admirer's side. "He struck me as being very intelligent," she said; "of course he was trying very hard to be grand and grown up, poor sweet, but when he was just himself he was very sensible, I thought."

His mother had gone out to do some shopping and Toby was alone in the house doing his prep. on Monday evening when something rather heavy fell through the flap of the letter box. Toby, going into the hall, picked up the large envelope addressed to him and carried it up to his own room before he opened it. Judy had kept her promise. There she sat as he remembered her, laughing and carefree, on her trapeze. Gratefully yours, Judy Merle. And with the picture there was a half sheet of notepaper with a few words scrawled on it.

"I am going down to Somerset. Wish me luck. J.M."

"Cool," said Toby. He put the picture and the note away very carefully in the drawer where he kept his treasures before he went down again to finish his Latin exercise.

He, Toby Fleming, aged thirteen, had started that ball rolling. Or perhaps not a ball but a stone, one of those stones that, in the end, may bring an avalanche crashing down into a quiet valley.

Chapter VIII
SARD MANOR

THE new building estates on the outskirts of the town had been left behind when the bus stopped.

"This is where you get out, Miss," said the conductor, and pointed to a lane on the left. "Follow that for half a mile and you'll come to the entrance."

It was a long half mile, and Judy noticed that she did not pass any house on the way, but she had been prepared for that.

The plan by which she hoped to gain admittance to Sard Manor was very simple. It depended for its success on the shortage of servants willing to accept situations in remote country houses. On reaching Bedesford, the nearest town, she had asked her way to a domestic agency, and presently was climbing a dark flight of stairs to a dingy office where the presiding deity, a thin, acid woman who had either been born a pessimist or had pessimism thrust upon her, had brightened a little when Judy described herself as a maid seeking a place.

"Would you be prepared to live in?"

"Yes."

"Dear me. That's unusual nowadays. Can you wait at table?"

"Well I'm more of a house than a parlour maid," said Judy, "but I'm willing to learn."

"That's unusual too—if you really mean it."

"And I don't mind being out of the town." Judy took a chance. "I did hear they were wanting somebody at Sard Manor."

"Who told you that, I wonder? But it's true. Mrs. Ramblett was in again only yesterday. Girls won't stay there. It's not a hard place, but it's dull, in winter especially. The last girl I sent there complained of the noise the animals make at night. They've got a private zoo, you know. It isn't everybody's cup of tea. Now there's the wife of the vicar of St. Jude wants a housemaid—"

"I wouldn't mind trying Sard Manor," said Judith. "I don't mind animals. In fact I'm fond of them."

"In that case I'll send you along. What about your references?"

"The lady I was with has gone to India, but she gave me a good reference. I've got it here," said Judy glibly, but with some inward qualms as she passed over the letter she had written herself the evening before.

"H'm. Yes," said the manageress of the Agency in a manner that indicated that she had known there would be a snag somewhere. She looked Judy up and down rather carefully before she went on. "It will be for Mrs. Ramblett to decide if she considers this sufficient." She wrote on a card "Give her this from me. The bus goes from the market square. They'll tell you where to get off."

Luck, thought Judy, as she trudged down the lane. Beginner's luck. She came at last to a five-barred gate with a board nailed on to it. Wild Life Sanctuary. Entrance one shilling. Car park free.

The gate was only latched, and she passed in and walked up an avenue bordered by a double row of limes and by a high fence of galvanised iron netting with a curved top. On the farther side, in a rough pasture field on the left, a pair of shaggy buffaloes were browsing. On the right, beyond some patches of undergrowth she caught a glimpse of a herd of small white Shetland ponies who were being boarded out there, no doubt, by some circus proprietor during the winter season.

The avenue sloped gently upward for another half mile and ended on the crest of the hill with a patch of level ground which was evidently used for a car park though no cars stood on it now. A gate on the left with a notice "Private" opened on a drive. On the right there was a wooden kiosk and a turnstile, both badly in need of a coat of fresh paint. The kiosk was closed. Beyond it a gravel path went on between unkempt laurels. A wooden shed blocked any more distant view. While Judy stood, hesitating, she heard something that might have been the howling of a dog, and she noticed a faint, musky smell.

Understaffed, she thought. She was turning towards the other gate when a rough-looking man wearing khaki leggings and a torn singlet emerged from the shed and shouted to her.

"Hi! What do you want?"

He came down the hill towards her and she waited for him.

"What are you doing here? Some of the animals are dangerous."

"They're all behind bars, aren't they?"

"It isn't open to visitors, only in the summer. We don't get enough this time of year to make it worth while, so you'd better go back the way you came," he said belligerently.

Judy withdrew a little as he leaned across the turnstile. His breath was definitely beery. She guessed that he had been asleep in the shed when he should have been working. A slacker, she thought contemptuously, and probably dishonest. He had a shifty eye.

"I've come for the place," she said crisply.

"The place?"

"Yes. They want a maid, don't they, up at the house?"

"Do they? I daresay. The other girl went. All right. Through that gate."

She was conscious that he stood watching her suspiciously until the turn of the drive, winding between high banks of ever-green shrubs, hid her from his sight.

She came to the house, a gaunt, barrack-like, four-storied building with a Doric portico. A few remaining leaves of a Virginia creeper covering one side wall were like splashes of blood on the grey stucco. The gravel sweep before the entrance was enclosed by a thick screen of trees and shrubs which had been allowed to grow, as Judy guessed, to ensure the privacy of the household during the summer when the zoo was open to visitors. In the wintry dusk the general effect was bleak and unfriendly and the girl's heart sank a little as she rang the bell and stood waiting.

The door was opened eventually by a woman no longer young, who had evidently once been very handsome. Her hair had been dyed a reddish brown and it hung in untidy elf locks about her face. Her lemon-coloured jumper and brown tweed skirt were dirty and her black rubber boots were crusted with mud.

"Sorry," she said, "I've been gardening. What did you want?"

"I've come about the place."

"Oh—come in, please. I am Mrs. Ramblett. Who sent you?"

She led the way into a shabby dining-room and bent to poke the dusty coal fire struggling to burn up in the old-fashioned grate.

Judy proffered the card that had been given her at the Domestic Agency and Mrs. Ramblett glanced at it without much interest. Her manner was weary and indifferent and the girl thought she looked ill. Her skin was very sallow under the carelessly applied rouge on her thin cheeks and her lips seemed parched.

"There's plenty of work in a house like this, but we don't have late dinner. You can have a couple of hours off every evening after six as well as the usual weekly half day. Of course we are out of the town, but if you have a bicycle and are not nervous—some girls don't like riding up the avenue after nightfall. It's very silly. The animals can't get out." She sat for a minute, staring at Judith with lack-lustre eyes as if she had forgotten what she had been going to say, before she resumed. "We are four in family. My stepson is an invalid and has his own suite of rooms at the top of the house. You wouldn't have to take up his meals or do anything for him. I attend to that. Then there is my daughter, Helen, and Mr. Bateman, my secretary and business manager. He sleeps in a bungalow in the grounds and comes in for his meals. We keep three maids, the cook, Mrs. Lacy, and her niece, Mattie." She paused again before adding, "Mattie is not quite—, but she's good for the rough work. You could have a pound a week."

"Yes, madam. I think the place would suit me. I would try to give satisfaction."

Mrs. Ramblett smiled for the first time with a curious bitterness.

"How unusual. I can only hope you mean it. When can you come?"

"I've been staying with an aunt while I was out," said Judy. "She'll take care of my luggage if I come for a month on trial. I'd just bring a few things."

"Very well. And when?"

"To-day if you like, ma'am. I can go back to the town to fetch my suitcase."

"Very good," said Mrs. Ramblett, yawning. "Do that. We've been without a housemaid for nearly a fortnight, and it's tiresome for my daughter, Helen. Go round to the back door next time. Mrs. Lacy will look after you and put you in the way of things. You can let yourself out."

The man Judy had seen before was still leaning over the turnstile when she came back to the avenue, but he was no longer in his shirt sleeves. He had put on a coat and was smoking a pipe. "Have you got the place?"

"Yes."

Well, there's no accounting for tastes," he said obscurely. "We'll be meeting again then. What'll I call you?"

Judy had decided on a change of name, so she was not taken unawares.

"Mary," she said. "Mary Morris."

"My name's Bowles. Mr. Bowles, the head keeper. If you go interfering with the animals you'll have me to deal with." He took his pipe from his mouth and grinned, showing discoloured snags of teeth.

Judy was fortunate in not having long to wait for a bus at the cross roads. She had left her suitcase at the station and she had come prepared for her adventure with two brown linen frocks and an adequate supply of muslin caps and aprons.

On her return journey she was the only passenger in the bus, and the conductor was inclined to be talkative.

"In service, and going to Sard Manor? Why, a sister of my wife's was there once, but she left after four days. What with the wolves howling and one thing and another it fair gave her the creeps. It don't pay, not the zoo, I mean, only for a few weeks in the height of summer, and it's all falling to rack and ruin, I've heard. The Rambletts are a good old family, mind you, but the old man lost most of his money and sold the farms, and after he died the son got the notion of turning the park into a zoo. And then—what do you think he did? He married the same woman twice.

"How did he manage that?"

"Easy. He divorced his first wife. Three girls he had by her. He married again, and the second wife died leaving one child, a boy, the one that's an invalid now, though my sister-in-law said he was strong enough when she was there. Then he re-married the first one, and not so long after that it was his turn to hop off the perch. She runs the show now with a chap called Bateman. Well, if you don't like it you can always come away, can't you?" He rang the bell to stop the bus. "Here you are."

The way seemed even longer now that she was burdened with a heavy suitcase, and she felt and looked hot and tired when she reached her destination. She had hoped that the cook would be stout and jolly but Mrs. Lacy was a wizened little woman with an anxious, hesitating manner, who greeted the newcomer in a sibilant whisper, while her niece, a clumsy girl with a large red face and the piggy, expressionless eyes of her type, said nothing but only stared.

Materially, however, the welcome was warm enough. A good fire blazed in the kitchen grate and the table was laid for tea with mounds of toast and hot cakes and jam, and Judy, for the first time for weeks, was really hungry.

After the meal Mrs. Lacy took her round the house. "Mattie does the washing up and preparing the vegetables and the cleaning of the kitchen and scullery. You have the upstairs rooms and laying the meals for them and clearing away. Mrs. Ramblett, and Miss Helen if she's in, have a cup of tea about four, and then there's a high tea, a kind of supper at half-past six, and nothing more after that. I'll come up with you to-night and show you where the china and silver's kept. There's a butler's pantry up there, where you'll wash the silver and the glass. Everything else comes down for Mattie to deal with."

There was a large hall on the ground floor, with two rooms on either side, those in front darkened by the thick screen of trees and shrubberies that shut the house and garden off from the park, while those at the back had a fine view across the valley. A baize-covered door shut this part of the house off from the servants' quarters in the left wing.

"On the first floor only three of the bedrooms are in use at present. Mrs. Ramblett in front, on the right of the landing, and Miss Helen on the left."

"And Mr. Bateman?"

Mrs. Lacy looked down her nose. "Mr. Bateman has his meals with the family, but he don't sleep on the premises. He has a bungalow in the gardens, though he did come in for a week or two last winter when the snow was on the ground. Now I'll show you your room. It's on the ground floor, but you needn't be nervous. Mattie and I are next door to you."

"Don't they use the top floor?"

"Not since Master Oliver has been ill. He's got to be kept very quiet. You've no call to go up there, Mary, and you're not supposed to. It's his nerves, and he can't bear to be looked at."

"Has he been like that long?"

"Some time now."

"How old is he?"

"Nineteen or twenty. Come along now. I've fish to fry for supper."

They went down again to the dining-room and Judy laid the table under Mrs. Lacy's supervision. At half past six she sounded the gong.

Mrs. Ramblett and her daughter arrived together. Helen Ramblett had inherited her mother's beauty. She was a big, dark girl with a skin like a ripe nectarine and brilliant dark eyes, but she looked very sulky and discontented. Mrs. Ramblett still wore her dirty tweed skirt, but she had draped an orange silk fringed shawl over her woollen jumper and exchanged her rubber boots for bedroom slippers of red felt very much trodden over and edged with mangy fur. She smiled at Judy. "So you really have come? Helen, we've actually got a housemaid. I've forgotten her name. So you can have a rest."

"Thank God!" said Helen, but without a smile. "You needn't wait. We look after ourselves. We'll ring if we want anything."

"Very well, Miss."

"What is your name?"

"Mary."

Mr. Bateman was coming into the dining-room as Judy went out. He was a middle-aged man with small, neat features. He was in evening dress with a dinner jacket and black tie, and his spick and span appearance contrasted very oddly with that of Mrs. Ramblett. She exclaimed at the sight of him petulantly. "Going out again, James?"

"To the Farwells to play bridge. Do you mind?"

"Of course not. Your evenings are your own. But I thought she was ill."

"She's better again, it seems."

"It's queer how often doctors' wives are sickly."

Judy closed the door very carefully and lingered a moment, but she could hear nothing now but a murmur of voices.

That night when she went to her room she sat for a while on the side of her bed thinking over every incident of a crowded day. She had succeeded, so far, beyond her expectations. This was the family that had everything to gain from the death of Mr. Fallowes. Evidently their connection with him was not known in the neighbourhood, or it would certainly have been mentioned as an item of interest, by the bus conductor who had told her so much of the local gossip. It was plain, by the state of the house and grounds and by their manner of living, that they needed the money badly. But they would not profit equally. Oliver Ramblett was the sole heir, unless, of course, he died before he reached his majority, in which case the money was divided among his half sisters. Judy thought of Helen, handsome, sullen, brooding over the fire as she had seen her when she went into the drawing-room to ask if there was anything more she could do. She had answered rudely, "Nothing," without turning her head. Three of them. That would be thirty thousand pounds each.

Yes, but lots of people talked and thought, more or less vaguely, of their expectations from their wealthy relatives, who would shrink, appalled, at the word murder. If David's story was true the murder of Mr. Fallowes had been carefully planned and carried out with devilish ingenuity. A cold-blooded crime. Judy shivered. She did not like this house. There was something queer about all the people she had met so far. Mrs. Ramblett with her ravaged beauty and her soft, well-bred voice and the dirt in her nails; her handsome, discontented daughter; the cook, with her furtive glances and her habit of dropping her voice to a whisper, and the silent, lumpish Mattie. Mr. Bateman—Judy had not placed him yet. In that slatternly household he had looked surprisingly clean and well groomed. He had given her a very sharp look as he passed her in the doorway. Mrs. Ramblett had described him as her secretary, but her manner to him had not been that of an employer.

Judy yawned. She was very tired and it was getting late. She took a letter pad and her fountain pen from her case. She had two people who would be expecting to hear from her, and there would be no time in the morning.

> "Sard Manor,
> "Nr. Bedesford.

"DEAR AUNTIE APPLE,

"I've got in here as housemaid. It was easy as pie. Servants are always leaving this sort of place. Miles from everywhere and one of those old-fashioned houses. I haven't heard anything said about them coming into money yet. The son is an invalid and has the rooms on the top floor. His meals are taken up by his stepmother, and I've been warned not to be snoopy. The cook says he hasn't always been that way. He's the one Mr. F. left his money to. I mean to have a peep at him by hook or by crook, but I've got to be careful. There may be nothing in it at all, but with David's life at stake I can't leave anything untried, and I don't feel quite so awful as I did when I was just sitting with my hands folded. Don't tell Ben Levy about this if he calls. Just say I've gone away to stay with friends. He's been so good to us, but I can't like him the way he wants. I'm sorry. When you answer this address me as Miss Mary Morris, and be careful what you say. I'll try and let you know how I'm getting on, but I shan't have much time for writing.

"God bless you. Your loving

"JUDY."

Her other letter was addressed to Master Fleming.

"Sard Manor,
"Nr. Bedesford.

"MY DEAR TOBY,

"I've been taken on here as a housemaid. Your friend was right. The place certainly looks as if they could do with some cash. I don't much like what I've seen of the family, but they may be all right. Oliver is ill. It's some kind of nerves and he doesn't like people to look at him. We wondered about his age. I hear he is nineteen or twenty. I'll write to you again later on if I find out anything. Don't answer this, as letters may get into the wrong hands. Oliver is living at the top of the house and the stairs leading up to that floor have a door which is locked. I got a chance to try it when I took hot water up to the rooms. I suppose if he's loopy the rest of the family would have the use of his money—or would he be what they call a ward in chancery? It may be in the family. Mr. F. was eccentric. My name here is Mary

Morris. I shall always remember what a nice time we had at the Zoo. I had been so miserable and you cheered me up. I hope you liked the photo.

> "Yours sincerely,
>> "JUDITH MERLE."

Having finished her letters Judy slipped out of her clothes, blew out her candle, and got into bed. The night was very still, but once before she dropped off to sleep she heard a clatter of iron bars followed by a long drawn snarl. Judy laughed to herself and thought, "No wonder they can't keep maids." She had travelled with a menagerie, and such sounds did not trouble her. She was very fast asleep when, a little later in the night, the handle of her door turned very slowly for an inch or two. But the door did not open. There was no key in the lock and Judy, with some experience of cheap lodgings, had wedged the knob with the back of a chair. The knob slipped back with a very faint click. Judy's head moved on the pillow, but she did not wake.

CHAPTER IX
A HOUSE DIVIDED

JUDY had been kept busy all the morning. No cleaning had been done since the departure of the last housemaid and the vacuum cleaner was out of order, so she raised clouds of dust with a brush. After the midday meal she had to wash and dry the glass and silver, and she was slow over the unaccustomed work. She was still in the butler's pantry when the front door bell rang. She was about to go and answer it when she heard the click of Helen's high heels running down the stairs and across the hall. Mrs. Ramblett, she knew, had gone up to her room to lie down and Mr. Bateman had returned to the gardens where he was superintending the making of a new enclosure for the bears. Mrs. Lacy and her half-witted niece were in the kitchen. Judy opened the pantry door an inch or two and went on rubbing the glasses.

The visitor had been admitted. There was a noticeable silence, followed by a murmur of voices, Helen's voice and a man's. Were they going into the drawing-room? No, they were still in the hall and moving towards the stairs. Judy, listening hard, heard the man say, "You must be patient. Promise you'll wait." The answer was inaudible. She waited a few minutes before she ventured to leave the pantry. There was nobody in the hall then. In the kitchen Mrs. Lacy was sitting with her stockinged feet on the fender and her skirt turned up over her knees listening to her portable wireless.

"There's a visitor," said Judy. "I didn't let him in. Miss Helen did."

The cook answered without interest. "That would be the doctor. Doctor Farwell. He calls two or three times a week to see Master Oliver."

"I've got some letters to post. Would there be time for me to run out before tea? Where's the pillar box?"

"Down the avenue and turn to your left. It's a longish way. Leave them on the hall table and they'll get posted. Bowles goes down on his bicycle twice a day."

"I'd like a breath of fresh air," said Judy.

"All right," said Mrs. Lacy good-naturedly; "if they ring for tea before you get back I'll take it up." The new girl seemed willing, and she was anxious not to be left alone with Mattie again.

"Stay out a little longer if you like," she said when Judy came into the kitchen again in her outdoor things. "Walk round the place and have a look at the animals. I don't fancy them myself, but some people feel different. And don't be surprised if you meet a black man."

It was muddy underfoot in the avenue between the drifts of dead leaves that filled the ditches on either side. Beyond the railings on the right a buffalo, after standing still for a moment to stare at Judy as she passed, lowered his huge shaggy head menacingly and began to paw the ground. Sard Manor was well guarded. It would certainly be dangerous to attempt to approach the house or to leave it by any but the recognised method. Judy had nearly reached the lower gate, which was standing open, when a lorry turned in. She moved to one side to allow it plenty of room to pass and saw that the load was a dead horse partly covered by a tarpaulin, and that the lorry driver was a negro. He touched his cap as he passed her with a friendly grin.

She had posted her letters and was going back up the avenue when the doctor's car passed her. He was driving fast, and he made no attempt to edge farther to the left to give her room so that she was obliged to back almost into the ditch to avoid being run down. She had meant to have a good look at him, but the light of a stormy sunset was in her eyes and she saw nothing. As she reached the closed kiosk and turnstile she heard a chorus of snarling and yapping.

Judy went a little way up the drive and followed a winding path through the shrubberies that the cook had told her of to the gate which was used by Mr. Bateman going to and fro from the gardens to the house.

She found herself on the crest of the hill. The ground sloped gradually to the valley and had been laid out with intersecting paths, roughly asphalted, that led to wooden outbuildings and rows of cages where the animals were kept. Farther down the hill dark shapes flitted about in the undergrowth where willows grew about a spring. The leafless branches of the trees were like coarse black lace against the fiery red in the west. In the waning light the strong wire netting that surrounded the copse was not visible.

"Don't be frightened, Missie." The negro had come up behind Judy unnoticed. He had a soft, crooning voice, like thick honey, and his strong teeth flashed in his face as he smiled down at her. "Them's the wolves, but they won't hurt you. I'll show you round. What'll you see first? The monkeys, or the hyena?"

"I don't mind. Are you one of the keepers?"

"There's me and Bowles, and old Curie. Bowles tends to the cat house and the wolves, all the critters what eats meat, with Curie to help him. I look after the monkeys and the deer and Sukey, the elephant, before she was sold; all grass eaters, see?" He lowered his voice. "If you want to know the reason," he whispered mysteriously, "I don' like blood. No, sir. It's that way with me."

Judy scarcely knew why, but this confession, muttered in her ear in the gathering dusk on that bleak hillside, was the reverse of reassuring. The fear he expressed had begun to creep along her nerves. But she only said, "It's getting dark. I shan't have time to go round now, but I might just take a peep at the monkeys."

"Sure."

He led the way into the monkey house. Several of the cages were empty and he told her that some of the more valuable species had died and had not been replaced. She could see that his charges were fond of him. They chattered excitedly and reached tiny hands through the bars to clutch at him as he came near.

"They need a more even warmth," he said. "Artificial sunlight and all that. I bring 'em grapes and titbits. I don't like to see 'em pine. It takes a lot of money to run a place like this. 'Tisn't nobody's fault we haven't got it. The boss—that's Mr. Bateman—does his damdest, repairing the old cages and painting them up. He says to me, 'I'd like to have everything of the best, Jerry, as good as Whipsnade on a small scale, or better. I got ideas if I could only carry 'em out,' he says. Come along any time, Missie and I'll show you round."

It was quite dark now outside, and she turned off from the main path too soon and instead of coming to the gate opening into the shrubberies was brought up short by wire netting and a mephitic smell. Something sprang at her out of the shadows and the steel net clashed and sagged under the strain. Judy withdrew hurriedly. The next turning proved to be the right one, but she was still rather white when she came into the warm, brightly lit kitchen and Mrs. Lacy glanced at her critically.

"You don't look much better for the air. You can go up now and lay the supper. There'll only be the two of them, Mrs. Ramblett and Mr. Bateman."

"Where's Miss Helen?"

"She's dining and spending the evening with Dr. and Mrs. Farwell. She often does."

Supper, Judy noticed, was a very silent meal. Whenever she went in to change the plates Mrs. Ramblett was leaning back in her chair and blinking drowsily at the ceiling. She hardly touched the food on her plate. Mr. Bateman, on the contrary, ate heartily, but he looked tired and harassed and as if his thoughts were elsewhere. When Mrs. Ramblett seeming to rouse herself from some waking dream, got up and trailed vaguely out of the room he pushed back his chair briskly, said something under his breath and followed her across the hall into the drawing-room.

Judy cleared the table and carried the tray of silver and glass into the pantry leaving the door ajar. As she turned off the tap after running hot water into the sink she heard the man's voice raised in anger in the drawing-room. She hesitated. Would it be safe to go and listen? Not at the door. The risk was too great. The pantry window was over the sink. She opened it and swung herself up with the effortless ease that had delighted audiences watching the Flying Merles going through their act. She landed on gravel, closed the window, but not so tightly that she could not pry it open again with her fingers, and crept round the side of the house.

The drawing-room was at the back, with french windows opening on a stone-paved terrace and looking across the valley. The curtains were drawn, Judy had drawn them herself. Light shone through one crack, but the crack was not wide enough to enable her to see into the room. She could not see, but she could hear.

Mrs. Ramblett was speaking, not sharply, but with an accentuation of her habitual weary indifference. "I can't help it. She does what she likes."

"You ought to be able to stop it. Send her away for a time."

"She wouldn't go. What does it matter to you anyway?"

"I should have thought her mother would have some feeling in the matter."

"She's twenty-two. I can't stop her making a fool of herself."

Bateman had moved towards the window. His voice, shaking with suppressed fury, sounded alarmingly near the listener.

"If you can't, I will."

Mrs. Ramblett was roused at last. She answered on an unexpectedly harsh note. "You'll do nothing of the sort. Don't interfere. I depend on him."

"For your filthy drugs. I know."

The silence that followed seemed ominous to Judy as the breathless pause after a thunder-clap. Mrs. Ramblett's answer, when it came, was uttered in her usual drowsy manner. "That's a lie. Don't talk to me like this again. You'd better leave the room."

Judy heard him go out, banging the door after him.

It was time to get back to the pantry, but when she reached the window she was horrified to see the shadow of a man's head on the frosted glass. She guessed what had happened. Bateman, crossing the hall, had seen the pantry door ajar, had pushed it open, and had found nobody there. Her mind worked quickly. She ran on down the path to the back of the left wing and the kitchen door. Luckily Mrs. Lacy had not yet locked up for the night. Mattie was in the scullery fumbling in her purblind way over the plates and her aunt was in the larder. Judy went through unnoticed and ran along the passage to the baize-covered door that shut off the servants' quarters from the hall.

Bateman was still in the pantry. He turned to face her as she went in. A little steam was still rising from the water in the sink.

He stared at her suspiciously. "How is it you haven't done the washing up yet? You're very slow. It's nearly ten."

Judy replied with a meekness that might have surprised him if he had known her better. "I'm sorry, sir. I had to go to my room for a minute. I shan't be long now."

"Very well." He was turning away when she said, "Am I to wait up for Miss Helen?"

"No. I have some work to do in the office. I will let her in. You can go to bed when you've finished here."

"Yes, sir."

"Didn't I see you coming out of the monkey house with Jerry this evening?"

"Yes, sir. The cook said I might go and see the animals."

"Yes, of course. And Jerry's not a bad chap. What's your name?"

"Mary Morris."

He looked at her for a moment doubtfully, as if there was something more that he wanted to say. The angry flush had faded from his face and he looked tired and harassed, as if the recent scene with Mrs. Ramblett had sapped his vitality.

He may be wicked, thought Judy, but he's not flourishing. She breathed more freely when he had gone. Was he in love with

Helen? It seemed so. In love with her, and jealous of the doctor. Judy remembered the car that had forced her into the ditch. A man who drove like that would be a formidable because a ruthless antagonist. He was a married man, but his wife was an invalid. Mrs. Ramblett depended on him. Judy, going over the quarrel she had overheard, remembered the man's fierce contempt.

"For your filthy drugs. I know—"

Drugs. That would account for Mrs. Ramblett's drowsy indifference to everything that was going on about her, for her slatternly habits, her lack of appetite, her momentary and otherwise inexplicable flashes of energy. Judy knew something of drug addicts. The wife of the proprietor of a circus they had travelled with two years earlier had been one. No one knew how she got the stuff. Her cunning was phenomenal. The dreadful craving had eaten into her body and soul. There was nothing she would not do to allay it. In the end, when the source of supply was stopped, she had killed herself with a pair of scissors.

The tragedy had left Judy with a horror of that vice. Its slaves were, she thought, capable of anything. She no longer doubted that Mrs. Ramblett might connive at her daughter's intrigue with a married man. There might be worse things.

She put away the silver and set the breakfast trays, two for the mother and daughter, and the third for the sick boy shut up in his rooms at the top of the house. Beyond taking up his meals no one seemed to do anything for him or pay him any attention.

Judy, taking down the dinner tray when she found it on the table in the hall during the afternoon, had noticed that the meat and vegetables lay untouched on the plate in a horrid pool of congealed gravy. Evidently his appetite was uncertain, yet he was not being given an invalid diet. Mrs. Lacy had referred vaguely to some nervous trouble. Judy was beginning to feel that there might be something sinister about that hidden figure cut off from them all by a flight of stairs and a locked door. Suppose he had, with the dreadful ingenuity of a warped mind, planned and carried out the murder of his uncle, following it with the ghastly masquerade that had ensnared David? He might have betrayed himself to his family on his return. If he was mad he might even have boasted of his cleverness. They would have had to choose between giving him up to the authorities, and shutting him up where he could do no more harm. Would they, simply to avoid scandal, allow an innocent man to hang in his stead? Judy, from the little she had seen of Mrs. Ramblett and her daughter, did not think either of them would have many scruples.

She had heard Mrs. Ramblett go upstairs to her room. The cook and her niece went to bed about nine. Judy switched off the light in the pantry. She had been asleep some time when she was roused by the sound of a car reversing. She looked at her watch. It was five minutes past three. She slipped out of bed, put on her dark dressing-gown and crept down the passage to the baize-covered door. She opened it an inch or two. Yes, that was Helen's voice, high and excited.

"I shall come in when I choose."

"Helen—"

"I won't be bullied!"

"It's for your own sake, Helen. That fellow's a rotter."

Judy heard the unmistakable sound of a blow. The silence that ensued was followed by the closing of a door.

CHAPTER X
RHODA DROPS A BRICK

SOON after ten the next morning Mrs. Ramblett came into the kitchen, in an incredibly dirty dressing-gown, to tell the cook that her married daughter, Rhoda, and her husband had rung up to say that they were coming to lunch.

"It's very tiresome, giving us such short notice," she complained, "but it seems that they are going to South America or somewhere. He's got a job at last. Make a list of things you'll need, Mrs. Lacy, and Bowles will fetch them from the town on his motor-cycle."

The cook pursed her lips and eyed her mistress doubtfully.

"The fishmonger sent in his account again yesterday."

"You mean they won't let Bowles have anything if he doesn't pay ready money? It's difficult just at the moment, but we shall have plenty quite soon. Couldn't he tell them that?"

Mrs. Lacy shook her head.

Mrs. Ramblett sighed. "Perhaps I can borrow a pound or two from Mr. Bateman. Do your best, cook."

"Yes, ma'am. Lemon soles and a brace of pheasants, and an apple soufflé. Shall I tell Bowles to get a bottle of whisky?"

"Yes. Whatever you think." Mrs. Ramblett, sick of the subject, wandered towards the door followed by the cook.

"Mrs. Ramblett, ma'am'."

"Yes, what is it?"

"The water's lovely and hot if you'd like a bath. I'd put on your green dress if I was you," said the old woman anxiously.

Mrs. Ramblett stared at her for a moment vacantly before the sense of this warning penetrated her dulled brain. Then she said, "Because of Rhoda? Perhaps I had better."

Judy was kept busy for the rest of the morning. Mrs. Lacy insisted on her turning out the bedroom that had been Rhoda's before her marriage. 'She may be staying the night. You can't tell. Anyway, you'll take her up there when she arrives to take off her hat and coat. Don't forget to put a clean towel and to take her a jug of warm water."

Judy, from the landing above, heard Helen telephoning.

"G. O. C. 528 . . . yes . . . is that you? Helen speaking. Don't come over to-day. Rhoda and Gilbert will be here. . . . Oh, only for lunch, I hope and trust. . . . I don't think she would . . . better not. I mean it. . . . Good-bye."

Mr. and Mrs. Lisle arrived a few minutes before one. Mrs. Ramblett and Helen came out of the drawing-room as Judy opened the front door

Rhoda kissed them both, and Gilbert shook hands. Rhoda had not her sister's dark beauty, she was hardly even good looking, but she had a pleasant voice and manner, and Judy liked her at once. Judy took her upstairs and brought a can of hot water.

"Have you been here long?"

"Only a few days, madam."

"Old Lacy is here still, I suppose, and her loopy niece?"

"Yes, madam."

"Well, I hope you'll be able to stick it for my mother's sake. She doesn't look well. I hadn't seen her for a year."

"Shall you be ready if I ring the gong now, madam?"

"Yes. Ring away."

Bateman was waiting in the dining-room when the rest of the family went in. His gloomy face lit up as he shook hands with Rhoda and her husband. Rhoda greeted him warmly. "Lovely to see you again, Batie. How are your beloved animals? Is Oliver still as keen as ever? Where is Oliver, by the way?"

Her mother overheard and answered the question. "Oliver isn't at all well, Rhoda. He developed some obscure form of nerve trouble and he's having to undergo a treatment."

"Poor Oliver! What a shame! Is he in a nursing home, or what?"

"He's upstairs. But he has to be kept very quiet. Do tell us more about your plans. Are you really leaving England quite soon?"

"The day after to-morrow. Our passages are booked. Buenos Aires. It's an agency. Gilbert was lucky to get it. We shan't have a leave for four years, so it's rather a long good-bye, I'm afraid. I've been frightfully busy, we both have, getting clothes, and selling our furniture and sub-letting our flat, but we felt we must just run down and see you before we went. Pheasant? Oh, yes. I love game." She helped herself to the vegetables handed by Judy. "I say, wasn't that a ghastly business about great uncle Joshua? What luck that we were none of us dragged into it to give evidence of identity or anything. Not that I could have done that—though I believe father did once take me to see him when I was quite small. I have a dim recollection of sitting in a chair with a very slippery seat and eating sweet biscuits, and I believe that when Oliver was at school he sometimes got asked over for the day. It wasn't too far for him to get on his bicycle. Awful to think that the poor old thing was murdered. Was Oliver very upset about it?"

"We all were, of course," said her mother. "Do you mind not speaking about it."

Gilbert Lisle, who had been very silent hitherto, leaving his wife to do the talking, joined in unexpectedly. "You'll forgive me if I say that's a mistake, Mrs. Ramblett?" he said earnestly, gazing at her through his horn-rimmed glasses like an amiable young owl. "It's the way to get inhibitions and all that."

"We'll risk that if you don't mind," said Helen coldly. "Have you seen anything of Alice lately?"

"No. She wrote on my birthday to say she couldn't afford to send me a present. That husband of hers has started a filling station somewhere. It will fail, of course. Bob Newbery never succeeds at anything—except touching his friends for a fiver. Though I remember the last time I did meet Alice—we lunched together at the Regent Palace—she told me he failed with Great Uncle Joshua. He went down specially from London to try to interest him in some scheme, but the old gentleman was not having any. Bob thought he might stretch a point for the husband of his eldest great niece, especially as he was known to be in the habit of making presents to perfect strangers picked up in the street. A born murderee really. He was asking for it, wasn't he." She glanced about her and seemed puzzled by the lack of response.

"Have I dropped a brick, Gilbert?"

"Obviously, my sweet," said her husband with a faint grin that belied his previous solemnity. "Oh, no, we never mention it, its name is never heard. But seriously, Mrs. Ramblett," he addressed his mother-in-law, "you're all missing a lot by being hush hush about it. I don't know much about county reactions, but Rhoda and I have never been so popular in our lives as since we made it known that we were mixed up, so to speak, in one of the juiciest murder cases of the season. Not only cocktails, good square meals have we consumed at our friends' expense just for that."

"How perfectly foul," said Helen.

Her elder sister looked at her. "Perhaps you're right, but you can't afford to be too particular when you're as hard up as we've been. After all, Great-Uncle Joshua never did a thing for us when he was alive. Of course it was dreadful that he should be murdered, and it's a good thing they got the man who did it, but after all, he was getting well into the sere and yellow, wasn't he? He couldn't have carried on much longer, and, strictly between ourselves,

Oliver will find the money very useful." She helped herself liberally from the glass dish of trifle proffered by Judy.

Nobody said anything, and Rhoda sailed gaily on. "I expect all your big pussy cats will be given new collars, Batie? Oliver was always the only one of us to share Daddy's enthusiasm for his old Zoo. He'll have lots of fun. I shouldn't be a bit surprised when we come home to find this room turned into a parrot house."

"So you're giving us a foretaste. How thoughtful of you," said Helen. "We'll have coffee in the drawing-room, Mary."

Rhoda laughed. "You always could be ruder than anyone I know, darling. You certainly haven't lost the knack. I suppose Oliver rests in the afternoon? I'd better run up and see him now he settles down."

"You can't see him, Rhoda," said her mother.

"Why not?"

"I told you he had to be kept very quiet. The least thing excites him. He's not allowed any visitors."

Rhoda's rather defiant and factitious high spirits wilted.

"I say! Is it really as bad as that? I'm awfully sorry. Oliver and I always hit it off pretty well. I wanted Gilbert to meet him. How did it come on? Did he have a shock or something?" She spoke to Bateman, who shook his head. "Not to my knowledge. I noticed he was getting very listless and losing interest in things. I was away, having a few days' holiday, when he got worse, and your mother called in Doctor Farwell. He's giving him some kind of treatment. He had been moved to the top floor when I came back, and I haven't seen him since."

"Poor old Oliver. How long has this been going on?"

"About two months."

"Perhaps it was a shock then—hearing about the murder. Oliver—yes, I suppose you could always have called him highly strung. Is it—is it mental? Gosh! Great Uncle Joshua was eccentric. Does that mean there's a family taint?"

"Certainly not," said her mother angrily. "If there is Oliver gets it from his mother so it wouldn't affect you girls."

"What does the doctor say?" asked Gilbert.

"You know doctors don't commit themselves. He talks about obscure nervous lesions."

"Is he any use?" asked Rhoda. "Oughtn't you to have a second opinion? It doesn't sound too good to me. After all, I suppose he's only the local G.P. Is it old Fraser? I remember him coming when we had mumps. A bird with whiskers."

"No. He died. It's a new man, named Farwell. He's very clever and we have every confidence in him," said Helen repressively. "I daresay you mean well, Rhoda, but you can't think how irritating it is to have outsiders butting in with unasked advice. We're on the spot and we're doing our best."

"I'm not exactly an outsider, Helen. Oliver is my half brother, too, remember. And, as it happens, I get on with him and you don't. I don't believe it would hurt him to see me for a few minutes."

Mrs. Ramblett's haggard face had begun to twitch. She looked ghastly. "Please, Rhoda, we must obey the doctor's orders. Can't you stop her, Gilbert? My nerves won't stand it."

"Oh, all right, Mother. I don't want to upset you. But I must say I'm disappointed. I was looking forward to seeing Oliver."

She was silent for a moment, stirring her coffee. Her husband glanced surreptitiously at his watch. This visit to his wife's relations was not being a great success.

"We ought to be going, old girl. We've got a longish drive before us."

"Okay," she said briskly, "but we must just run round and see the animals. You'll take us, Bade? There was a monkey with a behind like a sunset that was the apple of his eye when I was here last."

"Bimbo!" said Bateman. "He's gone. I sat up three nights with him. No one else could persuade him to touch food. He was holding my hand when he died." He cleared his throat. "Come along, then," he said gruffly, "if you really want to see round."

"You'll excuse me, I'm sure," said Helen, "and mother ought to rest."

Rhoda ran upstairs to fetch her hat and coat and joined her husband and Bateman, who were waiting for her on the gravel sweep in front of the house.

She took Bateman's arm and squeezed it. "I'm so glad you're sticking it. If you weren't here to run the show I can't imagine what would happen. I'm worried, Batie. Mother looks terrible. She's aged twenty years since I saw her last. And there's something wrong with Helen. She's so bitter."

"It's been a struggle to make ends meet," he told her. "We're understaffed. Everything's shabby, out of repair. When the animals die there's no money to replace them. I don't know what your father would say if he could see the place now. It would break his heart."

"It matters a lot to you, too, Batie."

"Yes." He set his teeth. "I'm not a good loser. I hate to fail."

They had entered the grounds by the path through the shrubberies and were passing a row of cages of which only one was occupied by a mangy-looking hyena prowling ceaselessly to and fro.

"We had to sell the elephant. She cost too much to keep."

"But it's going to be better now if Oliver is still keen," said Rhoda. "He'll spend some of Great Uncle Joshua's money on doing the place up and getting fresh stock and what not, won't he?"

"Well—I hope so," said Bateman slowly, "but your mother and Helen wouldn't agree. All this means less than nothing to them. They'd like everything to be scrapped."

"But Oliver can do as he likes when he's twenty-one," cried Rhoda.

"Yes. But he's ill. If he got worse—"

"Then—oh dear, do you think Oliver is"—she dropped her voice instinctively—"is insane? Please tell me the truth, Batie. I do hate mysteries."

An antelope came tripping daintily to the bars, hoping for tit-bits. Bateman fished in his pockets for some crumbs of biscuits.

"I don't know, Rhoda. He's being treated. I'm employed here to look after things. I'm only an upper servant actually, though I'm allowed to take some liberties. Do you see this?" He touched a small patch of black sticking plaster on his right cheek bone.

"Yes, what is it?"

Nothing much. A cut and a bruise, the result of not minding my own business. The doctor comes three times a week, sometimes more often. He's supposed to be clever. I daresay he is. You'll have to be satisfied with that, my dear."

They stopped before the tiger's cage. Its occupant was lying with his head on his paws. His emerald eyes were fixed on some point above their heads.

"Magnificent," said Gilbert. "You can't say he isn't in the pink. Look at his fur."

"He hasn't had to go short yet," said Bateman, "have you, Selim, old man?"

"Is he tame?"

"No. He hates us all. But he's not like a leopard, spitting and snarling. He's a prince of the jungle. He merely ignores us."

"I thought all the animals loved you, Batie," said Rhoda.

He shook his head. "He doesn't yet. I haven't had him long enough. But I haven't given up yet.

I spend some time every day talking to him."

"Wish you luck," said Gilbert, "but look here, old girl, we really must be going."

They began to walk back towards the house.

"I suppose you still find it difficult to keep servants?" said Rhoda.

"Yes. It's dull, too far from the town, and they don't like to hear the wolves baying at the moon."

"I rather like the look of the new parlour-maid."

"Do you?" said Bateman grimly. "I don't. I think she listens at doors and reads letters if she finds them lying about. If I catch her snooping around she'll go."

"Even if my mother wants her to stay?"

Bateman reddened slightly. He had been taken off his guard.

"She wouldn't. She resents any kind of inquisition, anything that could be described as spying,"

"I see. Yes. Naturally. Anyone would," said Gilbert rather hastily.

Bateman did not go back into the house with them. He had arrears of work to get through. They shook hands with him and went on together.

"Rather a sinister sort of blighter," was Gilbert's comment.

His wife protested. "Oh, no. He's been with us donkey's years. Father thought a lot of him. He's devoted to the animals."

"I could see that. But it doesn't prevent him from being rather sinister," the young man persisted. "Hidden fires and all that. I didn't care for the way he scowled at your sister more than once during lunch."

"That's nothing. Helen's the sort of person anyone would scowl at. He was probably trying to stop her from snubbing me."

Gilbert laughed at the recollection. "Your conversation was more than usually devastating, my sweet. I wondered when you'd begin to grasp that they really didn't want to talk about the murder."

"I grasped it all right. I'm not a moron. But I thought it would do them good to release their what is its. Why, you told mother yourself that it was wrong to bottle things up. Gilbert, I'm not happy about Oliver. He was the flower of the flock, you know. Much the nicest person in the family. I hate to think that he's actually there in the house, and I can't see him."

Her eyes filled with tears. Gilbert, who was very fond of his wife, slipped an arm through hers. "Don't—he's having every care."

Mrs. Ramblett and Helen were in the drawing-room awaiting their return. Gilbert once again explained that they had a long drive before them, and they were not pressed to stay.

"We could have stopped the night, really," said Rhoda rather sadly, as they drove down the avenue, "if they'd asked us. After all it's my home—or was—and my mother. She—she wasn't always so aloof and indifferent, Gilbert. Poor mother, I suppose she's really worn out with worry, and Oliver's illness."

"They've got a nurse in the house, I imagine," said Gilbert, slowing down to take the turn into the lane. "You generally hear them rustling about, but I didn't see hide or hoof of her." He was frowning a little. Though he would not say so to Rhoda he had felt rather acutely that there was something amiss at Sard Manor. But there was nothing they could do about it. Within forty-eight hours they would be leaving England. In a way he was glad of it. He did not care for what he had seen of his relations by marriage.

Helen meanwhile, had gone to the telephone.

"G.O.C. 528. Hello . . . is that you? Yes, they're gone, thank goodness. Mother says you will be coming round to-night? She's taken the last of those powders and she always worries so if she's without them . . . you can't? Well, the first thing to-morrow? Do try . . . I'll tell her."

She hung up the receiver and went back to the drawing-room where her mother was lying on the sofa drawn close up to the fire. She turned her head restlessly as her daughter entered.

"Is he coming?"

"He can't to-night. You've got to remember, Mother, that he has other patients, and Myra gets very fretful and tiresome if he goes out in the evening."

"You told him I had taken the last of my powders?"

"Yes." Helen hesitated. "They do you good, I know, but aren't you replying on them rather too much? I mean—it doesn't do to form habits, and there isn't really anything the matter with you, is there?"

"I have dreadful neuralgia," said Mrs. Ramblett plaintively. "I—I can't think why he didn't come this morning as usual."

"I told him not to."

"You told him? Why?"

"I felt sure he wouldn't get on with Rhoda. She's so pushing and so frightfully tactless. It would have been difficult for him if she'd insisted on seeing Oliver. I mean—you could just say no, but he would have had to be polite."

"Yes. I suppose you're right. I shall have to try to manage to-night. There's Oliver's medicine, too. He always has a dose the last thing. Oh, well—ring for the tea, Helen. Don't turn on the light. I can't stand the glare. I wonder what James said to them. I couldn't prevent them going round with him."

"Of course not. It didn't matter."

Mrs. Ramblett sighed. "Have you rung for the tea?" She spoke more sharply. "Why don't you answer me?"

"You didn't give me time."

"Nonsense. I've been waiting ages."

Chapter XI
AN AFTERNOON OUT

That night Judy wedged her door handle with a chair back before she began to undress. She was very tired, but she meant to write down all the information she had picked up during the day before she slept. Her room was cold, and there was no table to write on, so she sat up in bed with her old tweed coat over her pyjamas and scribbled away with her pad on her knees by the dim light of one candle. There was no electric light in the servants' bedrooms.

Judy's eager little face was flushed and her eyes were bright with excitement. She had made full use of her opportunities during lunch and felt that she had learned a good deal from Rhoda Lisle's indiscretions. Bits here and bits there, pointers and possibilities. It would all have to be sorted out.

Mrs. Ramblett. Age about fifty. Has been good looking. Very moody and queer and generally seems half asleep. I think she dopes, and people like that will do anything to get the stuff.

Helen Ramblett, the unmarried daughter, rotten temper and the type men go mad over. Hates being here, but too grand and too lazy to go off and earn her own living. N.B.—This may be unfair. I don't like her. Bateman quarrelled with her mother about her last night. He's jealous of the doctor.

James Bateman, age about forty, but I'm not really a good judge of ages. Has been here a long time as a sort of foreman manager of the zoo. Grumpy, disagreeable manners in the house, but seems to be good with the animals. I think he's in love with Helen and when middle-aged men fall for girls they get it badly.

Mrs. Lacy has been in service here for some time. Furtive sort of manners and a nerve-racking habit of starting at any unexpected sound and looking over her shoulder. Speaks so low that I can hardly hear her. I don't think she knows anything, but she's frightened. One might get like that if one lived here some time. The house is so large and dark and cold, with long, draughty passages and some of the trees are so close that their branches scrape against the walls when the wind blows, and at night one hears the animals. The wolves are howling at this moment.

Mattie, the kitchen maid, is Mrs. Lacy's niece. She's got a broad, red face, quite expressionless, and little piggy eyes, and she never speaks, but she seems to understand what her aunt says to her. When she isn't scrubbing floors or washing dishes or peeling Potatoes she sits by the kitchen fire doing nothing. I think she's quite harmless, anyway I hope so, but her aunt says she sometimes walks in her sleep.

Bowles is the head keeper. He's rough, and looks a brute, but I suppose he's all right with the animals or Bateman wouldn't keep him on. He drives the lorry and also a motor-cycle and takes letters into the town to post, but I wouldn't trust him.

Curie is his assistant. I've only seen him in the distance ; a wiry old man with bow legs, and looks horribly dirty.

Jerry is the other keeper. I like him better than anybody else here. He's good-natured, but I'm afraid he's not very brave.

Rhoda Lisle is Mrs. Ramblett's married daughter. She and her husband came to lunch. They are leaving for South America the day after to-morrow. They talked so openly about the murder that I'm sure they had nothing to do with it. Everyone else seemed very uncomfortable. She spoke of the other daughter and her husband. His name is Bob Newbery. He is always hard up, and he went to see Mr. Fallowes and tried to borrow money from him a year ago. He's running a filling station now. None of these people have anything to gain directly from the death of Mr. Fallowes, but all the money goes to Oliver Ramblett, and they may be relying on him to help them out.

Oliver Ramblett had everything to gain by his great uncle's death. He's young—twenty—but not too young to plan and carry out the crime if he has that sort of mind. I haven't seen him. His sister Rhoda wanted to, but they wouldn't let her. The door at the foot of the stairs leading to the top floor is kept locked. I try it whenever I'm up there and there is nobody about, but I don't know if I should have the courage to go up. They talk about nerves, but that may mean anything. People aren't kept shut up like that for any ordinary illness. The doctor comes three *times a week and Mrs. Ramblett takes up his meals. He must be alone there for hours and hours. A boy of twenty. He used to be all right. I could tell that from what Rhoda said at lunch. But I suppose if he's gone right off there may be a frightful change. I had a nightmare last night. I dreamt I was looking through a keyhole and I saw him crawling about the floor and gnashing his teeth and snarling, and I woke and just for a second I thought I really had heard something like that, and that there was a sort of padding, shuffling noise in the passage just outside my door. The best way to get that sort of bogy out of my mind is to really see him, but I don't know how I'm going to manage it. I must do it because I think that he may be the criminal, and that he's since gone quite loopy, and that his family are keeping him shut up rather than give him up to justice. They are the kind of people who might do that, very hard and self-centred. They wouldn't care a hoot about poor David. Perhaps they aren't really quite sure that Oliver murdered his uncle, but only have strong suspicions. They might salve their consciences that way.*

Doctor Farwell has called since I've been here, but I haven't seen him yet. He nearly ran me down in his car as I was coming up the avenue. Helen dined with him and his wife, and he brought her home very late, about three o'clock. Bateman was in his office doing accounts and he let her in. They had a row, and she smacked his face and cut his cheek with one of her rings. He had a bit of sticking plaster on it the next day. She rang him up this morning. I didn't know who it was at the time, but I heard the number and I looked it up afterwards in the book. Fortunately it's the old-fashioned kind of telephone, where you call the number instead of dialling. I think she told him not to come while her sister, Rhoda, was here. I hope to find out a little more about him before long.

Judy folded the four pages closely covered with writing and slipped them into an envelope. She was beginning to be very conscious of the disadvantages of working alone, but there had been no alternative. The forces of the law were against her. First the police and then the judge and the jury were satisfied that the murderer of Mr. Fallowes had been found. The evidence against him had been overwhelming, so much so that no other possibilities had been considered. In her heart Judy had very little hope that the judges of the Court of Appeal would reverse the verdict. That could only happen if fresh evidence was put before them, evidence that had not been available at the trial. Such evidence might exist at Sard Manor, but could she obtain it alone? If these people were in collusion to save one of their number from the gallows they would hardly hesitate to silence her by any means that occurred to them if once they discovered that she was there as a spy.

To whom should she send these notes which might be valuable later on? Ben Levy was a good sort but he was in love with her. Judy did not want to take advantage of his feeling for her to drag him into what might prove a very dangerous business. Besides, he was a very busy man. No, not Ben. Auntie Apples? No. There was nothing she could do. Reuben might have helped, but Reuben had gone off with Lil to join a circus abroad under another name. She knew that Reuben, though he had never said so, had very little doubt that his brother was guilty. Only one possible ally remained, and that was Toby Fleming. He was a child, he couldn't really do anything himself, but—She wrote a hurried postscript.

"DEAR TOBY,

"I've no one to help me, and this is a last chance to save David. Will you tell your stepfather all about us and show him these notes I have made?

I am sure from the way you spoke of him that I can trust him, and you said he was high up at Scotland Yard. Yours, J.M.

It only remained to address the bulky envelope to Master Christopher Fleming before she slipped out of bed to put away her writing materials.

She was in the kitchen waiting for Mrs. Lacy to make the coffee for the breakfast trays when the latter told her that she might have that afternoon for her weekly half day.

"Thanks. Suits me."

"You'll be catching the bus and going into the town to the Pictures, I expect. I wonder if you could match some wool for me. I want another two ounces for that jumper I'm making for Mattie. They've got it at Woolworth's."

Mrs. Lacy fussed over the two trays. Brown bread and tomato juice for Helen, dry toast for Mrs. Ramblett. The tray for Oliver went up later, when Mrs. Ramblett was dressed and ready to take it up to him.

Helen slept with her windows open and the blinds up, but her mother always had her curtains closely drawn. She moaned as Judy pulled them back. "Must you? The light hurts my eyes."

"You wouldn't be able to see."

Judy, setting out the bed table, noticed that Mrs. Ramblett looked very ill and that her hands shook so that she could hardly hold her cup.

"Mary, I—I'm far from well. I need my medicine. Will you ring up the doctor and tell him I must have it. Don't tell Miss Helen. She thinks I ought to be able to wait. The number is G. O. C. 528. Do it as soon as you've taken her tray. Don't let him put you off."

"Very well, madam."

She took Helen's tray to her. The girl was lying with her face to the wall and her bedclothes pulled right up and she ignored Judy's entrance.

Judy closed the door after her rather carefully and ran down to the hall. The line was clear and presently she heard a man's voice, curt and authoritative.

"Who is it. What do you want?"

"I am speaking for Mrs. Ramblett, at Sard Manor. She isn't at all well this morning. She says can you send up her medicine now?"

"I've no one to send. I'm coming over this afternoon and I'll bring it with me."

"She said I was to tell you she can't wait. She's very shaky and queer."

She heard him mutter something below his breath.

"I didn't catch what you said, sir."

"All right. I'll prepare one dose, if she can send somebody to fetch it during the morning. That's all I can do."

"Very good, sir. I'll tell her."

Judy went upstairs to deliver her message. She found that Mrs. Ramblett had drunk her coffee, all but half a cup that had been spilt on her satin quilt, but she had not touched her toast. She was crying, tears running down her sallow cheeks and dripping on to her abominably dirty and ragged dressing-jacket. Judy found her a clean handkerchief.

"What did he say?"

"He said he had no one to send this morning, but that he would have a dose made up if you can send someone to fetch it."

"Oh dear, I can't ask James or the keepers. There would be such a fuss. And I don't want to ask Helen."

"I would go for you, madam," said Judy, trying not to sound eager. "If I had a bicycle it wouldn't take long."

"A bicycle? You could take Helen's. She hardly ever uses it. You'll find it in the shed next to the wash-house. The doctor's house is on the main road just before you get to the town. It's called Sunnyside. On the left as you go. You can't mistake it."

"Am I to go now, before doing any more work?"

"Yes. You may even be back before Helen notices. That would be best."

"I'll be as quick as I can," promised Judy.

Mrs. Lacy stopped her as she was passing through the kitchen to go to her room.

"Where are you off to?"

Judy explained. "She said I might take Miss Helen's bicycle. I won't be long."

"You'll catch it from Miss Helen when she hears," whispered the old woman, "but you'd best go, I suppose."

Judy pulled on her beret without stopping to look at herself in the glass on her chest of drawers, and hurried into the yard, buttoning up her coat as she went. She had slipped her letter to Toby into one of the patch pockets. The bicycle was rusty, and she had to spend five minutes pumping up the back tyre, but she was off at last. She had rather dreaded meeting Bateman or the head keeper, but there seemed to be nobody about. She went carefully through the drift of fallen leaves in the avenue, but once in the lane that led across the valley to the main road she put on speed.

Sunnyside was a detached villa residence. It had been recently painted, and the front garden was neat and well cared for.

The door was opened by a sandy-haired young woman, who said curtly, "The doctor's started on his round. Mrs. Ramblett's medicine? Here it is." She gave Judy a small packet done up in white paper and labelled, *Mrs. Ramblett. One dose to be taken as directed.*

Judy took it and went back to her bicycle. She made one stop on her return journey where she had noticed a stile leading into a field with a right of way. She went into the field and, kneeling on the wet grass in the shadow of the hedge, she succeeded in opening the packet without tearing the paper.

It contained, as she had expected, a little white powder. She took the refill out of her powder compact case and shook a very little of Mrs. Ramblett's medicine into the box. Then she fastened the packet up again and went on her way.

Bowles was at the top of the avenue changing a tyre on the lorry. He stared very hard at her as she passed, but said nothing. She wished him good morning and he replied with a grunt.

She left the bicycle in the shed and reached her room unchallenged. She had posted her letter to Toby in the pillar box at the end of the lane. She was crossing the hall on her way upstairs when Helen came out of the drawing-room.

"Is that you, Mary? Where the hell have you been? The fire went out. I've been ringing and ringing."

"I'll get wood and paper and relight it, Miss. I'm sorry."

"You haven't answered my question."

"I'm sorry, Miss. I've been out on an errand for Mrs. Ramblett."

"An errand. What errand?"

"To fetch her medicine, Miss."

Helen bit her lip. She looked angry. "Why didn't you say so at once?"

Judy was tired of fencing. She answered with equal bluntness. "Mrs. Ramblett didn't want you to know."

"Did she say so?"

"Yes."

"You can't have been to Doctor Farwells and back in the time."

"I rode your bicycle. Mrs. Ramblett told me to."

"Damned cheek. Don't you dare touch my bicycle again."

"No, Miss."

Judy went on up the stairs. Helen watched her go. Judy, glancing back as she reached the turn, was suddenly sorry for her. Did she or didn't she know that the doctor was supplying her mother with dope? Judy thought not. She looked puzzled and unhappy.

Mrs. Ramblett was still in her room, but she was up and dressed.

"You've got it!" She almost snatched the packet out of Judy's hand. "Get on with your work now."

Judy was thrust out, and she heard the key turn in the lock.

The rest of the morning passed uneventfully. Judy was off as soon as she had washed the glass and silver after lunch. Mrs. Lacy told her that she might stay out until ten. "That's if you don't mind walking a mile in the dark after you get out of the bus. Don't forget my wool."

Judy had laid her plans. She had several purchases to make.

She was going to miss the doctor again, but that could not be helped. She hurried along the lane and was just in time to catch the bus into the town that passed there every hour. She went first to the post office where she sent off a small parcel. After that she did some shopping in the High Street. She bought a ball of fine twine and a bow and arrows at a toy shop, and then at an oil and colour shop she got sixty feet of fine but strong cord. It made rather a large parcel, and the assistant who served her offered to send it, but she preferred to take it with her.

She was in a grocer's shop and waiting to be served when her attention was attracted to the lady standing next to her by the owner of the shop, a fussy little man, who came forward to speak to her.

"Mrs. Farwell, isn't it? We haven't had the pleasure of seeing you in the shop lately."

She answered in a low voice, "I haven't been well. Your man calls for orders."

"Certainly, certainly, I hope you are satisfied."

"Oh, quite." She glanced round at the shop in a flurried manner before she said, "I—I want a tin of mustard. I'll take it with me."

"Very good, madam. Shall I put it down?"

"Oh no. I'll pay for it now."

She fumbled agitatedly over the coppers in her purse.

The little grocer looked on with unconcealed surprise and concern.

"You're hardly fit to be out alone, ma'am. Perhaps you've walked a bit farther than you meant. I believe I saw Doctor Farwell's car standing a little farther down the street half an hour ago. Shall I send one of my lads to see if he can find him?"

"Oh no, please. I'm quite all right really. Good afternoon and please don't—I mean—"

If her manner had not been so strange Judy would hardly have noticed her. She was one of those thin, neutral-coloured women who are apt to remind unsympathetic observers of chewed string. Her features were good, she might have been a pretty girl once, but the freshness of youth had faded and there had been nothing to replace that evanescent charm.

The grocer turned to Judy. "What can I do for you?"

"A quarter of acid drops, please."

CHAPTER XII
JUDY TAKES A CHANCE

"A POT of tea, Miss, and a poached egg on toast."

Judy arranged her parcels on the chair beside her. She had got all she wanted and meant to spend the rest of the evening in the cinema across the road. Meanwhile she was pondering over the odd little incident of Mrs. Farwell and the tin of mustard. It was queer, thought Judy, however you looked at it. Ill, perhaps. But it looked more like sheer fright. Those gloved fingers fumbling over the purse, the fluttering, breathless voice. "Oh, no, I'm all right."

She had not always been like that, thought Judy, or the grocer would not have been so surprised. What was Mrs. Farwell afraid of? She did not live at Sard Manor, where the wolves woke you in the night and you heard the boards creaking, if you listened long enough, under what might be a stealthy footstep.

Judy finished her tea and went over to the cinema, where she slept through two pictures and a newsreel and woke when the lights were turned on just in time to hurry out and scramble into the last bus.

The only other passenger got out on the outskirts of the town and she was left alone with the friendly bus conductor.

"I remember you taking this trip last week," he said, "going to Sard Manor. How do you like the place?"

"It's all right so far."

"You've got stronger nerves than my sister-in-law then. Been doing a bit of shopping?"

"Yes."

He eyed her parcels curiously. She was worried about them herself.

If only she could get them to her room unnoticed, the bow and arrows could be hidden under her mattress and the cord could be locked up in her suitcase.

He stopped the bus at the turning to Sard Manor and helped her down.

"Gosh, that's a heavy lump to carry. You're not afraid to go up that lane in the dark? Good night!"

The bus rumbled away down the road and its lights vanished round the next corner. Judy looked after it wistfully. She hated going back to Sard Manor. Only the thought of David, sitting in his warm, bright, dreadful cell, playing draughts with a warder; David, who would never be alone now until he died, nerved her to it. She trudged on until the black bulk of the house loomed up before her in the dim starlight. Ten o'clock, but only one light in the kitchen window. Mattie had gone to bed but Mrs. Lacy was sitting up for her with a pack of greasy cards spread out on the table.

Luckily she was absorbed and did not look up as Judy passed behind her. "Going straight to bed? Take your things off and come back for a cup of cocoa."

"Thanks, I will."

Judy disposed of her burdens and returned to the kitchen.

"Ought I to go to the drawing-room?"

"No. The doctor rang up. He was kept by a case and couldn't come after all, so Mrs. Ramblett and Miss Helen have both gone to bed early. I saw that the lights were all out and looked to the fastenings myself. The cocoa's in the saucepan and you'll find some biscuits in the tin."

"Are you doing a Patience?"

"No. I tried one, but it wouldn't come out. Miss Helen came in and bothered me to tell her fortune. I didn't want to, but she made me. I didn't tell her all I saw, but even then she wasn't pleased. I can't help the way the cards come out. The king of spades over and over again—and the ace."

"Is that bad?"

"Yes. She said it was all damned nonsense and I ought to be burned for a witch," Mrs. Lacy droned on. 'All right, Miss Helen,' I said, 'but there it is, and swearing won't alter it.'"

Judy stirred her cocoa thoughtfully. "What about Mr. Oliver when the doctor doesn't come?"

"That's what Mrs. Ramblett said. 'He won't sleep without his drops,' she said. That's when I took up her hot water. She talks to me sometimes when she's in the mood. I said 'What's the matter with him really?' She began to cry. 'He's very ill Mrs. Lacy,' she said, 'and I wish I was dead.'"

She collected the cards and pushed them into the table drawer. "If it wasn't for Mattie, I wouldn't stay," she said. "I couldn't have her with me anywhere else, and I promised my poor sister—well, good night, Mary."

Judy went to her room. She was still undecided. The plan she had evolved depended for its success on the fact that she was a trained acrobat. She had had a tiring day and it might be better to delay the enterprise for another twenty-four hours. But she wanted to get it over. She was going to take far greater risks than she had ever run with her brothers high up in the roof of the big circus tent. Quite unconsciously as she sat on the end of her bed she was rubbing her feet on the floor as she had rubbed them so often in the chalk before running into the ring. No lights to-night, no music, no applause, no net to catch her if she fell. Not yet, of course. She must wait until midnight. Meanwhile she could make all ready. She undid her parcels and fastened an end of string to one of the arrows. She changed into her practice clothes, canvas shoes and a dark bathing suit, and slipped on her tweed coat for warmth over a woollen cardigan which she wore for the sake of the pockets.

She had only a few inches of candle left. She blew it out to save it. "I won't sleep," she thought, but after a while she dozed off, waking with a start and the fear that it was too late. She switched on her torch and looked at her watch and was reassured, it was only twenty past twelve.

Half an hour later she had to admit that she had underrated the difficulties she had to overcome. Again and again the arrow carrying the string had fallen back. She had climbed easily enough to the fork of a beech tree growing close up to the house, but, seated there astride with her back to the trunk hampered her in drawing the bow. In the daylight she might have succeeded, but the darkness made it impossible for her to take aim. At last the arrow and the string were hopelessly fouled among the upper branches of the tree. She tugged desperately but uselessly, her plan, which had been to get the string and then the cord round one of the chimney stacks had to be abandoned. The only other way to reach the roof was to climb up by the rain water pipe. She had gone round the outside of the house the previous day on the pretext of cleaning the windows, and she knew there were pipes at each corner to carry off the water that ran off the roof. She chose the south-east corner and began to climb. She had fastened the cord round her waist. If she succeeded in scrambling on to the roof the cord fastened with a slip knot round one of the chimney stacks would solve all her difficulties. Fortunately Sard Manor was an old house and everything about it was solid and made to last. It was too dark to see anything clearly, but the dim projection of a windowsill showed Judy that she had reached the first floor. The rooms on this side of the house were unoccupied. Mrs. Ramblett and Helen's rooms were some distance away, luckily, for Judy's progress was far from noiseless as the pipe creaked under the strain of her weight, and once a bird roosting in the ivy flew out with a loud squawk and startled her so that she nearly lost her grip.

She came to the mouth of the pipe and a cold trickle of water from the gutters ran over her fingers as she stopped to consider her next move. To an observer, if there had been one, her position might have seemed almost hopeless. Her problem was to lift herself over the projecting eaves. Once on the roof it might be possible to crawl up the sloping gable and down the other side into the comparative safety of the cleft that divided it from the second gable. Judith never cared to recall that final struggle, in which every ounce of her strength and every nerve in her supple young body were involved. To fail meant to fall and break every bone on the stone pavement of the terrace forty feet below. She paid for the effort with a momentary suspension of consciousness, and came to to find herself lying face downwards and drenched with sweat on the sloping roof, with a chimney stack between her and the edge of that abyss. The weight of the cord which had unrolled behind her as she climbed threatened to drag her down She unfastened it from about her waist and managed to make a running loop and slip it over the stack. That done she felt happier. She and David had raced each other from the roof of the big circus tent to the ring below scores of times and up again, climbing hand over hand on the swaying ropes.

Her climb had been prompted by the fact that on her first evening at Sard Manor, when she was coming back in the dusk after her visit to the monkey house, she had happened to look up and see a dimly lit square patch on the inner slope of the south-eastern gable. That meant that either the top landing or one of the rooms up there was lit by a skylight. She was crawling in the direction where she thought it must be when it was suddenly illuminated from below. It was much nearer than she had imagined, its wooden framework within a few inches of her hands. One pane was partly opened by means of a pulley and cord and she could hear movements within, footsteps and the scraping of a chair.

Judy's heart thudded against her ribs. She craned her neck to peer into the room below, and was startled to see an upturned face within a foot of her own. The light was behind it and she could not distinguish the features, but it was framed by a tousled mass of dark hair, and it was that of a young man, wearing pyjamas and a dressing gown, and standing on a chair.

A faint and husky voice said, "Who is it? What are you?"

"I'm a friend. Are you Oliver Ramblett?"

"Yes. But I haven't any friends."

"Are you better? They told me you were ill."

He answered doubtfully, and still gazing up through the glass at her. "I'm better to-day-I think—my head's clearer somehow. Unless I'm dreaming this."

"No. You're awake."

"You're a girl, aren't you?"

"Yes."

"How on earth did you get up there?"

"I climbed. It was quite a job."

"I should think so. Are you staying in the house?"

"Yes."

"I see. At least, I don't quite. Do you mind if I get down from this chair? I'm beginning to feel giddy. It's rotten to be like this."

Judy watched him step down and sink on to the end of his bed. His movements were weak and uncertain. She could see his face more clearly now, and was shocked by its waxen pallor. The room was comfortably though plainly furnished, and had been fitted with a washstand supplied with hot and cold water taps, but there was something queer about the walls. They were covered with some dun-coloured material and seemed to sag in places.

"It must be very dull only having a skylight," she said.

He looked up at her. "Yes. But it's safer. I'm queer, you know. This is a padded room. If I became violent they could take out all the furniture except the bed, which is clamped to the floor. The padding is a hundred years old. They kept the wife of an Oliver Ramblett, who lived towards the end of the eighteenth century, up here until she died." He paused and said with an evident effort and with rather dreadful distinctness, "She was mad."

"How awful," said Judy faintly. It seemed so strange to be crouching on the roof and looking down through the open skylight at the mysterious occupant of the top floor. She no longer thought of him as sinister. And yet—

"She wasn't my ancestress. You must not think that. She had no children, and after her death her husband married again. So you see it's not an inherited taint."

"You've had a nervous breakdown. That's all. People often do and they get quite all right again," said Judy, trying to speak cheerfully. "It can't be good for you to be shut up here. If I were you, I'd ask the doctor to let me go out a bit every day. It's jolly out of doors even in December, the smell of leaves and earth and wood smoke and a robin singing in a thorn bush."

"Don't!" he said, and to her horror she saw tears running down his cheeks. "You don't understand. I can't go out. I promised I wouldn't. The time has seemed very long to-day, but that's because I was awake more than usual. I sleep a lot. It's the medicine, I think."

"Yes, but why can't you? Why should you make such a promise?"

"Because of something I did in a dream—at least a kind of dream. I don't remember anything about it, not a single thing, but the fact remains. It's what they call dual personality, the doctor, thinks, sort of Jekyll and Hyde. One part of me, the part that's talking to you now, is ordinary and fairly decent, and the other—"

"Yes."

"If I tell you will you swear never to repeat it?"

"Yes."

He looked up at her mournfully. "I killed somebody."

She was silent, appalled.

"I can't remember, I can't remember." He held out his hands palms upwards. She noticed that they were beautiful hands, with long, tapering fingers. "There's a name for that too. Amnesia, I think. If I knew when it was coming I might struggle against it. I don't. You see now, don't you, that they are right to keep me shut up here where I can't do any more harm?"

So this was the end of her search for the actual murderer of Mr. Fallowes. Or was it? It was hard to believe that this boy could have been capable of that carefully-planned and cold-blooded crime.

"I suppose you shrink from me now? I fill you with horror."

"No. It's so strange. But I think it's wrong to hide. You say you killed someone. Who was it, and when?"

"An old man. My great uncle. They say I went off on my motor-cycle and was away all night. When I came back in the early morning there was blood on my clothes. I couldn't tell them where I had been. They put me to bed. I slept round the clock and woke with a splitting headache. They knew by that time that my great uncle had been murdered. The doctor broke it to me. He's been jolly decent to me. I mean, some people would have shrunk from me, knowing what he knows. He said 'Oliver, I'm sorry, but if you're not watched and guarded it may happen again.' I said the best thing would be for me to give myself up to the police, but he pointed out how rotten that would be for my stepmother and my sisters, and he was right about that, of course."

"Would you go so far as to let another man be hanged in your place to spare the feelings of your family?"

"Don't be silly. Of course not. But Farwell says I left no clues, and that it will be one of the unsolved mysteries."

"He's a liar."

"He's not. I said I had no friends, but I was wrong. I've got Farwell, he's been jolly decent to me all through, and I'm grate-ful," said Oliver hotly.

"He's lied to you. A man was arrested for your uncle's murder and he was tried and found guilty. So now what?"

"I don't believe you."

"It's the truth."

"Farwell would have told me. Go away."

"Oliver," she said urgently, "I'm going. I've stayed too long as it is. Think over what I've said. I don't want to hurt you. I'm sorry for you. Every word I've said is true. I swear it. Will you promise not to say anything about me to Mrs. Ramblett or the doctor? If they knew I'd climbed up here it would be bad for me. I'll come again to-morrow night and bring a newspaper with an account of the trial. Perhaps you'll believe that. And please don't think I'm your enemy, you poor boy."

"All right," he said confusedly, "but you've muddled me. My head's often bad. I thought I liked you at first. You seemed kind."

"I want to be, Oliver."

"Come again then—and I won't say anything."

"That's right." She spoke soothingly, as she would have spoken to a child. "Put out your light now, and get back to bed."

She stopped to rest a moment and looked back when she reached the ridge of the roof, and she saw that the light had been extinguished. She had been motionless for some time crouching on the edge of the skylight in the bitter cold of the December night with only her tweed coat and a cardigan over her bathing suit, and her teeth were chattering. She had cut her knee on the sharp edge of a tile, but her flesh was so numb that she felt no pain. She sat down by the chimney stack to massage her hands and arms before starting on her descent. Already the stars were fading and the faint glimmer of the false dawn showed in the eastern sky. Her small hands, sunburned, sinewy, with calloused palms, gripped the rope. She slid gently over the edge of the roof. Three minutes later her feet touched the ground. She tucked the swaying end of the rope in among the ivy, praying that it would not be noticed, and switched on her torch to look for her bow. It was lying close at hand, and she picked it up. The arrow with the string attached was somewhere among the branches of the beech tree, where she would have to leave it.

Her bedroom window was open as she had left it. She climbed in. She was dead tired, too tired to think.

CHAPTER XIII
THE CHARMER

MYRA Farwell walked quickly up the High Street, glancing nervously from side to side as she went. The tin of mustard had been pushed into her handbag where it made a bulge. Somewhere on this side of the road there was a brass plate attached to the pillar of a Doric portico, the entrance of what had been a private house now turned into offices. It was months since she had walked by it last, but she remembered it quite well. Anson, Clough and Anson. Commissioners for Oaths. Just beyond these shops. There were several people about, young women pushing perambulators—she smiled absently at a baby whose round blue eyes met hers—middle-aged women like herself. "I'm not very noticeable," she thought hopefully—and then her heart seemed to miss a beat as a hand was laid on her shoulder.

"My dear Myra, how very imprudent."

Her lips moved, but she said nothing.

Her husband looked down at her smilingly. "I think I can guess why you slipped out unbeknownst, my dear. You wanted to buy a present for my birthday, didn't you? Yes, I thought as much. Very sweet of you, but I would far rather you did not risk catching a fresh cold. I've got my car here and I'll run you home."

She grasped the life line he had thrown her. "Yes, I—I wanted to get you some little thing a—a leather note case or something. It—it was to be a surprise."

"I'll take the will for the deed, Myra. You've really got to be careful this winter." He helped her into the car and tucked the rug round her knees.

"You're not angry with me, Ambrose?" she faltered.

He had settled himself in the driving seat and he turned to look at her before letting in the clutch. She blinked a little. It was a long time since he had troubled to exert for her benefit the charm that had overcome the underlying common sense that should have prevented her from marrying a young ship's doctor met on a Mediterranean cruise. She was nine years older, but he had made her believe that it did not matter. She was a woman of means and she had been able to buy him a practice. He had not kept it long. There had been some trouble, hushed up, about one of his women patients. He was clever, a brilliant surgeon; clever but unstable. Myra was not clever at all, and she knew it.

"Angry? Of course not." The brilliant gay blue eyes were reassuring. "You funny little mousey thing. I've been worried and over-worked lately, and I haven't had enough time to give to my mouse."

She flushed a little at his use of the pet name he had ceased to use soon after the end of their honeymoon. She had lost faith in him, but could not help feeling thrilled. She had never expected to be made love to again. She had never been pretty, and no man had paid her any attention before she met Ambrose. Perhaps, after all—she had read novels about errant husbands who had realised at last that their true happiness was with the wife they had neglected.

"What have you been worried about, Ambrose?" He accelerated to pass a lorry, and she caught her breath.

"Isn't it rather dangerous to do that on a bend?" she ventured.

"One must take a few risks or one would never get anywhere. Money worries chiefly," he said after a minute. "Paying interest on loans.'

"It's no use my asking my trustees to sell out any of my capital, Ambrose. I did that before, you remember, and they wouldn't."

"I know, I know. I'm not blaming you, mouse, you've done your best to gnaw through your lion's net."

"What's that?"

"One of Aesop's fables. Never mind."

"We might cut down expenses," she said. "We don't really need Miss Briggs." She tried not to sound too eager.

He laughed. "Get rid of our invaluable factotum? Poor old Briggsie. I couldn't do that, Myra. She's a trained dispenser, she looks after the garden and can drive the car; she nurses you devotedly when you're laid up. No one can say Briggs doesn't earn her salary. But you don't like her, do you?"

"Yes, I do," she said hurriedly.

"I tell you what," he said still in that caressing voice she had never hoped to hear again. "I've only one more call to make and I'll cut that. They can do without me until to-morrow. We'll go on a little jaunt together. I'll run you up to London and we'll dine together and do a show. Do you feel equal to it?"

"I—I think so. But I couldn't go in this old coat."

"We'll stop at the house and you can get your fur. I shall have to give Briggs some instructions."

He stopped the car outside the gate of Sunnyside. "Run in for your glad rags, and tell her to come out to speak to me."

Miss Briggs came out of the surgery as Mrs. Farwell crossed the hall. Her rather prominent pale blue eyes were bright with anger.

"Fancy you going out like that without telling me. I don't know what the doctor will say."

For once Myra heard the sharp scolding voice without flinching.

"It's all right," she said cheerfully. "I met him in the town. He's outside and he wants to speak to you."

Miss Briggs stared after her as she ran up the stairs. Then she went out to the gate and crossed the pavement to speak to Farwell sitting at the wheel of his car.

"What does this mean? I thought you'd be furious."

"I was surprised," he said coldly. "I thought you were supposed to be looking after her."

"I couldn't help it. She slipped out somehow. I saw her from the window and I would have run after her, but a bus was just passing and she stopped it."

"Yes, I see. Well, I've been busy and worried and I'm afraid I've rather shelved the problem of Myra. A little change will do her good. I'm taking her up to Town for a treat. We shan't be back until late."

Her light lashes flickered. "Very good, doctor," she said formally. "What about your patients?

"Ring up Sard Manor and say I've an urgent case and can't get over there before to-morrow. There's no one else. Ah, there you are, Myra, good girl not to keep me waiting."

Miss Briggs stepped back to allow Mrs. Farwell to enter the car.

The doctor smiled. "Doesn't she look a duchess in that fur coat?"

"Don't be absurd, Ambrose."

Myra was a little out of breath. She had changed not only her coat but her handbag, and had made time to push the tin of mustard well down under the scarves and handkerchiefs in her top drawer.

"I hope you'll enjoy yourselves," said Miss Briggs mechanically, and walked back to the house. Farwell looked after her stiff, retreating figure. "Just a minute, Myra. There's something I want to tell her."

He got out of the car and caught up with her just as she reached the door. She half turned. "Well?" she said harshly.

"Not jealous, my dear? You needn't be."

Myra enjoyed her jaunt. Ambrose was affectionate and considerate. It was like a lovely dream. As she sat during the interval of the third and fourth act eating the chocolates he had bought her she even dared to hope that she had been utterly mistaken when she had entertained those growing fears and suspicions. He was worried about money matters, and, for the rest, her nerves were to blame. She was very tired when they left the theatre and she slept in the car most of the way home. It was past one o'clock when he drove the car into the garage. There was a light in the dining-room. Miss Briggs had been sitting up for them.

"I cut the sandwiches, lettuce and tomato. Shall I make some coffee, Mrs. Farwell? It won't take a minute. The bottle in your bed is quite hot. I didn't put it in until about half an hour ago."

"I'm afraid she's tired out," said the doctor. They both looked at Myra as she sat drooping in her chair.

"It's been too much for her," said Miss Briggs. "I was afraid it might be."

Myra tried to rouse herself. "It wasn't. I loved it. Thank you, Ambrose darling, for a lovely time." He laughed the hearty laugh of the dominant male, and putting an arm about her lifted her to her feet. "Not coffee. You might heat some milk, Miss Briggs. She can drink it in bed. Come along my dear, I'll help you up the stairs."

Miss Briggs looked after them with a stony face as they left the room together.

The next morning Myra did not feel at all inclined to get up.

"It's those pains again, Ambrose. That food at the restaurant. It was nice, but too rich for me."

He and Miss Briggs had their breakfast together. He treated her as he always did when Myra was not present, with an easy familiarity which she did not resent.

"How is she?"

"Not so well. That gastric trouble. We'll keep her in bed for a few days. She won't give you the slip again."

"Shall you be in to lunch?"

"I don't think so."

"Mrs. Ramblett rang up twice yesterday evening."

"What about?"

Miss Briggs smiled, not very pleasantly. "Her medicine. She's got to the stage where she'd go through hell for it. You'll slip up one of these days, Ambrose. Why do you do it?"

"Mind your own business." He set down his empty cup and took a cigarette from his case. For an instant she saw him as he really was, and she was startled. "Ambrose, what is it? You look hag-ridden?"

"I'm in a mess, Milly. I'll get clear, but it's a bit complicated at present. Keep Myra quiet for me that's a good girl. I trust you. You'll stick to me, I know."

She nodded. "To the end. But for God's sake be careful. I don't know what you're up to at Sard Manor. I don't want to know. But it's dangerous, isn't it?"

"Damnably."

"Can't you stop?"

"Not now. Too late for that."

At ten o'clock he started on his morning round. He had not many patients and he had lost several lately. It wasn't his fault, he thought bitterly, that old Colonel Grant's daughter had made a fool of herself over him. He had only just been civil. She had not appealed to him. Too long in the tooth. The Grants had left the neighbourhood, but the harm was done. Then there was the fuss over that overfed little beast of a Pekinese he had run over. A fresh start. That was what he wanted, a fresh start. He left his call at Sard Manor to the last, knowing that Helen was expecting him to stay to lunch. Another woman to be smoothed down and kept in a tolerably good temper, but she was worth it. She was in the hall and opened the front door when he rang, but she drew back when he would have taken her in his arms, and laid a warning finger on her lip, and a moment later Bateman came out of the room on the left that was used as an office. He nodded to Farwell unsmilingly. The two men did not get on together.

"Is lunch ready, Helen?"

They were moving towards the dining-room. Mrs. Ramblett's voice was heard from the floor landing summoning the doctor.

"All right," he said. "I won't be a minute." James Bateman followed Helen into the dining-room. "Your mother's been like a cat on hot bricks all the morning," he complained. "This medicine she's so keen on doesn't seem to be doing her much good. I wish I felt as convinced as you do that he's handling Oliver the right way. If I had any say in the matter I'd get a second opinion."

"Well, you haven't."

Farwell joined them before he could say anything more, and he relapsed into a sulky silence, leaving the other two to carry on a conversation. They were leaving the table at the end of the meal before he spoke again.

"I'd like a word with you, Doctor, before you go."

"Very well. I've got to see my patient. After that. Where will you be?"

"Somewhere about the grounds if you don't mind coming out there."

"Not at all," said Farwell, smiling; "it's some time since I saw my friend Selim."

"He's no friend of yours," growled Bateman as he went out.

Farwell shrugged his shoulders. "What a bear that fellow is. I wonder how you stand him, but I suppose he's useful."

"Like your Miss Briggs," said Helen.

"Exactly. I wonder what he wants to say to me. Something unpleasant, obviously."

"He's getting fussed about Oliver." They had gone into the drawing-room, and Farwell had an arm about her shoulders. They moved hastily apart as Judy came in with the coffee tray. Farwell looked at her sharply as he took his cup, and kept her waiting while he selected a lump of sugar of exactly the right size.

"That new maid of yours has a very bad cold. She looks to me as if she might be sickening for something," he remarked when Judy had gone out again.

"I hope not. She's only been here a few days. I believe I did hear her sneezing this morning. What a nuisance servants are."

"Come here!" He set his cup down on the table by his easy chair and drew her down on his knees. "You lovely thing," he said softly. "Your cheek's like a nectarine, your neck like flower petals." He drew a finger gently down the fine curve from her ear to her chin.

"What are we going to do, Ambrose? We can't go on like this."

"Be patient a little longer. How did the family party go off? Your sister and her husband leave England to-day, don't they?"

"Yes. It was awful. Rhoda dropped a load of bricks. She always does. She wanted to see Oliver. We had the greatest difficulty in heading her off. I believe she and Gilbert expected to be asked to stay the night. I'm certain there was a suitcase in the back of their car. Bateman showed her round the gardens. Rhoda and he were awfully very thick. She calls him Batie."

"You call him Jim, don't you?"

"Sometimes. Do you mind?"

"I do rather. I bar that chap. I can't help fancying that you used to lead him on at one time."

"Rubbish. He's always been here. He was my father's assistant."

"He's in love with you."

"Don't be silly, darling. He's wrapped up in his job, his animals. He's looking forward to getting money from Oliver to make the place like it was in my father's time."

"I see."

"Ambrose"—she bent her head to look into his face—"Oliver is going to get better, isn't he?"

He hesitated for a moment before he said, "I'm afraid not. You know his trouble is mental?"

"I had gathered that."

"Well, the cause is an inoperable tumour on the brain. When that breaks he'll die. I'm telling you this, but don't repeat it."

"All right. I won't. Poor old Oliver. Then—if he dies—Rhoda and Alice and I get Great Uncle Joshua's money."

"Do you? I hadn't grasped that. Shall you spend your share on buying new cages to please Bateman?"

"I might. You never know," she said teasingly. They kissed lingeringly, expertly, and then he released her and rose himself reluctantly. "I must go up to him now."

Half an hour later he came down the path towards the small deer enclosure where Bateman was painting the railings.

"You wanted to speak to me."

"Yes." Bateman straightened his back and wiped his hands on an oily rag. "How is Oliver?"

"About the same."

"You know he'll be twenty-one a week from now?"

"No. I didn't know it. But what of it? The poor boy's not in a fit state for any kind of celebration."

"You are doing the best you can for him?"

"Naturally."

"Well, I'm not satisfied," said Bateman bluntly. "Will you agree to his being seen by a specialist if I bring one down from London at my own expense?"

"I have always been willing to have a second opinion if Mrs. Ramblett wished it, but she has every confidence in my diagnosis. I don't admit that you have any standing in this matter, Bateman. You are out to make trouble for reasons of your own. I resent your attitude to me."

"I see." They were moving slowly along the path together and from a distance it might have seemed that they were engaged in amicable conversation. Bateman stopped to fill and light his pipe.

They passed the hyena, prowling incessantly to and fro behind the bars, and paused before the cage of the tiger. Selim's emerald eyes rested on Farwell for an instant before they became fixed majestically on some point beyond him.

"I don't care about zoos, but I like this fellow," said the doctor critically. "Hell let loose if he got out, eh?"

"Probably."

"That striped coat of his. You can't beat it. Death in motley."

He flicked the end of his cigarette into the cage. The tiger snarled.

"I must come round some time and spit in your surgery," said Bateman conversationally.

Farwell laughed. "I'm sorry for your disappointment."

"I'm not disappointed. I expected you to take up this position. I agree that it's a strong one. I can't combat your influence over Mrs. Ramblett. You give her what she wants. But I tell you this, Farwell. If Oliver dies you'll sign the certificate and everything in the garden will be lovely. But I go straight to the Chief Constable and the coroner and ask for a post mortem and an inquest. You know best how well you'd come out of that. Remember. I mean it. Oh, there you are, Jerry." The latter had just come out of one of the outbuildings. "Just show the doctor the nearest way out, will you."

Jerry grinned. "Dis way, doctor."

CHAPTER XIV
"SO THAT'S YOUR GAME—"

JUDY went about her work listlessly, struggling with the combined effects of her exertions during the previous night and a heavy cold. Mrs. Lacy gave her a dose of peppermint and hot water and advised her to go to bed as soon as she had cleared away the supper. Judy went, but she could not sleep. She had promised Oliver to visit him again that night, and he would be expecting her. She had hoped to borrow Helen's bicycle and ride into the town to get a back number of a newspaper, any newspaper with an account in it of David's trial. Nothing else, she felt would convince Oliver that she had told him the truth. But the cycle shed, when she went to it, was locked, and the cook, coming out after her, had told her that Miss Helen had said her bicycle was not to be ridden again.

"You couldn't even if you found a key to fit the lock. She let the air out of the tyres and took away the pump," she added. "No one can say Miss Helen isn't thorough when she's roused, and even when she was little she couldn't bear anyone to make use of anything of hers. No one must touch her toys."

"A selfish little cat, in fact," said Judy bitterly.

Mrs. Lacy, as her habit was, looked uneasily over her shoulder before she whispered, "I always did like Miss Rhoda best."

Judy realised that she would have to wait for her next half day to get her newspaper. Auntie Apples would send her one if she asked for it, but she did not feel that it would be safe to have it come through the post.

Time, she was working against time. What was she to think about Oliver Ramblett? Was he abnormal, a homicidal maniac as he himself believed? Or had the account of his great uncle's murder given him a shock that upset his mental balance, and was all the rest a delusion? There had been nothing brutal or terrifying in his appearance. But his eyes—Judy recalled that there had been something queer about his eyes.

When she went to bed she meant to get up again later and repeat last night's performance. It would be much easier since the cord looped round the chimney stack still dangled hidden by the green cloak of ivy growing up the wall. She sat up for a while and wrote a letter to Auntie Apples. She would be able to post it some time the following day in the pillar box.

"DEAR AUNTIE," she wrote,

"I was right to come here, but I've found out all I can by myself, and I need outside help and advice so I've practically decided to leave to-morrow or the next day. Expect me when you see me. I've got heaps to tell you, and I shall be glad of your advice about what to do next. I'm longing to get away. This house gives me the creeps. I've got a frightful cold which has got me down, but don't worry about me. Your loving JUDY."

She addressed the envelope to Mrs. Sturmer and slipped it into the drawer of her dressing table. It wouldn't be safe to start on her expedition before midnight at the earliest. She shivered at the prospect and a moment later she was so hot that she had to turn down the blanket. "I've got a temperature," she thought. "Gosh, I mustn't be ill here."

Her legs and her back were aching. "I'd better take a couple of aspirin," she said aloud, and was startled by the sound of her own voice. She swallowed the aspirin and lay down again. After a while she slept. When she woke with a start and the certainty that there was something that she had left undone her head was still aching. "I believe I feel worse," she thought despairing, and faced the fact that she was not physically fit to go out into the December night and climb hand over hand up forty feet of rope. "Flying Merle. Crawling more like." Again she was surprised by the echoes of her own voice. "Oh, hell, if I'm delirious I shall give the show away. I must keep my mouth shut. What time is it, anyway?"

She struck a match and looked at her watch lying on the chair beside her bed. It was ten minutes past six. She did not remember anything very clearly after that.

Heat, and confusion, and voices sounding over her head, Mrs. Lacy's voice and Mrs. Ramblett's.

She was crawling over the skylight upside down like a fly on the ceiling, and there were stars overhead, but in the room below something dark and motionless, waiting to spring. David was there and the rope hanging from the chimney stack, and a white chrysanthemum trampled into the mud and the broken stalk of a dead rose. The petals had fallen, but the thorns remained. The brotherhood of the rose. But you're too young, my dear, to ride out after dragons.

Handsome. She had known he would be that. The kind women fall for. Sensual lips and a heavy jowl. Keeping her standing there with the tray while he looked her over. She tried feebly to push away the hands that unfastened the front of her pyjama jacket.

"A rash on her chest. Keep her warm and let her have plenty of barley water to drink. A nurse? No, she doesn't need nursing. Where's Mattie? Let Mattie look after her."

"Well?" said Mrs. Ramblett when the doctor came back to the drawing room.

He shrugged his shoulders. "She has a temperature of a hundred and three and there's a rash. It's probably measles. Helen had better keep out of the way if she hasn't had it. The cook and her niece can look after her between them. How's Oliver?"

"More restless than usual. He asked for you."

"I'll go up to him now." He looked thoughtfully at the slatternly figure huddled on the sofa. It was an opportunity to be frank since Helen was not there. "Has Bateman said anything to you about having a second opinion?"

"Yes."

"I won't have it. You understand? Don't put it to me. You must say that you won't have it. You don't want to endanger your regular supply of medicine, do you?"

She gazed up at him imploringly. "Oh, no."

He went upstairs, unlocking the door at the foot of the staircase leading to the top floor from a bunch of keys he carried in his pocket. The door of Oliver's room was locked too on the outside. Oliver looked up eagerly as he entered. "Oh, doctor. I'm so glad you've come."

Farwell was smiling as he patted his shoulder, noting through the material of the dressing gown he wore over his pyjamas how pitifully thin it was.

"Are you, my dear boy? Why? Is there anything I can do?"

"My mind has been doing funny things again. At least I suppose it's my subconscious. I had the queerest dream. It must have been a dream, though at the time I was sure it was real, but it's been like that with me for some time now."

Farwell nodded. The effect of the drugs he had been giving the boy. Nothing in fact.

"I dreamt—never mind that. There was something about a promise," said Oliver confusedly. "What I want to know is are you quite sure no one has been arrested for that—that murder?"

The doctor had taken out his cigarette case. He paused in the act of picking out a cigarette. "Dear chap, of course not. It was agreed, wasn't it, that in that case you would give yourself up."

"You're quite sure?"

"Absolutely. You trust me, don't you, Oliver? It's for the sake of your people as well as your own that we're keeping you shut up here. It wouldn't be very nice, would it, for your sisters, to have you sent to Broadmoor."

The boy shuddered. "No, Farwell—if only I hadn't done it. It's so horrible. I never wanted to kill things."

"Don't excite yourself. I'll give you something to make you sleep. Who put this idea in your head?"

"A girl. She looked through the skylight—in my dreams." Farwell's face changed slightly. He had been listening with easy contempt. Now he gave Oliver all his attention. But the boy did not notice it. He was leaning forward with his elbows on his knees and his head in his hands staring miserably at the floor.

"Don't worry about it, my dear fellow. Just an unusually vivid dream. Forget it. I've brought you some stuff to quiet your nerves. In this bottle. If I leave it with you can I rely on you not to take more than the marked dose?"

"Yes—I think so. Perhaps mother had better give it to me. I get so muddled. I've lost my sense of time—or else it's my watch. Sometimes the hands race round."

He took the glass the doctor gave him. It was nearly full of an opalescent liquid.

"It's more than usual," he said doubtfully.

"You need a good sleep."

"All right. I suppose I do."

He drank the medicine and handed back the glass before he lay back on the bed. Farwell drew a quilt over him and waited. In a few minutes his heavy, rather stertorous breathing showed that the narcotic had taken effect.

The doctor did not leave the room directly. He stood on the chair under the skylight and pushed the window open as far as it would go. He looked out on the slope of the opposite gable, but he was more interested in a tiny scrap of material caught in a splinter of the wooden frame. He detached it and saw that it was dark blue stockinette. He also noticed a small smear of blood.

Mrs. Ramblett was still alone, dozing on the sofa by the drawing-room fire, when he went down. She sat up, yawning. "Oh, it's you, doctor. I thought you'd gone. Perhaps you'll stay to tea now. Helen will be back soon."

"Where has she gone?"

"To the hairdressers to get a permanent wave."

"I won't stay. But I think I'll have another look at that new maid of yours before I go. I think she's sickening for measles, but I'm not quite satisfied."

"Oh dear," said Mrs. Ramblett vaguely, "I don't think Mattie is really up to nursing people. It's very tiresome. Could she be taken off somewhere in an ambulance?"

"No. No, that wouldn't do at all. She'll be all right here."

The kitchen door leading into the passage running the length of the servant's wing was open. Miss Lacy was busy making pastry.

"I'm just going to have another look at the patient," he explained as he passed. He went into Judy's room and closed the door. Judy was tossing and turning in her bed. Her eyes were bright with fever and she did not seem aware of his entrance, After a brief search he found the key of her suitcase among the handkerchiefs in the top drawer of the dressing chest.

He went through her few possessions and slipped the letter addressed to Mrs. Sturmer into his coat pocket. Then, when he had replaced everything as he had found it, he went over to the bed and stood looking down at the small, restless figure under the crumpled sheet. "So that's your game, is it," he said softly. "Spying."

Mrs. Lacy looked up from her pastry board when the doctor returned along the passage. He paused at the door.

"You look comfortable in here," he said pleasantly.

"How's poor Mary, doctor?"

"Is that her name? About the same. Your niece can look after her. See that she has plenty of barley water to drink. Don't let anyone else go near her."

"And who's to do her work?" lamented Mrs. Lacy. "We don't get much luck in this house."

"What do you know of her? Is she a local girl? Did Mrs. Ramblett have any references with her?"

"As to that I couldn't say, but she's a quiet, well-spoken girl, and willing. She's no friends in the neighbourhood, I fancy, she writes letters and likes to post them herself."

"I see. Well, don't let anybody go near her. That's important. She's highly infectious at the moment. Your niece can do all that is necessary." He glanced, coldly smiling, at the face of Mattie. It was like a lump of red flesh with two pebbles for eyes. "You can, can't you, Mattie?"

"No use you talking to her, doctor. She only listens to me," said her aunt, not without a touch of pride.

CHAPTER XV
A ROVING COMMISSION

INSPECTOR Collier, of the C.I.D., had spent nearly three months in the States. He had been sent there at the urgent request of the Federal police to help identify certain members of a gang of forgers. He had been detained to give evidence at their trial, much to his annoyance, for he was now a married man, and the garden of the house into which he and Sandra and his thirteen year old stepson Toby had moved needed attention, He landed at Southampton on the twenty-third of December. Looking down from the deck he had seen Toby and his mother in the little crowd that had braved the raw cold of the winter afternoon to meet their friends coming ashore.

The next three days were fully occupied. He had to report at the Yard, elude his family while he bought them Christmas presents, help Toby decorate the tree and Sandra, who was temporarily servantless, to cook the dinner. On Boxing day they all three went to the pantomime at Drury Lane. It was a jolly Christmas, but Collier, glancing now and again at his stepson, was beginning to wonder if there was something on his mind. He and Toby were excellent friends, and he hoped the boy would come to him if he was in any trouble. He was prepared, therefore, when Toby, abandoning a half-hearted attempt to finish a jigsaw puzzle, said, "Hugh—I want to ask you something." Sandra had gone up to her room to lie down for an hour before tea and they had the dining-room to themselves. Collier laid down his newspaper and set about filling his pipe.

"Carry on. What is it?"

"While you were in America did you read about an old man who was murdered by an acrobat? He was rich and eccentric and lived alone."

"Yes. I read about it. What of it?"

"That acrobat was one of the Flying Merles. You remember that circus we went to in August at Seaton. You came down for the week-end and took mother and me—and I went again with another boy to the evening show because it was so awfully good?"

"I remember."

"The Flying Merles were first class. There were two men and a girl. They were all quite young. There was another girl, but she didn't do much. When I saw that one of them had been arrested for this murder I felt pretty rotten about it, and so did Fatty Dyson, who saw their show at Sidmouth. And when he was found guilty we got all worked up because we thought the defence had been pretty slack and—and I wrote a letter to the girl and sent it care of the theatre where they were performing when all this happened, and I asked her to meet me at the zoo to talk things over, and she wrote back and said she would."

"No one can accuse you of lacking initiative," said his stepfather. "Did she turn up?"

"She did. She wasn't as beautiful as she looked in the ring in that silver dress, but she was jolly nice. No swank or anything," said Toby earnestly, "and I could see she was awfully unhappy about her brother. It's absolutely ghastly for her, of course. I told her I was sure he hadn't done it, and she was a good deal bucked, because other people were kind, but she could see they thought he had. We had tea opposite the Mappin Terraces and talked and talked, and I told her what Fatty's chauffeur had found out at Somerset House about Mr. Fallowes' will and who the people were who came into all his money, and she decided to go off to their place and do a bit of snooping." Toby paused for breath, and Collier, who had been listening with growing interest, produced a pencil and a notebook.

"This isn't very clear. You must learn how to make a report, Toby, if you're going to be a policeman. You think Merle is innocent. I read the accounts of the trial and I must say that the evidence against him seemed overwhelming."

"I wish you'd been here, Hugh."

"Thanks for the bouquet, but I couldn't have done anything. The local police handled the case. The Yard wasn't called in."

He paused a moment and then he said, "I'm afraid you did rather a cruel thing, Toby, if you raised this girl's hopes."

"Wait until you've heard all I've got to tell you, Hugh."

"All right, I will. Go ahead."

"I thought it was a frame up, just as David Merle himself said, partly because there were too many clues. His finger-prints on the silver, for instance. Why should he bother with the silver? He might as well give himself up at the station as offer it to a local pawnbroker—it was Fatty's chauffeur who said that, but Fatty and I agreed—if David had really done it he wouldn't have been such as ass as to leave the bundle of notes in his coat pocket to be found when he was searched. It was all made too easy for the police."

"There is something in what you say, Toby; it's a point. What's your theory, if you have one?"

"Well, it seemed to me that the defence ought to have looked about for any other people who might gain by the death of Mr. Fallowes. He was supposed to be very rich. We found out about his will. He left ninety thousand pounds to his great nephew, a chap called Oliver Ramblett. If Oliver died before he was twenty-one it was to be divided equally among Oliver's three half-sisters. It said where they lived. Sard Manor, near Bedesford. Fatty had even been to the place. They run a sort of private zoo like the one at Maidstone, but not nearly so good. It's rather a bum show actually, Fatty says."

"How do you know that the police didn't make a few discreet enquiries about Mr. Fallowes' heirs?"

Toby's face fell rather at this suggestion, but he combated it vigorously. "Not they. They were too jolly pleased with them-selves. They'd got Merle. Why bother to look for someone else when he filled the bill?"

"Human nature, Toby. You're probably right again. The Ramblett family certainly had a good deal to gain. What has Miss Merle done about it? Did she go to a detective agency?"

"No. She hasn't much money and she wanted to do something herself. She went down to Bedesford and got taken on at the Manor as a maid. She wrote to me twice from there, but I wasn't to answer because it might not be safe. I've got her letters. The second one was a sort of descriptive list of all the people she'd met there. They sound a pretty poisonous crowd, and it looks as if she's bitten off more than she can chew. She asked me to show you her letters and get your advice. I've been hoping to hear from her again, but I haven't. And there was one of those little powder boxes girls use for their noses, with hardly any powder in it, but I've lost that. It fell out of my pocket or something."

"I'd be glad to see the letters."

"I've got them upstairs in my room. Half a mo."

Collier took them from him and examine the envelopes carefully before looking at their contents.

Toby watched him with breathless eagerness. "Why do you do that?"

"Routine, Toby. You get the postmark, place and date and sometimes you can see if an envelope has been steamed open and stuck down again. In the latest written of these the writing is very straggling. I should say it was written in a hurry and under some stress of emotion. Now I'll just read these through before I say anything more."

One of the two Cairn terriers curled up in their basket got up and came over to climb on to Toby's knees. Toby played with his ears inattentively. He was watching his stepfather's face.

"Why didn't you tell me all this before, Toby?"

"I wanted to, but I haven't been able to get you alone. I didn't want Mummie to be worried. And—you see I didn't tell her at the time—about writing to Judy I mean—I didn't want to look an ass. Mother wouldn't have laughed, but still—if you don't tell things at the time it's always more difficult," mumbled Toby.

Collier nodded. "Quite. I understand. I don't blame you, old chap. But the time factor—we've lost three days," he said half to himself.

"I'm sorry," faltered Toby.

"Don't worry. What's this girl like? How old is she?"

"Smallish, with brown hair. Sort of natural, not painted up. She told me she was nineteen."

Collier looked at the clock. "Tell your mother I'm sorry I shan't be in for tea. I should have been going back on duty to-morrow in any case. I think I'll go along now and talk this over with the Superintendent."

"Ooh! Will the Yard take it up?"

"I can't say about that. But I have a certain responsibility in the matter because it was through you that this girl went to Sard Manor. Don't discuss this affair with anyone, Toby, not even with your friend, Fatty Dyson, and that very useful chauffeur of his." He was in the hall by this time, struggling into his overcoat. Toby and the terriers went with him to the garden gate and saw him catch a bus at the corner of the road.

Superintendent Cardew was working placidly as usual in a thick fog of tobacco smoke. He received Collier cordially.

"You weren't expected before to-morrow morning. Why this excess of zeal? Glad to see you anyway. Sit down."

"It's that boy of mine, young Toby. I'm inclined to think he's unearthed something. That murder case at Holton, an old man named Fallowes—"

"I know. A nasty business. His head was bashed in with a stone taken from the rockery by a young fellow he'd asked to supper."

"You were sure of his guilt?"

"There didn't seem to be any room for doubt. But we didn't have the case. The locals got on with it."

"Well, that kid of mine thought otherwise." Collier's pride in his stepson was a source of some amusement to his friends at the Yard, and Cardew grinned. "He's solved the mystery, eh? Out of the mouths of babes—"

"I know it sounds unlikely, Superintendent, but he got into touch with the sister of the condemned man, the only person, apparently, who has always been convinced of his innocence, and between them they've raked up a few facts that will bear looking into." He repeated what Toby had told him of the Ramblett family's connection with the murdered man, and laid Judy's two letters on the Superintendent's desk.

Cardew read them. "You're right. It sounds fishy. The last is a week old. Merle's appeal has been dismissed. Did you know that? He'll be hanged, barring miracles, in a week or two, I suppose. Why have you come to me, Collier? What do you want me to do?"

"I'd like a roving commission. There's enough here to justify it."

Cardew fingered the letters doubtfully. "Is there? Some wouldn't think so. But with a man's life at stake one can stretch a point."

"It shouldn't take long to vet the place."

"No. Borders of Somerset and Devon, isn't it? I seem to have heard of Bedesford lately—and Sard Manor. Wait a minute." He reached for the crumpled remains of that morning's *Daily Telegraph* lying under his writing table. "Here you are. Fatal accident at a private zoo. The mangled body of Mr. James Bateman was found yesterday evening in the tiger s cage. No one was about at the time that the tragedy must have occurred, as the zoo is closed to the public during the winter month and both the keepers had gone out with the lorry to fetch the daily supply of meat for their charges. On their return their attention was attracted by the snarling of the tiger and the terrified cries of the other animals who were all, apparently, aware that something was amiss. It is supposed that the unfortunate man, who had been trying to tame the tiger, had ventured into the cage. The inquest will be held to-morrow."

"That settles it, I think," said Cardew. "You can go down for that. It will give you an opportunity to give some of these birds the once over."

"Shall I get into touch with the local police?"

"I leave that to you. Use your own judgment. Make sure the girl is safe. If the murder of old Fallowes was a put up job and Merle a scapegoat there's a very cunning and completely merciless mind at work."

"I'd like to run down to Holton first. I might pick up something on the spot."

Cardew reached for a time table. "Not a bad notion. There's a train at 6.10, a fast one. But could you make Bedesford in time from there? The inquest is pretty sure to open at eleven."

Collier was running a finger down the page. "Can do. Toby wrote to this girl care of the Palace Theatre of Varieties at Holton, and they evidently forwarded his letter. That looks as if somebody on the theatre staff is keeping in touch with her. These stage folk are pretty good to one another when times are hard. Well, goodbye, sir, and thank you for giving me this chance."

Collier reached Holton soon after eight and went straight from the station to the Palace Theatre. It was raining, and he was not sorry to get out of the cold, wet streets into the brightly-lit vestibule. The girl in the box-office warned him that the first house would be over in forty minutes. He thanked her but paid for a stall. He had only looked in, he said, to see the trapezists. He had a weakness for acrobats.

"Too bad," she said. "You must have been looking at last week's bills. We've no acrobatic turns this week. They get engagements in panto at this time of year."

"You wouldn't get many as good as the Flying Merles."

"They were good, weren't they," she said. "I don't like to think of them now. Such a nice-looking boy he was. Nice manners, quite the gentleman always, and to think of him shut up in a cell and going to be executed. It gives one the creeps." She lowered her voice confidentially. "Our manager, Mr. Levy, was sweet on Judy Merle. He got as much time off as he could during the trial to be with her and her aunt. I saw him myself taking them across the square to the court. And he's looked very down in the mouth ever since."

She broke off as the commissionaire, who had been outside, came into the vestibule, and Collier took the hint and found his way to the bar. There he was supplied with a gin and it by a young woman whose head reminded him of corrugated iron painted daffodil yellow. He asked her if Mr. Levy was anywhere about.

"Mr. Levy? He was here just now. Oh, Mr. Levy, this gentleman was asking for you."

"Pleased to meet you, sir. What can I do for you?" Ben smiled expansively, but his dark eyes were anxious.

Collier suggested a drink, but he declined. "No time. I've got to go round to the back."

Collier drew him aside. "You are a friend of Miss Merle, aren't you?"

"I am. What of it?"

"You know where she is at present?

Ben eyed him doubtfully, but there was something about Collier that invited confidences, and poor Ben had been longing to unburden his soul to some sympathetic listener.

"It's queer you should ask that. I'm her friend, I'd do anything for her, and she knows it, but she hasn't trusted me. That's hurt me, see. Mrs. Sturmer—that's her aunt—but you know that if you're a friend of hers—Mrs. Sturmer wrote me that Judy had gone into the country to stay with friends. Then only the other day she wrote me again. Some other friends have taken her on a cruise, a long cruise until it's all over. Well, that took my breath away. Judy on a cruise, sun bathing and what not, while her brother is being hanged. Sounds cold-blooded, doesn't it. And not like Judy. I can't get it somehow. She—well, she'd been my ideal of what a girl ought to be, warm-hearted, straight as a die, loyal to her pals, and this cruise business has messed it all up. I mean, it's out of character, see."

"Did she write to you herself telling her plans, or did you hear from the aunt?"

"From the aunt. And that hurts too. She might have sent me a line."

"Is the aunt a reliable sort of person?"

"You haven't met her? I see. Oh, quite. Absolutely. I understood that Judy was to make her home with Mrs. Sturmer, and that seemed okay. She's not posh, you know, not class. She was in the show business when she was a girl. She married a German hairdresser and he was interned when the war broke out and died of 'flu just before the armistice. She turned the hairdresser's shop into a dress agency and she's been running it ever since. She brought up Judy and her brothers. I don't know what she thinks of Judy running off like this. Of course one can't blame the kid really," said Ben loyally. "She's been desperately unhappy. She wants to forget if she can. We ought to be glad she doesn't insist on waiting outside the prison to hear the bell toll."

"One never knows how people will react in such circumstances," said Collier. "I suppose nobody here doubts that her brother committed the murder."

"Poor devil. No. His wife was ill, and her mother was pestering him for money. She one of the witnesses for the prosecution. Gosh, how she hated him. Very prim and pi and as hard as nails. You couldn't make her see that she's driven him to it. If I'd only known he was so hard up I could have let him have a pound or two. Mind you, I'm sure the murder was unpremeditated. He saw the open safe and was tempted and then the old man caught him at it and he struck out blindly."

"His sister wouldn't admit that. She believes in his innocence."

"I know she does. Bless her. Poor little Judy. That's why that damned cruise sticks in my throat. I can't swallow it somehow. Well, good night. Pleased to have met you. Look in again—"

The assistant stage manager of the Palace had seen one of the usherettes trying to attract his attention. He shook Collier's hand warmly and rushed off, leaving Collier to finish his drink and consider his next move.

CHAPTER XVI
NO ADMITTANCE

COLLIER rang up Sandra and told her he might not be home for some days. He always kept a suitcase packed with everything he might need in his locker at the Yard and he had brought that down to Holton with him. After some minutes spent in studying a local road map he left the Palace Theatre and made his way through the drizzling rain to the rather ill-lit residential quarter of the town that had been the scene of the murder.

He had no difficulty in finding Laurel Lodge. The entrance to the drive bristled with house agents' boards. He fancied they would not easily find a purchaser. He walked from there to the station through tree-lined roads bordered with detached houses standing in their own grounds. Once he saw the red tail light of a car disappearing in the distance, but he did not meet a single pedestrian. He noted, too, that there was a side path leading up to the station platform as well as the main entrance. If there was a third person at the Lodge at the time of the crime it would evidently have been quite possible for him to get away unnoticed.

At the Station Hotel, where he had booked a room for the night, he went into the coffee room to thaw himself at the fire. Two commercial travellers who were there before him were bemoaning their fate at having to be on the road while traffic was still disorganised by the Christmas rush. From the elder of the two he learned to his dismay that it would be almost impossible to reach Bedesford before noon.

"The only way you could get there would be by getting the night mail to Salisbury. You'd be landed there round about 11.50, and get an early local train on to Bedesford."

Collier worked it out himself with two time tables and saw that the commercial traveller was right. He had been looking forward to a night's rest, but it could not be helped.

He was in the public gallery of the old Town Hall of Bedesford when the inquest on James Bateman was opened by the coroner, sitting with a jury, the following morning. He had enjoyed a hearty breakfast at the King's Head and had been refreshed by a hot bath and a shave.

Apparently very little public interest had been aroused in the neighbourhood by the tragedy. The gallery was sparsely filled by the local unemployed who had drifted in to pass the time and keep out of the rain. Under the new ruling the jury was not compelled to view the body, and the proceedings began with the calling of the manager of the South Western Bank, in the High Street, who gave evidence of identification. He had known the deceased since

1919 when he came to Sard Manor to act as the late Mr. Ramblett's assistant. Mr. Ramblett had a collection of wild animals and what had formerly been the park and pasture land attached to the estate had been laid out by him as a zoological garden. After his death a few years ago Bateman had been retained by Mrs. Ramblett to look after the place.

"Had he any means beyond his salary?"

"So far as I know he had not, but he lived in a cottage in the gardens and spent very little on himself. He banked his salary and never spent it all. He has quite a good balance."

"You were on friendly terms with him?"

"I knew him as well as anyone knew him, I think, but he wasn't a man to make friends. He never came into the town except on business. He didn't play golf or tennis."

"Did he ever mention any relatives?"

"He told me once that he was quite alone in the world."

"I see. Thank you."

The next witness, a rough looking man, was called and came to stand by the coroner's table.

"Your name is Tom Bowles, and you are the head keeper at Sard Manor?"

"That's right, sir."

"Will you tell the jury how you found the body?"

"Well, me and Jerry had gone over to Exeter that afternoon to fetch a plough horse that had dropped down dead the night before. The farmer rang us up, see. Our animals are fed mostly on horseflesh, and it's a bit of a job to get it. There's another chap working at Sard—old Curie—but he had a poisoned finger and Doctor Farwell told him to go along to the cottage hospital and get them to lance it, so he had the afternoon off. Mr. Bateman was alone there, see, from round about two until a bit after six. Jerry said to me, 'There's something wrong,' as soon as ever I'd backed the lorry into the yard where me and Curie cut up the meat and all that. I didn't have to be told. You never heard such a yelping and screeching. It sounded as if all the animals had gone mad. It was past their feeding time and normally they'd have been fairly quiet. I went into my cottage and fetched my old army pistol. I got a licence for it so I'm not afraid to mention it. And I got my torch and Jerry fetched a stable lanthorn. It was quite dark by that time. We went round by the wolves enclosure and they were all huddled together and yapping and snarling. It looked like fright to me. I'd got a notion by that time that the tiger had got out of his cage, and I didn't altogether fancy walking about in the dark with that beast loose on the hillside. As for Jerry, his teeth were chattering like the keys of a typewriter. We stuck together like glue, but we went on. The monkeys in the monkey house were whimpering like sick children and Jerry wanted to go to them, but by then I could hear Selim moving about in his cage. I thought 'Thank God!' and then I switched on my torch and I saw Mr. Bateman inside lying close to the door. He was dead. No mistake about that. He'd been badly mauled, especially about the head, but Selim wasn't guarding him as those beasts usually guard their kill. He was as far away as he could get and prowling up and down and grumbling under his breath. He wasn't frightened. You can't frighten a tiger. But he wasn't happy. I could guess what had happened. Mr. Bateman thought the world of Selim, and he was always talking to him and putting his hand through the bars to stroke him and kidding himself that he could be tamed. I warned him time and again, but he wouldn't listen. He loved animals, and he couldn't believe they'd hurt him. And, as it happened, in all these years not one of them had. I think Selim may have seemed more friendly than usual and Mr. Bateman thought he'd chance it and go into the cage, and Selim misunderstood him and sprang. Mr. Bateman fell and fractured his skull on the cement floor of the cage, and after a bit Selim stopped worrying and tearing and got a notion in his dim brain that there was something wrong. That's the way it looked to me anyhow. I made Jerry flash the light in his eyes while I opened the door and pulled the body out, but I didn't really think he'd go for me. I went up to the house then and told the cook to break it to Mrs. Ramblett and Miss Helen while I telephoned to the police, and within half an hour they'd come along with the ambulance and taken him away."

The next witness to be called was Gerald Courtney. The name was impressive, but its bearer turned out to be Jerry, the under keeper. His evidence corroborated that of Bowles in every particular.

"If it hadn't been for old Curie and his bad finger it wouldn't have happened, no, sir. I don' reck to deal with no dead horses, and any other day Curie'd have gone along with Mr. Bowles and I'd have been in the gardens and maybe I could ha' stopped poor Mr. Bateman from doin' anything so plumb foolish as walk into that pesky tiger's cage. But old Curie he's deaf as a post and he don't talk much, but he said to me only the day before, 'The doctor paints this finger o' mine with his stuff every time he comes and puts on a fresh bandage and it gets worse and worse. Half a mind to go to the hospital,' he said. And when he went they kept him."

"Yes," said the coroner. "Blood poisoning. I hear he's on the danger list. That will do, Courtney.

The police surgeon was the next witness. He had accompanied the ambulance to Sard Manor. He described the examination he had made of the body as it lay outside the cage and its terrible injuries.

"Did you make a post mortem of the organs?"

"No. It hardly seemed necessary. The cause of death was obvious."

"H'm. Yes. I just wondered whether he had any alcohol at lunch. It sometimes induces over-confidence. I don't want to bring any member of the Ramblett family here if I can avoid it. I understand that Mrs. Ramblett was seriously affected by the shock of this tragic occurrence. I will recall Thomas Bowles."

Bowles was brought back, and this time it seemed to Collier, watching from the gallery, that he betrayed some reluctance.

"Was Mr. Bateman a heavy drinker?"

"Not him. Hardly drank anything at all."

There were no more witnesses after the local police sergeant who described how he had been called to Sard Manor and had gone there with the doctor and a couple of men in the ambulance.

"There is just one point, Sergeant. The witness Bowles has told us that the animals were making a great deal of noise. How was it that the attention of the household was not attracted earlier?"

"That point occurred to me, sir. They don't seem to have noticed anything. But the wind was in a direction that would carry the sound away in the opposite direction."

"Thank you."

The coroner summed up. There seemed no doubt that the unfortunate man had been attacked by the tiger as the result of his own foolhardiness in venturing alone and unarmed into the cage. The evidence of the keepers showed that he had been planning to do this, and was not to be dissuaded. No blame attached to anybody else. The police had examined the cage and considered it adequate, and there was nothing wrong with the fastenings of the door. The jury consulted together in whispers and the foreman rose. "We say death by misadventure."

"I concur with that. And I shall not take upon myself to advise Mrs. Ramblett to have the tiger—no doubt a valuable animal—shot. The evidence of the keeper Bowles has shown that the poor beast can hardly be blamed for what occurred."

There was a murmur of agreement from the jury.

The inquest was over.

Collier, lingering under the portico of the Town Hall, which was built in the pseudo-classic style of the eighteenth century, to light his pipe, saw Jerry, crossing the square, and followed him into the bar of the King's Head.

Jerry ordered a double whisky. Collier asked for a bottle of tonic water.

"You've had a trying time," he said sympathetically.

He felt genuinely sorry for Jerry. The big man looked grey with cold. He seemed as forlorn as a lost puppy as he fumbled for his change and stood staring at his glass as if he did not know what to do with it now he had it.

"Trying. You said it. Things keep happening. Losing my monkeys with lung trouble, and Master Oliver ill, and now this. Looks like a hoodoo to me. I'll say it does. Way of the wind. But its gol darned queer all the same that nobody heard up at the house with all the animals raising hell the way they did. And everyone there was sighing and sobbing. They all loved Mr. Bateman. Sure.

Barring the hyena, maybe. He wouldn't care. And he was kind to me," said Jerry sadly.

The barmaid tittered, "What, the hyena?"

"No, ma'am, Mr. Bateman." He sighed and set down his glass, wiping his lips on his sleeve. "Got to be getting along."

"Mrs. Ramblett won't care to keep that tiger," said Collier. "I'm in touch with some of the dealers, as it happens. I might be able to make her an offer. But I'd have to see him first. Can't do much with an old animal, in poor condition."

"You won't see a finer tiger anywhere in a cage," boasted Jerry. "In the jungle maybe. But I don't know that she'll want to sell."

"No time like the present," said Collier briskly. "I'll come along with you, and if I like the look of him I can make her an offer."

But Jerry shook his head decidedly.

"Not with me. We aren't allowed to bring anyone in. Mrs. Ramblett don't like strangers about the place. Nobody can't stop you from coming, and maybe she'll see you, but I hope you won't mention that I got talking to you about the tiger. I don't want to lose my job."

"All right, I won't," said Collier easily, "and I may not come after all."

He let Jerry get well away before he left.

Collier smiled at the barmaid. "Do you know this zoo place he works at?"

"My boy took me there last summer. Awkward place to get to. Over a mile from where the bus stops. But he took me on the pillion of his motor bike. We didn't think much of it. Half the cages were empty. My boy and I kept on reading the labels over the pens, oryx something or other and all that, and throwing in gravel and scraping sticks along the bars to ginger the thing up, and lo and behold, there wasn't anything there at all. You can take it from me it wasn't worth the sixpence admission."

"Too bad," said Collier with a sympathy which, this time, was far from genuine.

Some other customers came in and he went out. He had decided that it might make a better impression if he drove up to Sard Manor in a taxi, and it would certainly save time. He had learned that the 'bus service was infrequent and he did not fancy a six mile walk in the rain. He engaged a taxi from the rank outside the station.

The driver stopped his car and turned in his seat to speak to his fare at the top of the avenue. The gate at the foot of the hill had been standing open.

"Can't get no further."

The road on the right leading over the crest of the hill was barred by a locked gate, a turnstile fastened with a chain and padlock and a kiosk with its windows closed. On the left the gate opening on a drive winding through dense shrubberies bore a notice No Admittance.

Collier got out of the taxi. "Wait for me here."

"All right, guv'nor."

The man Bowles emerged from a path at the back of the kiosk. He came towards them. His expression was distinctly unfriendly.

"What's all this? Don't you know this is private property? You left the public road half a mile back. There's no thoroughfare this way."

"I've come to see Mrs. Ramblett on business."

"Mrs. Ramblett isn't well. She don't receive visitors."

"I think she will see me."

Bowles grunted. "I tell you she isn't well enough. She's got to be kept quiet. Doctor's orders."

"Miss Ramblett then."

He took out his note case. Bowles eyed it thoughtfully. His tone changed slightly. "I got my orders. But you give me your card and a message and I'll take a chance and tell her."

The only cards Collier had with him were his own, and he did not want to reveal his identity. He slipped a ten shilling note into the keeper's ready hand. "I haven't got a card, and my name won't convey anything to her. It's Jarrow, Charles Jarrow. I thought of making an offer for that tiger."

Bowles nodded. "You wait here. I'll see."

He went up through the shrubberies on the left beyond which Collier could see the corner of a roof and part of a chimney stack dark against the darkening sky. Rain dripped from the laurels.

A long drawn howl added to the gloom. Bowles came back at the end of five minutes.

"Sorry, sir, but she won't see you. I was to say they have no intention of selling the animal."

"Well, if they won't they won't. I suppose I couldn't have a peep at him."

"I'm afraid not. It would be more than my place is worth. Mrs. Ramblett doesn't like strangers. I'll have to ask you to go now."

Surly brute, thought Collier, who had seldom got less return for an expenditure of ten shillings, but he knew better than to antagonize a man who might still be useful to him, so he wished him good day quite pleasantly as he climbed back into the taxi.

As he drove down the avenue he noticed the buffalo in the pasture on the right and the high curved wire fence on either side. It struck him that it would need courage to trespass in those fields. He did not know what to do next. Sard Manor was private property. He could not force his way in and he had no evidence that would justify him in applying for a search warrant. A gleam of red among the tangle of briars in the hedge a quarter of a mile farther along the lane gave him the needed inspiration. Judy posted her own letters. There was just a chance that she might come down later on. It would be his opportunity to speak to her. He stopped the taxi when it reached the main road and paid off the driver, very much to that worthy's surprise.

"I'll walk the rest of the way back. I need some exercise."

He turned down the lane again and tramped to and fro to keep himself warm where he could not fail to see anyone coming to the pillar box. When it grew too dark to see he could still hear even a light footfall, for the night was very still. But Judy did not come.

CHAPTER XVII
DISAPPEARANCE OF MRS. STURMER

SUPERINTENDENT Cardew listened attentively to Collier's account of the inquest and of his subsequent failure to penetrate the defences of Sard Manor.

"I don't see how you could do more than you have done. The Rambletts seem to be odd fish, but there's nothing we can take hold of. Did you agree with the verdict at the inquest?"

"Well—I should have preferred an open verdict myself. There was nothing to show how he got into the tiger's cage. The keepers said he had been hankering to make the experiment, but so far as I could see there was no actual proof that he wasn't pushed in, having previously been stunned by a blow on the head. The base of his skull was fractured. The police surgeon thought he was knocked backwards when the tiger sprang at him. Might have been, of course. My point is that no one saw it happen."

The superintendent grinned. "What a doubting Thomas you are. The three keepers have got good alibis, haven't they?"

"Curie has. I'm not so sure about the others. I don't like Bowles. He'd sell his grandmother for a fiver. The assistant keeper Jerry is afraid of him. Their story hangs together well enough. I can't say I doubted it at the time, but thinking it over in the train coming back to London I couldn't help seeing that it might be a put up job. I don't suspect Jerry of any violence. He's a big fellow, but constitutionally timid. I can imagine Bowles being taken to task for some neglect of duty, answering insolently, words leading to blows, and Jerry looking on, afraid to interfere until it was too late. It would have been easy enough to push the body into the tiger's cage and drag it out again when the tiger had done his bit."

Cardew stared rather hard at his subordinate. "Do you really think that is what happened?"

"I wouldn't go so far as that, but it might have been. Bowles is a nasty piece of work, and Jerry isn't at all happy."

"That's natural enough if he liked Bateman."

"Yes." Collier stared moodily out of the window, where a brown sailed barge was going down with the tide. "It's hell having to wait for a crime to be committed before you can go all out," he said.

"What's your trouble actually?"

"I didn't see the girl. According to the stage manager at the Palace theatre where the Merles were performing when the murder was committed, friends have taken her on a cruise. It puzzled him. He couldn't believe it, and I can't either."

"Why not? There are such things. I've seen the posters myself, blue skies and flying fish and young women in beach pyjamas playing deck quoits."

"Quite. But we know that only a week ago Judy Merle was working as a house parlour-maid, under a false name, at Sard Manor. She may have friends who can afford to take her on a cruise, but how did they get at her? Levy didn't know that, but he wasn't comfortable about it. He knows she's breaking her heart over her brother. He said it wasn't in character, and I should say he was a pretty good judge."

"How did he hear about the cruise?"

"From her aunt. That's an idea. I might get something from her. He mentioned her name. She lives in Cottingham and runs an old clothes shop."

The Superintendent was drawing noughts and crosses on his blotting paper, a habit of his when in doubt. He had learned to respect Collier's hunches. On the other hand he was apt to worry over any possible waste of the taxpayers' money.

"You still suspect a possible connection between this man Bateman's death and the murder committed in another part of England two months ago?"

"Yes. The Rambletts, or rather Oliver Ramblett, inherits his money. They had a motive, as good or better than Merle's. You know what some of these young people of the post-war generation are like. Amoral. If they're okay Judy Merle's safe enough. But if they aren't—I feel responsible. It was Toby's idea. He put her on to it, not realising the danger."

"Yes. I see. Well, see the aunt. She may be able to reassure you. If the girl is all right I don't see what more we can do." Cardew picked up a pen and laid it down again. He cleared his throat. "That's the worst of capital punishment. That young fellow—he'll be for it about a fortnight from now. Less than that. Ten days. Find out what you like after that, proof positive of the poor devil's innocence—you can't bring him back to life. All right, Collier. Carry on and good luck to you."

Collier went home for an hour. Toby was out. He had gone to the Pictures. "He's like a cat on hot bricks," said his mother.

"You and he were confabulating down here the other afternoon. I'd rather like to know what it's all about."

"Get him to tell you. I think he wants to really. It's about a girl."

Sandra looked startled. "My dear Hugh. Surely not already."

"Why not? Romance dawns early. I remember falling madly in love at the age of nine with one of the film stars of the silent days, Lillian Gish. She was lovely. I used to long to be the fellow who rescued her from fire and floods and the villainous attentions of bad men. Unfortunately the troubles of Toby's idol are real. I haven't time to tell you about it now, but will you tell him from me that I'm doing the best I can."

"Good Heavens, Hugh. Is she mixed up with the police?"

Collier laughed, in spite of himself, at her look of horror.

"Don't forget you're a policeman's wife. But don't worry. She's not a crook. Gosh! Look at the time—I've a train to catch."

"Can't you have something to eat before you go?"

"No. I'll get lunch on the train."

The train, however, as Collier presently discovered, had no restaurant car attached. He staved off the pangs of hunger with a couple of buns washed down with scalding hot tea from a refreshment trolley at the first stop. He reached Cottingham soon after three, went into the first stationer's shop he came to and got Mrs. Sturmer's address from the local directory. It was, as he had expected from the nature of her business, in the less fashionable business quarter of the town, in a dreary little street overshadowed by the smoke-blackened walls and towering chimneys of two factories, but the house itself, one of a row, had a neat appearance that contrasted favourably with its neighbours on either side. The woodwork had been recently painted, and the lace curtains at the upper windows looked clean. But the shutters were up over the shop window and though he knocked at the side door and rang the bell several times no one came to open it, and there was no sound of life within.

A stout woman in a soiled pink jumper came out on the doorstep of the little sweet shop across the street and shouted to him, "Hi, mister!"

Collier went over to her. "I can't make anyone hear."

"There's nobody there, that's why. Mrs. Sturmer went off on Christmas day in that bit of junk she calls a car, and she's not back yet."

"Isn't that bad for business?"

"Well, it is, and I'm surprised really. "I've seen a good few of her customers come along and try the door. My own girl was one of them. Her sent her a postal order for Christmas, see, and she thought she'd blue it on a new frock for some dance she's going to with her boy on New Year's Eve. Miss Sturmer gets some good stuff. She buys from the ladies' maids at big houses."

"Did she tell you where she was going?"

"No. She's not one to talk much about her doings. A bit reserved, if you know what I mean. But it was to do with her niece, the one that's been staying with her and was ill. She went away for a change into the country somewhere. Mrs. Sturmer said she'd had a letter from her, something about going off with some other friends. Mrs. Sturmer said she didn't know them and had never heard of them, and she wasn't altogether satisfied, and she was taking the opportunity of the Christmas holiday to go and see her niece, and maybe bring her home again."

Collier had heard enough. He thanked her, evaded her offer to give Mrs. Sturmer any message he cared to leave by saying that he would call again, and walked away. When he came to the main street he turned into a Cadena Café and ordered a cup of coffee.

He wanted to marshall the facts in his mind and consider all the possible implications. Allowing a whole day for the journey Mrs. Sturmer should have arrived at her destination the evening of Christmas Day. She would put up somewhere for the night and drive out to Sard Manor to see her niece the following morning. Or perhaps, as the girl was in service she would wait for the afternoon, when she might be allowed an hour or two off duty. She would start on her return journey the following morning. "The day before yesterday," thought Collier, frowning as he helped himself to another lump of sugar. He remembered the fat woman's jeering reference to Mrs. Sturmer's car as a bit of junk. There might have been an accident. On the other hand, if his suspicions, very vague and formless as yet, but existing nevertheless, of the people at Sard Manor, had any foundation there might be another and more sinister explanation of Mrs. Sturmer's prolonged absence from home.

Obviously he would have to go down to Bedesford again. He finished his coffee and went off to find a public telephone box and put through a call to Superintendent Cardew. His activities hitherto had been almost, if not quite, unofficial. His next step brought him down from the fence. He went to the central police station and sent in his card, asking if he might see the Superintendent. The members of the C.I.D. of Scotland Yard, though not always very heartily welcomed by their provincial colleagues, are seldom kept waiting, and Collier was shown almost directly into the Superintendent's room.

"This is an unexpected pleasure," said that official as he shook hands. "Anything we can do?"

"I am trying to discover the present whereabouts of a Mrs. Anne Sturmer, who runs a second hand clothes shop in Grace Street. She is a car owner and she drove away on Christmas morning and has not yet returned. I have some reason to fear that she may have met with an accident. I'd like a description of her car and the number."

"We can probably get that from her nearest garage. Wait a bit."

He took a book down from a shelf and turned over the leaves. "The Acme garage and filling station, proprietor Bert Hackett, is just round the corner from Grace Street. I'll ring him up." He made the call and passed the receiver over to Collier. 'Yon can question him yourself."

He listened with unconcealed interest to the one-sided conversation that ensued.

"Lucky first time?" he said when Collier had rung off.

The man from the Yard nodded. "He does her repairs and supplies her with juice. He says the car's a Ford—fifth or sixth hand, and she gave about eight pounds for it. It's not much to look at, but in his own words, there's a lot of kick in the old girl yet. It's a four-seater, painted dark blue, with talc windows. Registration number, GLP100042. I'm going to give the Yard that description, Superintendent. Whether they'll take all possible steps to trace it at once I can't say. The decision doesn't lie with me. But meanwhile I'm going to ask you if you can send a plain clothes man to Grace Street to watch Mrs Sturmer's house and report to you without delay if she comes home."

"Yes, I can do that." He hesitated. "Mrs. Sturmer has been known to us for a number of years. She had to register as the English-born wife of an enemy alien. Her husband ran a hairdresser's shop where she lives now. I often had a shave and a hair cut from him before the War. He was a quiet, harmless little chap, but of course he had to be interned, and he died before the Armistice. Mrs. Sturmer is a decent, hard-working woman, a bit of a character too. You've nothing against her, I hope."

"No. But she may be quite innocently involved in a way that threatens her own safety. I can't say more than that at present. I'm pursuing a certain line of enquiry," said Collier glibly. "There may be nothing in it."

"But you must explore every avenue and leave no stones unturned. I get you," said the Superintendent with a grin. "If she turns up safe and sound to whom do I pass on the information?"

"To Superintendent Cardew, at the Yard, and I'd be glad if you'd ring me up at the King's Head, Bedesford. Mr. not Inspector Collier, if you don't mind."

This time Collier was fortunate enough to catch a non-stop train to Salisbury, and after forty minutes' wait at that station he travelled in a slow local train that pulled up at every station for two or three passengers to alight to Bedesford. There he booked a room for the night at the King's Head and asked if there had been any telephone calls for him. There had not. That meant that Mrs. Sturmer had not yet returned to the house in Grace Street. He went down the street to the local police headquarters. The Superintendent was away and he saw the sergeant who had given evidence at the inquest on Bateman two days previously. Collier explained that he was looking for a woman, the owner-driver of a Ford car with the registration number G.L.P. 100042, who had probably driven down from Cottingham on Christmas Day,

"Ar," said the sergeant, "if you'd come an hour ago I'd have had to say we knew nothing about it, but we've got somebody here now who may be able to help you." He went to the door and called to a constable in the charge room. "Bring that gipsy fellow here, Atkins."

"Has she been found?"

But the sergeant was not to be hurried. "That's as may be. You ask young Boswell any questions you like."

The gipsy was brought in by the constable. He was a slim, swarthy youth, handsome in the Romany fashion, with restless dark eyes that roved from side to side and avoided those of his interlocutors. He was dressed in old and much patched riding breeches and a dirty pullover.

He seemed to have a grievance. "If I'd a known I was going to be jugged for doing a kind action blowed if I wouldn't have left her to rot. I saved her blooming life, see. And this is what I get for it."

"That will do, Boswell. You're not under arrest. You're merely being detained pending enquiries. Now I'm going to tell this gentleman what you told us when you were brought in, and if I go wrong you can correct me."

The sergeant, a slow mover as Collier had already noted with controlled impatience, produced a notebook to refresh his memory.

"Boswell and his wife and her mother are going about the country in their caravan selling clothes pegs and rolls of linoleum. They were encamped at Fairmile Bottom, twenty miles from here, this morning when one of my men who was patrolling that district on his bicycle was passing. Boswell hailed him, and told him they'd got a woman in the caravan whom they had picked up by the roadside about nightfall on Boxing Day. She was lying on the bank of a pond at the foot of a steep hill, and they thought she'd tried to drown herself and lost her nerve and crawled out again."

"She'd been in the water right enough," said Boswell. "Her clothes was soaked and caked with mud."

"Mrs. Boswell and her mother did all they could for her. They stripped her and rubbed her down and wrapped her in blankets and laid her in one of the bunks in the caravan. They thought she would be well enough in the morning to tell her story, but she did not regain consciousness. This morning, after a lapse of three days during which she might have been having skilled attention, they decided to inform the police. Our man rang us up from the nearest A.A. box, and we sent the ambulance and had her removed to the hospital, and we brought Boswell along. No need to worry, Boswell, your wife and mother-in-law can sell rolls of linoleum without you."

"I suppose," said Collier, "she had nothing of value on her?"

The gipsy answered promptly. "A wedding ring on the poor soul's finger. Nothing else."

Collier caught the sergeant's eye and thought he knew why Boswell had been detained. But if the Boswells had saved the woman's life the disappearance of a purse and a wristwatch might be conveniently ignored.

"Were there initials or laundry marks on her underclothing?"

The gipsy nodded. "Initials. A.S. My wife showed them to me."

"Thank you. That may be very useful. You acted very rightly, Boswell, in doing all you could for the poor woman, though it would have been wiser to have notified the police at once."

Boswell scowled. "I'm not fond of the police."

"He's been had up now and again for poaching," the sergeant explained with a fruity chuckle. "What time was it when you found her?"

"It was getting dark. I wouldn't have seen her but my old dog began to bark and make a fuss, and wouldn't come on, so I went back, thinking it might be a hedgehog, and there he was licking her face."

"Fine," said Collier, heartily. "I'm a dog lover myself. I'd like to pay his next year's licence."

"There's nothing to stop you," said the gipsy, with a flash of white teeth.

"Well, you can go back to your cell now," said the sergeant repressively. "May as well keep you overnight now you are here."

When he had been removed Collier turned to the sergeant.

"You know this country and I don't. About this pond. How is it situated?"

"Tang's Mere it's called, and it's at the foot of a steep hill. The road turns sharply just there. It's a nasty bit, dangerous to motorists, and they talk of making a by-pass some day so that it need not be used at all."

"Is the pond deep?"

"Very at one side and in the middle."

"If a driver lost control going down the hill he or she might fall into the pond?"

"That is so. I wonder it has never happened."

"I think it may have happened in this case. Can you have the pond dragged, with a breakdown gang from a garage standing by to get the car out if it's there?"

"It'd be a bit of a job," said the sergeant slowly. "Would some time to-morrow do?"

"No. I want it done to-night. Have you an ordnance map here? Thank you." He studied the map closely and saw that as he had expected Tang's Hill was on a bye road that would be a short cut from Sard Manor, rejoining the main road to Salisbury beyond the town of Bedesford.

The sergeant heaved himself out of his chair. "I'll have to speak to the Superintendent," he said. "It'll be a bit of a job-—you think the car fell in and she crawled out of the sunshine roof maybe?"

"Yes. And I'll tell you what." A formless suspicion took shape in Collier's mind while he was speaking. "If the car's there under water and they get her out, I want an expert to go over her. It's possible the steering gear or the brakes had been tampered with."

The sergeant seemed somewhat shaken at last. He promised to see to it, and Collier left him dialling the Superintendent's private residence. He asked the constable who showed him out the way to the cottage hospital. It was on the outskirts of the town, a sprawling, one-storied building of staring red brick with a big verandah on to which the beds of the convalescent patients could be wheeled when the weather permitted.

A chubby-faced probationer who reminded him of a little pink pig in crackling showed him into the visitors' room, and after some time the house-surgeon came to him.

"The patient who was brought in this afternoon by the police? It's concussion, rather bad. She may be unconscious for some time yet. There's a general shock to the system. She's not a young woman, you know, though she seems quite healthy apart from this. Are you a relative?"

"No. I understood that there was nothing on her that could lead to her identification?"

"Initials on her underclothing. A.S. She wears a wedding ring. One of her wrists is swollen, a slight sprain."

"Could that have happened while she was trying to steer a car that had got out of control?"

"I should say it could. Yes. Was this a car accident? I understood from the police that it was a case of attempted suicide. Her clothing has been rough dried by the gipsies who found her, but it stinks of stagnant water."

"We don't know yet," said Collier. "Will you ring up the police directly she recovers consciousness? I suppose her case is not hopeless? She will come round in time?"

"Too early to say. Sir William Maybury will be seeing her. To-morrow is his day."

Collier turned up his overcoat collar when he got outside. It was raining again. He trudged back to the King's Head. He was tired and chilled. It had been a long day and his work was not yet done, but he would have to wait for the result of the dragging operations in any case. He ordered dinner, and was pleased to find that he could have a table near the fire. He would relax for an hour. He asked for the wine list and chose a good French claret.

CHAPTER XVIII
NO GROUNDS FOR SUSPICION

COLLIER had finished his dinner and was enjoying a cigarette when he was called to the telephone. It was the sergeant.

"We've found the car," he announced. "It's going to be looked over but we can't get that done to-night, and Colonel Benson, that's our Chief Constable, would like a word with you. He's sending his car to take you to the Grange, and it'll be there anywhen now."

Collier smiled to himself. Evidently the sergeant regarded this summons as equivalent to a Royal Command. He would have to go, of course. He knew the importance of keeping in with the local authorities, especially in a case like this where his own position was still undefined.

He was still in the hall when a uniformed chauffeur came in from the street and spoke to him. "Excuse me, sir. Is it Mr. Collier? I've been sent to fetch you."

After a short drive, too short, Collier felt, to give him time to prepare his case to meet a possible challenge, he was taken through a hall hung with trophies, which showed the Colonel to have been a hunter of big game in his time, into a book-lined room. The Colonel, a little man, but very soldierly and erect, with a lean, tanned face seamed with a long scar from the ear to the jaw, rose from his chair beside the fire to receive him.

"Pleased to meet you, Inspector. Have a cigarette? A drink? No? Well, take a pew anyway."

"Thank you, sir."

"Now, I don't want to be unfriendly, but I try to keep the rules of any game I play and I expect others to do the same. We call on the Yard if we need help, very grateful and all that—but—"

"I'm here unasked. I am afraid that is so," said Collier with his most disarming smile. "I was coming to you, sir, but the fact is I'm being rushed. Time is of such frightful importance in this enquiry which, so far as I am concerned, has only just begun. I am being continually held up by the evasiveness or the disappearance of witnesses. And it's a matter of life and death."

"My sergeant reported that you suspected foul play in connection with this woman who was picked up by the gipsies?"

"I can't rule it out, sir. I've reason to believe that she had been to Sard Manor to visit her niece who is in service there."

"You don't suspect anybody there with tampering with her brakes? Why the devil should they?"

"It's a long story," said Collier, "and I'm not sure that it makes sense. The fact is, sir, I've no evidence to put before you—yet."

The Colonel looked at him shrewdly. "You mean that you don't want to."

"I may be on a wild goose chase. You know sir, that for every clue that leads to the discovery of a crime there are five hundred that lead nowhere. You'll forgive my asking if you have any personal acquaintance with the family at Sard Manor?"

"The Rambletts? I used to know John Ramblett pretty well before the War. We were young men together. Never very intimate, but we met in the hunting field and at dances and so forth. But I only came home from India last year, and he's been dead some time. That collection of animals was his hobby. He did one unusual thing. Married the same woman twice. He divorced the first wife. Three girls he had by her. Then he married another woman. She died when the boy was born. A charming girl, they say. I was in India and I never met her. After her death he met the other woman again. She was very attractive, I suppose. Anyhow they got married again at a registrar's office. I don't know how it turned out. They couldn't afford to entertain, and they rather dropped out. Now he's gone, and I understand that the widow is in very bad health and that the son, poor fellow, is a hopeless invalid. Very sad. That's all I can tell you, Inspector."

"Did you know, sir, that Mr. Oliver Ramblett inherits the estate of a Mr. Fallowes, who was murdered at the beginning of November?"

Colonel Benson stared at him. "Good Lord! No, I'd no idea of it. Fallowes. John's mother was a Miss Fallowes. I remember hearing the name now you mention it, but they don't belong to this part of the world. The Rambletts always went far afield for their wives. He was a wealthy eccentric, wasn't he? He used to ask performers at the local music hall to supper with him? Very odd. And one of them repaid his hospitality by smashing his skull with a stone. He was caught almost red handed, wasn't he? Has he been hanged yet?"

"Not yet."

"It's queer how some people are always getting involved in tragedy," mused the Colonel. "There was a man killed up at their place only last week. A fellow who had been in charge of the animals. Monkeying about in the tiger's cage. There had to be an inquest naturally, but it was all plain sailing. Death by misadventure. And now there's this woman, some relation of one of their maids, I think you said."

"A chain of misfortune," said Collier. He was wondering when he could get away. "It's a pity Mr. Oliver Ramblett is such an invalid. Do you know the nature of his illness?"

"Afraid not. I've heard rumours that it's mental. There's a kink somewhere, perhaps, though Ramblett as I recall him, seemed sound enough. But the only one of the three girls who's left at home is getting herself talked about. She's been seen a bit too often driving about with Dr. Farwell in his car and dancing with him at road-houses. Young people are very free nowadays, but he's a married man."

"Is he their doctor?"

"I believe so. There may be no harm in it. You know what these country towns are for gossip, I daresay. She's a good looking girl though I'd say she had a temper. But we're getting away from the point, aren't we? What are you going to do next?"

"Well, I thought of going over to Sard Manor as early as possible to-morrow morning to get the niece of this woman we're looking for to come over to the hospital and identify her. She's still unconscious—"

"Yes, of course. Would you like one of my men to go with you just to give an official touch?

"I should. I don't want to introduce myself as coming from the criminal investigation department at the Yard for various reasons. It sounds a bit pompous and it puts people off."

"Just so, just so," said the Colonel readily. It was obvious that he wanted to keep a finger in the pie. "I'll ring up the Superintendent. If you go over to the station any time after nine he'll arrange to have somebody to run you over in a car. You'll need a car if you're to bring the girl back to the hospital. That's all right. No trouble at all."

He saw his visitor through the hall decked with antlers and lifeless grinning heads of the animals he had shot, to the door, and took a very cordial leave of him, but Collier was amused to find that no arrangements had been made to take him back to the town. He set off on foot, but an omnibus came along when he had walked part of the way, and he hailed it thankfully.

His visit to the Chief Constable had not been altogether a waste of time. It had given him some fresh light on the Ramblett family.

He ordered an early breakfast and was over at the police station by nine o'clock. His friend the large sergeant greeted him.

"I'm going with you," he announced. "I was over there a bit last week when that poor chap was killed by the tiger, and they're used to me like. They're all women up at the house, barring the young gentleman, and he's ill in bed, they say. Women are easily upset. You've got to go easy with them."

The sergeant drove himself and made earnest efforts to pump his companion on the way. They parked the car at the top of the avenue and walked up the winding drive through the shrubberies to the house.

They were kept waiting for some time at the door, and Collier could hear people moving about and a murmur of voices within. The door was opened at last by a withered little woman with an earthen complexion and mouse-coloured hair who asked them in a whisper what they wanted.

Collier had been rather afraid that the sergeant meant to take the lead. He moved forward without giving the burly west countryman the time he needed to get under way.

"There is a Miss Morris in service here, I believe?"

"Yes, there is."

"Did her aunt come to see her on Boxing Day?"

"She did."

"I am sorry to be the bearer of bad news. I am afraid she met with an accident on her way home. She is now a patient at the Bedesford Hospital and on the danger list. Her niece would be able to identify her. I can run her over in a car so that she will not be kept from her work for more than an hour or so."

The sergeant thought it was time for him to take some part.

"We'll take good care of the young woman, Mrs. Lacy. You know me, don't you. Sergeant Treadgold. We don't want to cause any more trouble up here, so if you'll just call the young person and can take the responsibility of letting her out for a bit Mrs. Ramblett needn't know."

Mrs. Lacy shook her head. "Mrs. Ramblett's poorly and she's had quite enough to worry her lately, as you say. But Mary Morris can't go along with you. She's got measles. Her aunt came on Boxing Day, but she couldn't see her on account of the infection. Very disappointed she was too. She had a cup of tea with me in the kitchen before she left. The doctor happened to be here, and he saw her and told her Mary was getting on as well as could be expected considering that she'd got a bad chill on top of the rash like. My niece, Mattie, is looking after her. She isn't over bright, but she does what she's told, and that's more than you can say of some of the lively ones. Mind you, measles can be a nasty thing and this Mrs. Stern or something told me she had to be extra careful of germs in her business of selling second-hand clothing. 'If once an epidemic was traced to my shop,' she said, 'I should be ruined.' So 'Give her my dear love,' she said. 'And I'll come and fetch her away when she's fit to travel.' I'm sorry she's had an accident."

"Had Mary given notice to leave before she was taken ill?"

"Her aunt asked me that. She said Mary had written her something about going on a cruise with friends. She hadn't said anything to me. But she was one of the quiet, reserved kind; more in them than meets the eye, if you know what I mean, and a great one for writing letters, and always would run down to the pillar box to post them herself, so she may have made plans I know nothing about. Here is the doctor. He can tell you how she is."

The doctor presumably had left his car on the parking space at the top of the avenue as they had done with theirs, and had walked rather quickly up the steep winding drive, for he seemed short of breath.

"Hallo, who's this? What is it, Mrs. Lacy?"

Collier answered. "We wanted Miss Morris to identify a patient at the Bedesford Hospital who has met with an accident. We think it may be the aunt who came here to see her on Boxing Day."

"That's bad. Is she seriously hurt?"

"I'm afraid so. She's unconscious, suffering from concussion. She lost control of her car going down a steep hill—you may know it, Tang's Hill—and ran into the pond at the foot. The car was submerged but she managed somehow to crawl out by way of the sunshine roof before she collapsed on the bank. She was picked up later by some gipsies."

"Dear me. Tang's Hill. Dangerous at any time on account of the gradient and full of potholes. I warned her not to go that way, but it's a short cut and I suppose she was in a hurry."

"You saw her?"

"Certainly. I happened to be here. Didn't Mrs. Lacy tell you? Unfortunately her journey was in vain. She was not able to see her niece. She developed measles a couple of days earlier. The rash was well out and she was in a highly infectious state. She's been running a temperature of over a hundred, and has to be kept quiet. She must not hear of her aunt's accident, Mrs. Lacy."

"When will she be free from infection?"

"Not for another ten days. It's very unfortunate." The doctor was looking rather hard at Collier. "I know the sergeant here by sight. I was one of the judges at the police sports last summer. Your side did very well in the tug of war with Yeovil, Sergeant—but I don't remember you."

"I'm connected with the A.A.," said Collier. There was nothing in all this that he could take hold of, but he was not quite satisfied. He disliked Farwell's type of good looks. The fellow's hair looked as if it had been permanently waved, and he was just a shade too ready to impart information.

It struck Collier that he was the kind of man to have an almost hypnotic influence over women.

"The A.A.?" Collier fancied that the doctor was made rather uneasy by this reference to a famous organisation. "That hill is a death trap," he said. "There ought to be a by-pass."

"The brakes may have been inefficient. I'm having that looked into on behalf of the insurance company," said Collier.

"It was a fearful old rattletrap," said Farwell, smiling. "I'll run over to the hospital presently if you like. To-morrow is my day there actually. I should know her again. That will settle the matter of identification."

The sergeant saw no reason why this offer should be declined, and Collier was forced to agree. After all, he had now no grounds for suspicion. The mystery of Mrs. Sturmer's prolonged absence had been solved. He could not think of any valid reason to put forward for asking to see Mrs. Ramblett. When the sergeant said, "Well, thanking you kindly, and we'll be getting along," he was obliged to concur. Mrs. Lacy had already returned to her household duties. The doctor wished them good morning very civilly and closed the door on them.

CHAPTER XIX
ANOTHER WAY

COLLIER took the next train back to London. He had the report from the garage hand who had examined the sodden remains of Mrs. Sturmer's Ford saloon. The verdict of this expert was highly unsatisfactory. The car was a wreck. He could not exclude the possibility that the brakes had been tampered with, on the other hand there was no positive proof of deliberate sabotage. Collier, who had seen the mechanic, a bespectacled youth and evidently an adult school addict, recognised his style in the neatly penned report handed to him at the station when he returned there with the sergeant. He thanked everybody profusely and managed to leave them still completely fogged as to his real motive in visiting Bedesford.

From Waterloo he went directly to the Yard. Cardew received him with a grunt.

"Bringing your sheaves—or scalps?"

Collier gave a detailed report of his movements during the previous forty-eight hours.

"Well, that sets your mind at rest, doesn't it?" asked the Superintendent. "The girl's safe, recovering from measles. The aunt—not so good, but there's nothing extraordinary about a motor accident unfortunately. We haven't a ghost of an excuse for carrying on with this, my lad, and you know it. We can't reopen the Fallowes murder case. It was never our pigeon, and Merle was tried and found guilty on evidence that ought to convince anybody. I'm going to put you on to something else."

Collier said nothing for a minute. He was remembering the hot afternoon in August that he had taken Sandra and Toby to the circus whose tent was pitched in a field on the outskirts of the south Devon fishing village where they were spending their summer holiday. He had run down for a weekend before going to America. He remembered the Flying Merles' act, the light, shining figures darting to and fro high up in the roof, looking in the greenish gloom like silver fish flashing through still water. He remembered how the girl had laughed and flung the rose from behind her ear over the barrier as she ran out, and that Toby had caught it, and the boy's round, freckled face lit up with excitement. There had been something about that act that had caught his imagination too.

"I don't agree, sir. There's something wrong at Sard Manor. This illness of Oliver Ramblett's. What is it? I've studied the reports of the trial and I tried walking up from Laurel Lodge to the station. It was a wet evening, not very late, between nine and ten. I didn't meet a single soul. If it was Oliver, he used to ride a motor-cycle. I got that from the garage hand who vetted Mrs. Sturmer's car for me. Assume that Oliver planned the murder. Or perhaps he didn't plan it. Perhaps he rode over to see his uncle and try to borrow money from him. The uncle refused. There was a quarrel and the fatal blow was struck. Oliver had heard perhaps from the old man himself, of the fancy he had for asking music hall performers in to supper and presenting them with tracts and good advice. He worked out the idea of personating the murdered man and getting somebody into the house to act as his scapegoat."

"Where would he get the false hair and beard?"

"That's a point, sir. It must have been premeditated, a carefully worked out scheme, planned perhaps weeks in advance. Clever. Damnably clever."

"There's one objection to it being Oliver," remarked the Superintendent. "Wouldn't he have waited until he was twenty-one? He wouldn't get the money before."

"He could get an advance. As to the personation I learned from the barmaid at the pub where I stayed that there's a flourishing dramatic society at Bedesford. They put on plays for local charities several times a year. Oliver and his sister belonged to it for a time. I gathered that there was some unpleasantness for which the girl was responsible. So you see he might have some experience of theatrical make-up. I don't want to drop this enquiry before I've seen him."

"You and your hunches," grumbled Cardew. "How are you going to see him? You can't force your way in and insist on the family producing him. We don't play those totalitarian games in this country."

"You can't do that there here, in short," said Collier grinning. "I've thought of a way if I can pull it off. May I try?"

"Oh, go and boil your head," growled his superior officer.

"Thanks awfully," said Collier gratefully, and left the room rapidly before he could be recalled.

Three minutes later he was climbing on to a bus in Westminster Square on his way home.

Toby was in bed but not asleep. Hearing his stepfather's voice below and the welcoming barks of the terriers he came down in his dressing gown over his pyjamas to bounce up and down on the springs of the long-suffering sofa while Collier had his supper.

"Have you seen her? Is she all right?"

"I think she is, but I couldn't see her. She's got measles."

"What? At Sard Manor? How putrid for her. I say, Hugh, are you sure?"

"The doctor said so."

"Did you see Oliver Ramblett?"

"No."

"You don't seem to have done much, do you?" observed the critic on the hearth.

Sandra looked at him reprovingly. "Be quiet, Toby. You ought to be in bed."

"I'm going. But I say, look here, Hugh. What's the good of being in the C.I.D. if you can't make people talk? Anything may be happening there. Can't you do anything to stop it? You could tell in Judy's last letter that she was frightened. She asked for help." The boy was half crying.

Collier rose from the table and began to fill his pipe. Sandra, piling the dishes on a tray, glanced at him anxiously and was shocked to see how tired he looked.

"Don't, Toby," she said sharply, "he's simply worn out."

"It's all right, Sandra. Don't scold him. Toby, that's one of the hardest things in my job, the feeling that something is going to happen, and that we can't prevent it because we don't know who will strike the blow or where it will fall. I believe you are right about these people, but there's nothing to take hold of—yet."

"You're not giving up?"

"No. I'm going down there again to-morrow."

Toby brightened. "Good egg. I say, I'm sorry if I was rude just now. I didn't mean to be."

Collier lay back in his chair with his feet stretched out to the fire, comfortably relaxed. "I know you didn't. Try not to get too worked up over this, old chap. I'm sorry you got mixed up in it."

"What hopes if I hadn't?" said Toby, who was never inclined to belittle his own achievements. "I put the Rambletts on the map. Didn't you see any of them?"

"Only Mrs. Lacy, the cook, and Dr. Farwell."

"What's he like?"

"Very smooth spoken, with a toothy smile. Can't say I liked the blighter."

"They seem to go in a lot for being ill," said Toby thoughtfully.

"Toby, you really must go to bed," said his mother, coming in from the kitchen.

"Another five minutes. I'm trying to help. This is serious, you know, Mother. I mean—it's getting pretty near the time when—when Judy's brother—"

"Darling," she said gently, "you know what I told you. Pray for him. It's all you can do."

"Yes, Mother. Good night." He kissed her and gave her a hug that told her all he could not put into words. "Good night, Hugh."

"He's got this very much on his mind," his mother said with a sigh when he had left the room.

"I know."

"Will you be going off again to-morrow?"

"Yes. Early. Toby's right about the time. It's getting terribly short. Don't you get up, Sandra. I'll come down and boil the kettle on the gas ring."

"Nonsense. I shall get up and see that you have a good breakfast."

Soon after ten the following morning a clerk brought Collier's official card into the room where Mr. Freeman, of the old-established firm of Freeman, Vansittart, James and Freeman of Lincoln's Inn, was going through his morning mail.

"Scotland Yard? Dear me. Show him in at once."

Mr. Freeman was a man verging on sixty, a good lawyer of the steady, unenterprising, reliable type, who will see to it that his clients do not take unnecessary risks. His practice seldom took him to the Courts.

"Come in, Inspector. Take a chair. What can I do for you?"

"I'm sorry to trouble you, Mr. Freeman, but the name of your firm has come up in the course of an enquiry. The late Mr. Fallowes was a client of yours, I believe?"

"Yes."

"You are continuing to act for his heirs?"

Mr. Freeman adjusted his spectacles. "These questions are rather—but the matter is hardly confidential. Mr. Fallowes made a will which we drew up for him, in favour of his great nephew, or, failing him, of his three great nieces. He left a very considerable fortune and naturally there is a good deal to be done, but we are getting on with it as fast as we can."

"Did you have any visits from the police at the time of the trial, or before that?"

"No. My managing clerk went down to have the house and furniture valued for probate. The police had the keys, but they were most considerate. There was no difficulty about that. As Mr. Fallowes' relatives live in another county and he has seen little or nothing of them of recent years they have been spared the notoriety which—"

"Just so," said Collier sympathetically. "We've abolished the pillory as a legal instrument of punishment, but there's something very like it. Oliver Ramblett is still a minor, isn't he?"

"He will be twenty-one one day next week."

"Have you seen him since his great uncle's death?"

"We have not. We wrote at the time to advise him of the contents of the will and suggested that he should come up to see us. His mother replied for him. He was suffering from what appeared to be some obscure nervous trouble and had been ordered complete rest. I am afraid, from what I hear, that he is not much better. What is the purport of this enquiry, Inspector?"

Collier wondered rather uneasily if he had made a good impression. He realised that Mr. Freeman was of the type who would be adamant in the defence of his client's interests.

"I have not come here to make mysteries, Mr. Freeman. I have had occasion to visit Sard Manor twice in the last few days. I did not succeed in seeing any member of the family. I came away with a very strong feeling that there was something amiss there."

Mr. Freeman looked disturbed. "Can you put it more plainly?"

"Well—I'll say this. If I had any standing, if I were in any way responsible for or connected with Oliver Ramblett I would insist on seeing him. I happen to know that for some time past he has been shut away from the rest of the family in a suite of rooms at the top of the house, and has been seen only by his stepmother and the doctor who has been visiting him almost daily."

"Dear me. That sounds—that won't do. And yet—you don't allege any ill-treatment, Inspector?"

"I've no evidence as to that one way or the other. But I think if he is ill he should have trained nurses."

"I agree. But—hasn't he?"

"My information is that he is being nursed by his stepmother. That is, she takes up his meals and brings down the tray. Nothing was said of any further attention."

Mr. Freeman took off his spectacles with careful deliberation, wiped them, and put them on again.

"I cannot suppose that an Inspector of the C.I.D. would come to me with a—with a mare's nest. The terms of the will—no, I can't believe it."

"You have met Mrs. Ramblett?"

"No. We have been in correspondence. There have been papers to be signed and witnessed and so forth. She is empowered to act for her stepson during his minority."

"Have you advanced her any money on his account?"

"Yes. A small sum when one considers the amount he inherits. Five hundred pounds. I gathered that the family are in straitened circumstances. Land-owners nowadays—have you—have you anything against her, Inspector? Strictly between ourselves?"

"I have some reason to suspect that she is addicted to drugs."

"Good Heavens! I shall have to act on what you have told me, Inspector, but I don't quite see—what do you advise?"

"I should go down there, sir, making the excuse of some legal business which you want to explain to him personally or papers which must be signed by him in your presence. Don't announce your arrival. Make it a surprise visit. And insist on seeing him. Don't let them put you off."

"Yes, yes," said Mr. Freeman reluctantly. "I can see that it is my plain duty. I suppose you can't come with me to—to back me up if need arises?"

Collier, who had always meant to go with him, was glad that he had not had to make the suggestion.

"I might do that, sir, though I don't think I had better go up to the house with you. It might make things awkward for you if my suspicions turn out to be unfounded."

"Yes, I see that. You're right. I can go alone."

"No need, Mr. Freeman, if you don't object to my company. I am going down to Bedesford in any case."

"We can travel together then. I'll go by car, I think. I can give you a lift."

Collier thanked him. He had spent a good many hours in trains and railway station waiting rooms during the last few days and was growing rather tired of them.

"I suppose it should be fairly soon," said the lawyer.

"To-day if you can possibly manage it."

"Oh dear. I might—but I couldn't get off until after lunch. I have an important appointment at half past twelve. We shouldn't arrive until long after dark," Mr. Freeman objected.

"There's quite a decent hotel at Bedesford. The beds are comfortable and they know how to grill a steak."

"Very well. I must ring up my man and tell him to pack a bag and see that my car is ready for a long run. Dear me, how I do dislike being hurried. Not that I blame you, Inspector. Don't think that. Will you be here at two? Right. I'm much obliged to you."

CHAPTER XX
A MORNING VISIT

MR. FREEMAN and Collier had breakfast together in the coffee room of the King's Head before they parted. Collier had explained that he had business in the town.

"I shall stay to lunch if they ask me," said the lawyer. "I am hoping that your—ah—suspicions—are unfounded. But if I am not satisfied I should like to talk things over with you."

Mr. Freeman smoked a cigar and read his paper before he started, but he did not enjoy either as much as usual. He dreaded the coming interview with people who were strangers to him in a house he did not know. He often had to deal with strangers, but on his own terms, in his familiar office, with his law books ranged on the shelves. Mortgaging, conveyancing. Dry as dust, perhaps. But he liked things to be dry.

Mills, his elderly and taciturn chauffeur, had brought the car round from the inn yard to the main entrance.

"You know the way, Mills?"

"Yes, sir. It's only about three miles out of the town."

It was a dull day and the main road, bordered with new villas, was uninteresting. On turning into the lane soon after the last house had been passed they seemed to plunge into the depths of the country. The gate leading from the lane into Sard park was open. Mills drove the car up the double avenue of limes and turned on to the patch of level ground where the turnstile entrance to the gardens on the right and the high gate of the drive leading up to the house barred any further progress.

The lawyer put aside the rug that covered his knees and got out.

"You'll wait for me here, Mills."

"Yes, sir."

Mr. Freeman unlatched the heavy gate and let it clash to after he had entered. A bad approach, he thought, as he trudged up the steep, winding drive, and the house itself had a forlorn and neglected aspect. He rang the bell and waited.

Helen Ramblett opened the door. She had expected the doctor and her face fell when she saw Mr. Freeman.

The lawyer stiffened. Her dark beauty was undeniable, but he disapproved of the type. She reminded him of a young woman who had given one of his clients a great deal of trouble some years earlier. Mr. Freeman had managed to settle the case out of Court, but he retained a very unpleasant recollection of several interviews he had had with her.

He cleared his throat. "I am Mr. Freeman, of the firm of Freeman, Vansittart, James, and Freeman, who are acting on behalf of Mr. Oliver Ramblett. I have come down to see him on a little matter of business regarding the estate. As Mr. Ramblett will be coming of age shortly—"

He broke off, realising that he was saying much more than he need out of sheer nervousness.

The girl stared at him unsmilingly. "Oh—I am Helen Ramblett. You had better come in." She led the way across a hall that seemed very cold and into a long and almost equally chilly drawing-room where a fire very recently lit threatened to go out.

"I'll tell mother you're here," she said, and left him. He had been waiting rather a long time when Mrs. Ramblett came in. She looked very sallow and weary, and there were grey pouches of loose skin under her still magnificent eyes. She was wearing a velvet bridge coat over her old torn cardigan.

"How kind of you to come, Mr. Freeman. Do sit down. What a wretched fire. I tell Mrs. Lacy to pour some oil on it. But she's so silly. She says it's dangerous."

"So it is. You should never do that."

She shivered, crouching on the sofa and holding out spectral hands to the flickering flame. "When you're as thin as I am you feel the cold." She yawned and sat back, rubbing her fingers together to restore the circulation and gazing at him drowsily. The Inspector is right, he thought, she takes drugs.

"I've really come to see your stepson," he said "Mr. Ramblett."

"I'm sorry. That's quite impossible. Poor Oliver is very ill. He's quite unfit to see anyone. If you'd written to say you were coming I could have told you and saved you a useless journey."

"What is the matter with him, Mrs. Ramblett?"

"I think you had better talk to the doctor about that. He's here. He's just been up to him. He's been most kind and attentive," said Mrs. Ramblett earnestly. "I don't know what we should have done without him." She looked towards the opening door. "Here he is. Dr. Farwell, this is Mr. Freeman. He's come down from London to see Oliver."

"Very pleased to meet you, Mr. Freeman," said the doctor cordially.

The two men shook hands and the lawyer felt relieved. He preferred to have a man to deal with.

"I was just asking Mrs. Ramblett what's the matter with her stepson."

"And I said you could tell him better than I could," said Mrs. Ramblett, "and how splendidly you'd looked after him all these weeks and how grateful we are." There was something rather dreadful, rather slavish, in her eagerness to ingratiate herself with Farwell. It shocked Mr. Freeman. The doctor ignored her.

"As the family lawyer you have a right to know," he said. "We've been trying to keep it quiet for the sake of his sisters. He is suffering from delusions of which the chief is that he killed his great uncle. I have been hoping he might recover, but I am afraid there is no doubt that the cause of this mental trouble is a tumour on the brain, an inoperable tumour. The end may come at any time now. I haven't told you this before, Mrs. Ramblett, because I did not want to distress you, but I did warn Helen. I hope that now that you have been made aware of the facts, Mr. Freeman, you will not feel it necessary to see the poor boy. He is terrified of strangers."

"How very sad," said Mr. Freeman. He was a kind-hearted man and he was genuinely shocked. "What about getting down a specialist? Isn't there any treatment that could be tried? Money is no object, you know."

"No use, I'm afraid. I should be quite willing, of course. In fact, we have discussed it. But any movement, any emotion now would merely hasten the end."

"He's actually dying then?"

"I'm afraid so."

"Dear me." Mr. Freeman's hands shook a little as he wiped his spectacles. "A boy of twenty. It's very sad. With his life opening out before him."

Mrs. Ramblett yawned. The doctor gave her a hard look and she shrank a little.

"Then—I suppose I must leave it at that," said the lawyer doubtfully. "I must say that for my own satisfaction I should have liked to send down a specialist. No reflection on you, Doctor, but it's a great responsibility for you to bear alone."

"I agree," said Farwell. "From a purely selfish point of view I'd be glad of another opinion. But it would be torture for Oliver. He's in such a state now that he'd probably die of fright. So you see—"

"I see. Well, there's his birthday next week. Normally he could make a will after that. He'll be in control of the estate. But if his brain is affected we shall have to have him made a ward in chancery if he lives."

"I shall be very surprised if he is alive a week from now," said Farwell.

"Dear me. Well, keep me informed, if you please."

The door was opened and Helen looked into the room.

"You're wanted at the telephone, Dr. Farwell."

"Excuse me one moment," he said and went out.

Mrs. Ramblett sat blinking at the fire, which had begun to burn up at last, and pulling at a loose thread on her coat.

"There must have been a button here, I think."

Mr. Freeman observed her with growing distaste. Drugs. He wondered how she got them.

He had heard that they were peddled in the West End by street hawkers and in cinemas and night clubs, but surely in the depths of the country it would be more difficult. Perhaps the stuff was sent by post. Or—another possibility occurred to him that would account for her evident painful anxiety not to offend the doctor. But a doctor who would do that would be betraying a sacred trust. Such a man would be capable of anything. "No, no," thought Mr. Freeman, "I'm letting my imagination run away with me. This won't do. It won't do at all. And she may not be a drug addict. I've no proof."

But as he sat and waited and Farwell did not return he remembered, with growing discomfort, that the Inspector had warned him not to be diverted from the main purpose of his visit. He had come down to see Oliver Ramblett, and he was not seeing him. On the other hand he did not feel that he could insist after what the doctor had told him.

"He's a long time gone, isn't he?" he said at last.

Mrs. Ramblett made no reply. She had stopped playing with the loose thread on her coat and sat rubbing her fingers together and blinking sleepily at the fire. Apparently she had forgotten Mr. Freeman's existence. She reminded him of a mechanical toy running down.

He had half risen from his chair when he heard footsteps in the hall.

CHAPTER XXI
THE TRUTH AT LAST

COLLIER, when he left the King's Head, went first to a garage in the High Street, where he hired a motor-cycle for the day. From there he rode on to the hospital, where the same chubby probationer he had seen before showed him into the visitor's room. This time the house-surgeon did not keep him long waiting.

"You've come about the patient you were enquiring for when she was first brought in?"

"Mrs. Sturmer. Yes. How is she?"

"Definitely better. Sir William Maybury is hopeful. He does not think an operation will be necessary."

"There is a chance of a complete recovery?"

"Oh yes. It will take time, of course. But she's a very healthy woman. Sound as a bell. And that helps a lot." A slight change was perceptible in the young house-surgeon's brisk, efficient manner. "Look here—are you representing an insurance company, or the police, or what? You're not one of the locals, I know."

"I am Inspector Collier, of the Criminal Investigation Department at Scotland Yard."

"I see. Well, I've got something on my mind, something that happened here. I may have imagined it. Really I hardly like to mention it."

"It may be more important than you think," said Collier encouragingly, wondering what he was to hear now. "In any case you can rely on my discretion."

"All right. You shall have it for what it's worth. Dr. Farwell came over yesterday. He said a representative of the insurance people had asked him to see if he could identify an accident case that had been brought here."

"That's right. I did ask him."

"Well, I took him into the private ward where we were keeping her as comfortable as possible with various gadgets to prevent any movement until Sir William Maybury could examine her. Farwell brushed past me rather rudely, I thought, and bent over her. Of course he's senior to me and all that. I mean—the house-surgeon is dust under the feet of the visiting staff in a way. And if it had been Sir William, for instance, I would not have minded in the least. But Farwell's not much liked about here, though he's a marvellous surgeon—I'll give him that—a bit too inclined to take risks though. Anyway I got a funny feeling that the patient was in some danger and that it was up to me to protect her, and—well—I shoved him aside, getting between him and the bed, and said, 'She's not to be touched.' Gosh!" said the young man feelingly. "I go hot all over when I think of it. I mean—a fellow might be broken for less. He glared at me, but he never said a word. He just stooped and picked up something that had fallen out of his hand and rolled along the floor, and he went out leaving me still striking an attitude and feeling a damn fool. I haven't seen him since."

"What was it that he dropped?"

"I don't know. It was quite small."

"Could it have been a hypodermic syringe?"

The house-surgeon opened his eyes to their fullest extent.

"Good Lord! Yes. It could have been. I don't say it was. It was small enough to be hidden in the palm of his hand. It might have been something quite harmless. A stud, for instance."

"I am glad you told me," said Collier. He had turned rather white. "I have a good deal to thank you for. You have saved me from the consequences of a mistake I made. My job has this in common with yours, Doctor, that mistakes may be fatal." He held out his hand and the other shook it warmly. "You think I was right, then? That has bucked me no end. I've been shivering in my shoes since, looking forward to a hell of a row if Farwell chose to cut up rough."

"No. I think I can promise you that won't happen."

"I suppose you can't give me a hint of what is actually going on? Barring that accident at Sard Manor before Christmas I've heard of nothing likely to bring somebody from the Yard down here."

Collier shook his head. "I can't tell you anything. And don't mention this, please. I daresay you'll hear all about it before long."

"You're getting on, then?"

"Yes," said Collier grimly. "I'm getting on. Good-bye."

He rode back to the town, where he stopped at a chemist's to get Dr. Farwell's private address. Five minutes later he was ringing the doctor's bell, and noting as he did so the shining brass of the knocker and the well-kept borders of the front garden. The door was opened by a sandy-haired young woman in a well-cut navy-blue frock. Her rather prominent pale blue eyes were evidently weak, for she wore horn-rimmed spectacles.

"Could I see the doctor?"

"He's just gone out."

"When will he be in?"

"I couldn't say. His surgery hours are from six to seven."

"I see. Are you Mrs. Farwell?"

"No. I'm the doctor's dispenser. My name is Briggs."

"I'd like a word with you, Miss Briggs."

"I'm busy. You must call another time if you want the doctor."

She tried to shut the door, but he inserted his foot in time to prevent her.

"How dare you!" Her pale eyes blazed at him. "You can't force your way into a private house. I'll call the police."

"I am the police, Miss Briggs."

As she still tried to keep the door closed he exerted his greater strength, stepped inside, and closed the door behind him.

"Here is my warrant card to show you that I am a police officer. Now, Miss Briggs, please be sensible. There is no need for any fuss. I am here to ask a few routine questions, and there is nothing for you to get excited about. Who else is there in the house beside yourself?"

"Only Mrs. Farwell. She isn't up yet. The maid left last week and the daily woman we had has failed us."

"I see. Which is the surgery?"

"In here." Her anger had died down, and she was merely sullen.

He glanced about him. The room was well furnished and beautifully kept. "You seem to manage very well, without a maid."

"I do it," she said brusquely. "That's why I've no time to waste. What do you want?"

"The doctor keeps books, I suppose, a record of the visits of patients to the surgery and so forth?"

"Of course."

"Splendid. Then you can tell me if a patient, an accident case was brought in here between eight and nine o'clock the evening of the third of November?" He was watching her closely without seeming to do so, and he saw no change in her face. Apparently the date conveyed nothing to her.

"I don't remember it. There's another doctor farther up the road, you know. But I'll look in the book and make sure."

The book was very neatly kept, with lines ruled in red ink, and he could see that she took the same dour pride in it as she did in the shining floor and highly polished chairs and tables.

"It must have been Dr. Smith," she said triumphantly. "Dr. Farwell had taken a day off. He didn't see any patients on that day. He'd gone up to London to lunch with an old friend and he went to a theatre in the evening and didn't get home until the early morning."

"Thank you very much." He wondered if he should take possession of the book, and decided against it. Even if her suspicions were aroused later on she would hardly dare to destroy it.

"I'll try Dr. Smith," he said. "The police have to make all sorts of enquiries, you know, in these accident cases."

She was going with him to the door and they were in the hall when a weak voice called him.

"Are you the police? Please wait a minute."

He turned, but Miss Briggs was quicker than he. She ran to the foot of the stairs. "Mrs. Farwell, go back to your room at once."

She spoke so harshly that Collier was startled, but Myra Farwell paid no attention. She was half way down the stairs, looking very small and insignificant in her quilted dressing gown, which was an unbecoming shade of blue.

"Are you a policeman?" she asked again urgently. Her voice had a brittle quality. It was apparent to Collier that she was keyed up to breaking point.

"Yes, I am. Is there anything I can do for you?"

"Yes. Tell that woman to let me pass."

Miss Briggs gasped. "Don't be silly, Mrs. Farwell. I'm not stopping you. But you're not dressed and you haven't really got anything to say."

Myra would not look at her, she kept her eyes fixed on the face of the stranger. If he failed her it would be the end.

"Come into the dining-room," she said.

He opened the door for her and motioned to her to pass in before him. He glanced at Miss Briggs, and now he saw fear in her face.

"You must not mind her," she said. "She's not quite—she's a little bit touched. Persecution mania."

"Thank you for telling me," he said.

She backed away from him, turned abruptly and went into the surgery, closing the door after her.

He followed Mrs. Farwell into the dining-room.

The room was bright and comfortable, with a good fire burning in the grate and the remains of breakfast on the table. Collier saw that two places had been laid.

"Now, Mrs. Farwell," he said gently.

She came close up to him and clutched his arm with both hands.

"I thought he had changed and it was going to be like the old times when he loved me, but he was only pretending. I came out on the landing and listened to him talking to her. She knew him before I did and she was always in love with him. Briggsie he calls her, and makes use of her. He makes use of everybody. He's tired of me and tired of being here. Lots of people don't like him, I know. He ran over a dog and left it half dead on the road and there were other things. I know more than they think. I've been afraid for a long time. They both watched me. I couldn't go out alone or speak to the woman who came to do the cleaning. I did get out the other day. I thought I'd make another will so that he wouldn't gain anything—by my death. But before I could find a lawyer's office he came along and made me get into the car. That was the day he was so sweet to me that I thought perhaps I was mistaken. He can be sweet. But I got the tin of mustard—"

Collier watched the lined, sallow, middle-aged face twitching with nervous excitement, and wondered how much of truth there was in her whispered outpourings. He had learned to be careful not to rely on the statements of hysterical women.

"What was the mustard for?" He was genuinely puzzled by this unexpected detail.

"I thought I'd be able to make myself sick if he gave me anything. I've got it ready where I can find it in a minute. But now—for God's sake take me away."

He thought a minute. She was delaying him when everything might depend on his quickness of action. But it would be inhuman to leave her in her present state to be bullied by her husband's dispenser.

"Very well," he said. "Get dressed now. Be as quick as you can or I shan't be able to wait for you."

He stood at the foot of the stairs and listened to her scurrying about in the room overhead. He fancied he heard Miss Briggs speaking to someone in the surgery. He tried the door. It was locked.

It occurred to him that she might have been telephoning. Well, he could not help that, but it added to his sense of urgency. Mrs. Farwell came down dressed to go out and they left the house together.

He stood with her on the footpath, momentarily at a loss. He was going on to Sard Manor and he could not possibly take her with him. His problem was solved by the arrival of a bus. He shouted to the driver to stop and hurried her across the road.

"Have you any money? No? Take this," he thrust half a crown into her hand. "Go to the King's Head. Wait for me there." He went back to his hired motorcycle. He had learnt enough at Sunnyside to give him cause for acute anxiety. He liked what he had seen of Mr. Freeman, but the lawyer had not struck him as one who would exhibit great force of character in a crisis, and he had now no doubt that a crisis was imminent. His machine was noisy and smelly, but it had a pretty turn of speed. He roared down the main road and splashed through the mud of the lane. The shaggy buffaloes in pasture snorted angrily and tossed their huge heads as he rushed up the avenue.

Mills, Mr. Freeman's chauffeur, was sitting placidly in his master's car, reading the *Daily Mail*. The doctor's dark blue saloon was in front of him.

All set, thought Collier. They have not got rid of Freeman yet. There may still be time. He hastened up the drive between the dank green banks of overgrown laurels.

The front door stood open. Mrs. Lacy, that grey wisp of a woman, was sweeping down the steps.

"It's you again," she said fatalistically. "You're not the first. There's a lawyer gentleman, and the doctor. You'll find them in the drawing-room with Mrs. Ramblett. She don't like visitors, but see one, see all." She went on with her sweeping.

"How is Miss Morris?"

"I don't know. There's no key to her door, but she's pushed the chest of drawers up against it. We haven't been able to get in since yesterday morning. We might have through the window, seeing it's the ground floor, but there's inside wooden shutters and she's fastened those. I went and talked to her through the door. She said not to worry, and that she'd be all right. She's got the water in her bedroom jug to drink."

"Do you know why she's behaving like that?"

"I could make a guess," whispered Mrs. Lacy. "There's queer goings on in this place. It can't last."

The dead leaves that had collected on the lowest step fluttered away before her broom.

Collier entered the house and stood for a moment uncertain which way to turn. The hall was empty. He tried the first door on the right and found himself in the drawing-room.

At the far end a thin, dark, witch-like woman, crouched on a sofa drawn close up to the fire, remained apparently unaware of his entrance, but Mr. Freeman, sitting bolt upright on a gilt spindle-legged chair, seemed unfeignedly glad to see him.

Collier glanced at Mrs. Ramblett, and realised that she had reached the stage when all her faculties were concentrated on conserving the drowsy inertia that was the last agreeable phase of her reaction to her beloved poison. He had had some experience of drug addicts. For the moment at any rate she might be disregarded.

"Have you made any progress? Have you seen the boy?" he asked.

"No. The fact is, Collier, both Mrs. Ramblett here and the doctor think it inadvisable. I am sorry to say that the poor fellow is critically ill, suffering from a tumour on the brain—in fact, he is dying. He has delusions and imagines himself to be a fugitive from justice. I gather that the atmosphere of secrecy which has made such an unfortunate impression is due to the fact that he has to be humoured. He is terrified of strangers. Under the circumstances I could not insist."

"What does he think he's done?"

"Does that matter? The murder of his great uncle must have been a shock to him. He thinks he committed the crime."

"Where is the doctor?"

"He was called to the telephone some time ago now. I've been expecting him back."

"Good God! If only he hasn't—" Collier leant over Mrs. Ramblett. "Will you give me the key of the door to the top floor." He spoke very slowly and distinctly. "The key."

She answered in a dead voice, "Don't touch me."

"I won't if you'll tell me where it is."

"The pocket of my cardigan."

He turned out the pocket of her ragged pink woollen jacket and picked the key out of a varied assortment of pencil ends, bits of knotted string and crumpled envelopes of old letters. To Freeman, looking on in amazement, he gave an impression of controlled but none the less almost frenzied haste. He ran to the door, calling over his shoulder, "You come too."

The lawyer followed him, moving more quickly than he usually did, but by the time he reached the hall the other was half way up the stairs.

He was panting when he came to the second floor landing. Collier was fitting the key into the lock of the door at the foot of the last flight.

"Why such a hurry?" Freeman was inclined to be resentful. "I told you what the doctor said. Bursting in like this may do irreparable harm. The matter needs consideration."

"We can't afford to wait, sir. The point is that Farwell was almost certainly lying." He set his teeth.

If this isn't the right key I'll break down the door." But it turned as he spoke. The last flight was uncarpeted, and their progress was far from noiseless, but there was no sound or movement from the rooms above. Collier opened the door facing him across the landing. It was the same into which Judy had looked down from the skylight. The rug by the bedside was grey with dust. The body of a young man was lying in the bed, only his tousled dark head showing above a heap of blankets. Collier, bending over him, very gently turned back the coverings. He seemed to be asleep. A line of white showed under the thick black lashes.

"He breathes very heavily," said Mr. Freeman.

"Drugged," said Collier briefly. "Thank God we were in time. Touch and go, I fancy."

"What do you mean?"

Collier did not answer immediately. He was thinking hard.

"He should be safe enough now, but I don't like to leave him. Will you stay with him, sir, while I go down to telephone?"

"What am I to say to the doctor if he comes up? He'll be extremely angry. I very much dislike scenes."

"He won't come. If he does don't let him touch this boy."

Mr. Freeman gaped at him. "But—my dear sir, I can't prevent him from attending to his patient."

Collier looked at his well-meaning, bewildered face, flushed from his unusual physical exertions. "I'm sorry, Mr. Freeman. There hasn't been time to explain. There's no doubt now that this boy is the victim of a conspiracy. He wasn't meant to live to see his twenty-first birthday. I'm going to ring up for the police ambulance to take him to the hospital. I fancy they'll find that he's been kept under the influence of drugs, and that there's nothing else the matter with him."

"Good Heavens. Then the doctor—"

"He won't come. I was at his house before I came on here. I fancy his dispenser rang him up. He's been warned."

Collier ran downstairs. There was nobody in the hall, no sound or movement anywhere. He pushed open the baize-covered door leading to the servants wing. Mrs. Lacy was in the kitchen with her niece. Mattie was peeling potatoes. She stared vacantly at the intruder. Mrs. Lacy, who was chopping suet, laid down the chopper and wiped her hands on her apron. "Where's the doctor? Do you know?"

"He left the house a while ago with Miss Helen."

Collier nodded. He had rather expected that. He hurried back to the hall. The local police would have to jump to it. He picked up the receiver of the telephone and waited to be put through. The line was dead.

"Cut. I might have known that too," he thought. He did not like the idea of leaving the Manor, but there seemed no alternative. He could ride down the lane to the main road, speak to the Bedesford police station from the nearest A.A. box asking them to rush over reinforcements and the ambulance, and then ride back to await them. Or perhaps he could send one of the keepers with a message. Not Bowles. He was definitely suspect. He would rather trust Jerry. He was crossing the hall to the front door with some hope that Jerry might be somewhere at hand when the door was opened from outside and the head keeper stumbled in, closed it after him and leaned against it. Collier stared at him. "What's wrong?" he asked sharply. The keeper's answer was unprintable.

"Pull yourself together, man," said Collier. "Foul language won't help. What's happened?"

Before Bowles could speak he was answered by a long drawn snarl prolonged into a deafening roar, apparently only a few feet away.

Chapter XXII
STATE OF SIEGE

The echoes of that heart-searching sound had hardly died away when Mrs. Lacy rushed into the hall, dragging her niece with her.

"Oh, sir, what's happened? Save us!"

Bowles found his voice. "He's let 'em out, that's what it is. Selim and all. I was in the carpentering shed with the door open mending a feeding trough, and I saw him go by, walking very quick. I thought nothing of it. And then, after a few minutes, I saw something else out of the corner of my eye. It seemed to be a large dog skulking past. I turned my head just in time to see it plain before it slipped round the corner of the shed. It was one of the pair of big Russian timber wolves we've got in a separate enclosure. They gave me a fair turn, for those wolves are nasty customers. And then I heard a yell from Jerry and saw him shinning up a tree. I thought of staying in the shed, but there's no way of fastening the door. I say—are we safe in here?"

Collier had been wondering the same thing. "Better close the inside wooden shutters of all the windows on the ground floor. You take the back of the house, Bowles, and I'll do the front. Jump to it, Mrs. Lacy, I think you'll find Mrs. Ramblett in the drawing-room. Take her up to one of the rooms on the first floor. I'll join you as soon as I've seen to all the fastenings." Bowles, an ex-service man, responded to the note of authority. He ran from room to room, slamming the shutters into place and dropping the iron bars that held them into their sockets, to the accompaniment of an incessant flow of profanity.

Mrs. Ramblett, shaken out of her torpor by the hubbub, allowed herself to be led away.

The drawing-room had four french windows opening on the terrace. Beyond the terrace the ground sloped steeply away to the valley in open pasture land with a clump of trees here and there, and the avenue of limes leading down to the lane on the left. As Collier was closing the shutters over the last window he could see the buffaloes, whom he had noticed on each one of his visits, browsing in the field on the farther side of the high wire fence, lifting their great shaggy heads to snuff the air. The bull began to bellow and paw the ground. Was there something moving along by the hedge? Collier could not be sure. He closed the last shutter and left the room, stumbling against chairs and tables in the darkness.

Bowles was waiting for him in the hall.

"Quick work," he said, panting.

Collier mopped his brow. "Gosh. You're right. This is a new one on me. What about Jerry?"

Bowles grinned. "He's up a tree. Guess he'll stay there."

"Well, you'd better come upstairs with me."

They found the three women in one of the unused spare bedrooms at the end of the house, with one window looking out at the back over the valley and one at the side. Collier saw at once that Mrs. Ramblett must have taken another dose of her medicine. She appealed to him as he came in.

"Mrs. Lacy says you've come here to help us. Where is my daughter? Can you tell me that? Where is Helen?"

"I believe she's gone off with Farwell in his car, madam."

"With the doctor? I wish she wouldn't. It isn't right. But I can't stop them. James tried to. He was so jealous. He tried—and you know what happened to him."

Collier heard Mr. Freeman's voice, rather high-pitched and unsteady, calling him by name. He had almost forgotten the lawyer. He strode to the door and opened it.

"Here I am, sir."

Mr. Freeman came down the passage to him.

"He's sleeping soundly, and no one has been near us. What has happened, Collier? That roar, and then such a rushing about down below. I confess I felt greatly alarmed."

"Come in here, Mr. Freeman. You can safely leave young Ramblett. The doctor's probably twenty miles away by this time. He's got off in his car, and Helen Ramblett with him."

The lawyer, following him into the room, gazed in mild surprise at its occupants. Mattie sat in one of the armchairs smiling foolishly into vacancy, but the others were gathered at one of the windows. Mrs. Ramblett in her draggled tweed skirt and numerous coats, the cook with her sleeves rolled up and her arms floury, and Bowles in his dirty overalls and heavy boots crusted with mud.

They were all silent, listening to a confused volume of sound coming from the hillside beyond the thicket of evergreens that screened the house from the wired enclosures and the rows of cages.

"It's a good thing Mr. Bateman's gone," said Bowles at last. "This'd have broken his heart. He loved the animals, he did. That sort of shrieking, that's the monkeys. They go on that way when they're frightened. But they'll go up in the trees same as Jerry.

Only, if we don't get 'em back before night they may die of cold. It's the deer and the antelopes that I'm thinking about. They can outdistance the wolves, but they'll dash up against the fence, and then what?"

His rough voice was charged with unexpected feeling. No one had any consolation to offer, but Mr. Freeman touched Collier's arm to attract his attention. "What has happened exactly?"

"Farwell has bolted, taking Helen Ramblett with him. Before he went he cut the telephone wire. He then went into the gardens and opened all the cage doors. A risky thing to do, but I expect he was well away before they realised they were free. Remarkable for his ingenuity from the first. This final touch is quite in character. If he wasn't such a damnably cruel, cold-blooded brute I'd say he deserved to get away."

"Oh dear me!" said Mr. Freeman tremulously, "do you mean to say that we are, so to speak, surrounded?"

"I'm afraid so. How many of the animals are likely to be dangerous, Bowles?"

"It's hard to say. The wolves might not attack you, but then again they might. One of the bears is harmless enough, but the other's very spiteful. You see, they won't understand, and they'll be frightened and suspicious, and that's when they turn on you. And then, of course, there's Selim. I half hoped he'd draw the line there, but no. I had to pass near his cage as I was legging it over here and I saw it was empty. You don't see anything down there in the shrubberies, do you?"

They all peered down into the thick, dark tangle of privet and yew and laurel that grew up to within a few feet of the house.

"I can't be sure," said Collier at last, "but he must have been close behind you, Bowles, when you came in. That roar sounded near enough."

Bowles shuddered. "I don't want to end like Mr. Bateman, and that's a fact. Do you know what I think now? I believe the doctor pushed him into the cage that afternoon. He was here for lunch, and who's to say what happened in the gardens with me and Jerry gone to Exeter? They weren't on good terms, that I do know."

"Oh dear," said Mr. Freeman, "what about poor Mills my chauffeur. He's waiting with my car at the top of the avenue. He will be quite unprepared."

"You left your car on the little car park outside the entrance turnstile? He'll be safe enough there, sir," said Bowles. "There's wire fences and ditches on either side of the avenue. We had to be careful about that because of tradesmen and errand boys coming up. There's the turnstile, of course. Some of the animals could clear that easily, but it's an off chance they come that way."

Collier looked at his watch. "Ten past two. Could you get us some kind of a meal, Mrs. Lacy? You're not afraid to go downstairs, are you?"

"I don't fancy it much, being dark and all," she said doubtfully.

"I'll come with you. If you'll stay here, Mr. Freeman, we'll bring up something on a tray, and after we've eaten we can decide what must be done."

Once down in her own familiar kitchen and with the lights switched on Mrs. Lacy declared herself able to manage.

"You might speak to Mary through her bedroom door," she suggested. "It's at the end of the passage."

Collier agreed. He reproached himself for having forgotten all about Judy until now.

He tapped on the door. "Miss Merle—I am Inspector Collier, Toby's stepfather. I've come down to look into things."

He waited and heard somebody moving about within.

"Are you all right?" he asked anxiously.

She answered rather faintly. "Oh—I'm so glad you've come. I've been frightened. The doctors have found out I wasn't what I seemed. I could see he hated me, and I've been afraid to take the medicine he gave me. He said, 'You're a great climber, you'll be climbing up Mount Everest, you'll be climbing to the moon,' and I knew he was laughing at me. I've felt so helpless lying here covered with these beastly spots, and Mattie's no use. So I pushed the chest of drawers against the door and drank the water from the jug on the washstand. Has anything happened? I've heard a lot of noise."

"Yes. But you're all right where you are. Keep your shutters closed. We'll fetch you out as soon as possible. Be patient."

"Oh, please, Inspector—"

"Yes, what is it?"

"My brother David—"

"Don't worry. Don't lose hope!"

He went back to the kitchen. The cook had made coffee and cut sandwiches. He carried the tray up for her to the spare bedroom where Mr. Freeman paced restlessly to and fro while Mrs. Ramblett and the kitchen-maid sat inertly on the chairs, and Bowles stood at one of the windows staring gloomily down at the shrubberies.

"There's been something down there," he announced. "I heard it snarling and cracking bones."

The lawyer shuddered. Mrs. Lacy was pouring out the coffee. Collier noticed that two of the cups were of Crown Derby china and the rest of cheap white ware. It was a mixture typical of that strange household. He drank his coffee and ate a sandwich before he drew Mr. Freeman aside.

"This is an impossible position. I'm going to get help."

"How can you with these wild beasts at large. It would be a great risk. We must remain here, Inspector, until someone outside gives the alarm."

"The underkeeper and your chauffeur are both in some danger. We don't even know if Farwell closed the park gates after him. The animals may escape from the grounds into the open country. I must act, Mr. Freeman. There is Oliver Ramblett upstairs. His life may depend on his receiving skilled attention without any further delay. I have put it off," said Collier, "because I am the only person who holds all the threads in this case, and there is so little time. I've enough evidence now to go to the Home Secretary and ask for a reprieve for David Merle."

'Merle? He's to be hanged the day after to-morrow—or was it to-morrow? I'm not sure. I saw that in the paper this morning. It's been put forward because the executioner has to be in Lancashire at the end of the week."

"That settles it," said Collier grimly. "I'll get down to the gate somehow. The tiger's the only real danger. I don't believe the wolves would attack a man in broad daylight. They've probably wrought havoc among the deer and the antelopes, but that's another story. I'm going now. You'll remain here, sir, in charge, until the local police have cleared up the mess. Their Chief Constable was a great shikari in his time. His house is full of trophies. He'll be the very man."

"You'd better wait with us, Collier. It can't be long now."

"And chance some errand boy or tradesman with his van coming up the avenue and running into danger? I tell you I've got to go. I'll be all right—but if anything happens to me I rely on you, Mr. Freeman. Ring up Superintendent Cardew at the Yard, tell him I said I've proof of Merle's innocence. That execution must not take place."

"Then—who did murder Mr. Fallowes?"

"Farwell. I'm going now. Don't worry. I shall take no unnecessary risks."

"Good-bye," said Mr. Freeman tremulously. They shook hands. Collier asked Bowles to come into the passage. The keeper followed him out of the room.

"I'm going down to the gate," Collier said briefly. "I left my motor-cycle out there. There's no shorter way than by the drive?"

"There's a path through the shrubberies, but I'd keep to the drive."

"Have you actually seen the tiger?"

"No. There's been something scuffling about in the undergrowth but I couldn't see what it was."

"All right. You can shut the door after me."

"Take a stick with you. It's better than nothing." Their footfalls sounded hollow as they crossed the darkened hall. Collier took a stick from the umbrella stand. As a weapon it seemed inadequate, but it might give him the confidence of which he felt badly in need. He heard Bowles bolting the door behind him as he went down the steps to the gravel sweep. He glanced round uneasily at the surrounding shrubberies and walked rather quickly towards the drive. He had to exercise all his will power to prevent himself from breaking into a run. Some instinct warned him that if he was being watched that might be fatal. His heart was thudding against his ribs. There was no sound but the crunching of loose gravel under his feet and the rustling of dry leaves among the laurels, but he noticed a strong musky smell.

The great striped beast had killed a man only a few days ago. He had been prowling round the house, the proof of it that nerve shattering roar that had sounded only a few feet away.

"ANOTHER TRAGEDY AT WEST COUNTRY ZOO.
SCOTLAND YARD DETECTIVE MAULED BY
BENGAL TIGER."

How Farwell would laugh when he read those headlines in to-morrow's papers. It would mean that he had won his last and most desperate throw.

Collier was half way down the drive now. There was a sharp turn before him. Another hundred yards to go, and then the gate. But he was now convinced that he was being followed. Another sound had been added to the rustling of leaves. It was the snapping of dry twigs under a heavy weight. He dared not turn his head.

CHAPTER XXIII
A REPRIEVE

THE sequence of comings and goings at the Manor that morning should be remembered. Mr. Freeman was the first to arrive. Doctor Farwell in his blue saloon came very soon after him. Collier arrived on his motor-cycle some twenty minutes later. Mr. Freeman's elderly chauffeur observed the later comers without much interest. He was about to lay aside his *Daily Mail* when a girl in a fur coat came hurrying down the drive and got into the blue saloon. She was followed a few minutes later by its owner, also apparently in a violent hurry, who climbed into the driving seat, slammed the door, and drove away down the avenue at a pace which Mills, who knew the risk of skidding on wet leaves, thought very imprudent.

Mr. Freeman had not said how long he was likely to be, but Mills was used to waiting. He had brought with him a weekly publication which specialised in cross word puzzles and competitions, offering large sums of money for correct solutions. Mills had never yet won even a consolation prize, but he had not lost hope. He spent some time trying to think of a town in the United Kingdom beginning with B and ending with F, and filled in all the spaces in a puzzle called missing birds. Then he leaned back and decided to give his brain a rest.

He dozed for a while in the comfortable fug of the closed car, snoring gently from time to time, and woke with a start from a dream that had begun placidly enough to grow more and more menacing. The blue saloon had gone, but the battered motorcycle still rested on its frame by the road side. His eyes, still bemused with sleep, rested vacantly at first on the turnstile and the kiosk and the path inside mounting sharply to the crest of the hill where a more distant view was blocked by the backs of a row of cages. Something was rooting about on the farther side of the turnstile. He thought at first that it was a large dog, but while he looked it reared itself up with its forefeet on the iron arms of the machine. It was not a dog. It had small red eyes, and it looked shabby and dirty and misshapen. There were smears of blood on its jaws and on its chest. It was a hyena. Mills did not know what it was, but he did not like it at all. He sat, paralysed with fear, staring at it, but began to recover a little when he realised that it was not paying any attention to him.

"It must have got loose," he told himself. "They'll have to get it back to its cage. Just as Mr. Freeman's there, too. He'll be upset. That must be why he hasn't come back."

Then, after a while, his mind moved another step forward.

"Suppose it had happened sooner when that girl in the fur coat was coming down the drive." And then, "There's blood on his fur. I've been asleep. Anything may have happened up there." He began to wonder if he ought to do something. He had been in Mr. Freeman's service a long time and he was sincerely attached to him, but he lacked initiative. There were rules of the road. This was outside all rules.

And so it was the hyena who moved first, dropping with uncanny swiftness from his erect position and vanishing into the undergrowth behind the kiosk. The reason for his abrupt departure was immediately apparent. It was many years since Mills, who was not a frequenter of the Regent's Park Zoo, had seen a full grown Bengal tiger, and his jaw dropped as he gazed helplessly at that magnificent incarnation of the spirit of the jungle. Selim had appeared, only for a moment, where four paths crossed at the top of the hill. The huge, striped body was silhouetted against the incongruous background of English woodland just long enough to convince the beholder that he was not dreaming. Then it vanished as the hyena had vanished.

But the vision had had its effect. Mills was too frightened for coherent thought, but he knew he must act, and fortunately he did the best thing possible.

The burly sergeant was in the charge room, having just returned from his midday meal, when an elderly man in a chauffeur's uniform stumbled in and told his tale. He was taken into the Superintendent's room.

"The animals loose at Sard Manor?" They could hardly believe him at first. "I'll call the Manor and hear what they have to say." The Superintendent rang up the number without result. He called the exchange and was told that they were unable to get any answer.

"We'll have to do something. But what the hell—get through to Major Benson, Sergeant. He'll know better than we do how to deal with this."

The Chief Constable, luckily, was at home. He replied that he was coming along immediately bringing with him three of his rifles. "Two of your men are good shots, I know. Parker and Tregonwell. Better take as many others as you can spare, and Anderson with the ambulance in case there are any casualties." It was less than an hour after Mills had given the alarm that the first of the three police cars filled with uniformed and plain clothes men passed up the avenue.

Major Benson and the two men he had picked got out. The Major looked about him doubtfully. "Seems quiet enough. If this is a practical joke—" He flinched at the possibility. He and his men would be the laughing stock of the county. His companions glanced at one another, the same thought in their minds. The occupants of the other cars were getting out. The white painted ambulance, a recent acquisition and the pride of the Chief Constable's heart, was being backed on to the little car park. Benson was sniffing the raw December air, scented with wet earth and dead leaves, and detecting another odour. His face cleared. "I smell tiger. Keep your guns cocked. He may be anywhere. Tregonwell, stay with the others in case he breaks cover in this direction. Parker, you come with me. I must go to the house first."

As they moved towards the drive gate a man came rather quickly round the turn between the high banks crowned with laurel. Somebody shouted a warning and Major Benson fired, aiming at the undergrowth where his quick eye had detected some movement.

"Damn, I missed it whatever it was. What? You back again, Inspector Collier—"

The man from the Yard slammed the gate behind him. "He was following me. I'm uncommonly glad to see you, sir," he said, and meant it.

"What's happened here? A fellow who tells us he's the chauffeur of Oliver Ramblett's lawyer come down from London to see him, turned up with a hair raising yarn about wild beasts roaming at large."

"True enough. Farwell bolted this morning with Miss Ramblett, and before he went he opened all the cage doors. One of the keepers reached the house and the other climbed a tree. The tiger's the only customer likely to be dangerous to man, but I'm afraid there'll be a nasty mess. We've heard the wolves in full cry hunting the deer, and more than one death shriek."

"Farwell did this thing? It's incredible. I don't like the fellow— but still—what possessed him?"

"You shall have a full report later, sir. It's hardly the place here. I'm glad you've brought the ambulance. Oliver Ramblett ought to be taken to the hospital for observation. And there's a girl recovering from measles."

"Good Lord!" said the Major. "Coming down from the house must have tried your nerves a bit, what? You look a bit white about the gills. I don't blame you. Stay here. You wouldn't be of any use without a gun."

"Thank you, sir," said Collier. It was true that he felt rather muzzy. Somebody was holding his arm. He found himself sitting in the back of a car. A voice said, "Your head over your knees." Another voice said, "Poor devil, he's all out."

Then a long way off, as it seemed, he heard the sound of three shots in quick succession.

Chapter XXIV
TOBY'S CASE

SUPERINTENDENT Cardew looked across his desk at Collier as he hung up the receiver of the house telephone. "We're to go to the Home Secretary's house with the Chief Commissioner. Luckily he's in London. You can't be sure when the House isn't sitting. He's come down from Scotland to attend his niece's wedding. Sir George will be ready in ten minutes. Meanwhile have a look at the papers." He went on initialling reports while his subordinate scanned the front columns of the morning press.

"Amazing Scenes in a Private Zoo.

"Tiger at large in Somerset.

"Chief Constable and Police on Safari. Battle of wild animals in English Park."

Collier read the headlines and turned to the picture page. He had taken no part in the cleaning-up operations at Sard Manor and so had escaped the attentions of the enterprising local photographer who had cycled out from the town to get pictures, but Major Benson was there with some of his men grouped rather stiffly with the body of Selim, majestic in death, in the foreground.

The Superintendent laid down his pen. "We must be off. Pretty picture, eh? Fancy you playing hide and seek with that fellow."

"I'm sorry they had to shoot him," said Collier. "It wasn't his fault.

He followed the Superintendent down to Sir George Trant's room. He had been there earlier in the day to make his report. Since then the wires had been busy. Sir George was ready, and they went out to the car.

"Mr. Maclean wants to hear your account of this extraordinary affair, Inspector. I have told him that I believe we have evidence enough to justify him in granting a reprieve to David Merle, but I don't think he is convinced. It's up to you."

"I'll do my best, Sir George."

Mr. Maclean received them in the library. He shook hands with them all. Cardew he had met before and the Chief Commissioner introduced Collier.

"Pleased to meet you, Inspector. You won't be going down to the country again for quiet, I fancy. I've been reading about this affair in Somerset, and Sir George tells me it has some connection with a murder committed in another part of England two months ago. A man was arrested, tried, and found guilty of that crime, and he's to be hanged tomorrow. He appealed, and his appeal was dismissed. I've been going over the case since Sir George rang me up. The evidence against him is overwhelmingly strong."

"Yes, sir. But Merle's sister was convinced of his innocence. She assumed that the story he told in the witness box was true. That meant that the murder was done by someone who had planned it out very carefully in advance; someone who knew Dr. Fallowes sometimes asked music hall artistes visiting the town to supper with him, and who actually impersonated his victim, with the body lying on the bed upstairs. The question of motive arose. Merle was supposed to have attacked Fallowes in order to possess himself of a bundle of notes taken from the safe. Plain robbery, and almost certainly unpremeditated. Who, apart from him, stood to gain by the old man's death? His will supplied the answer. I don't want to appear to be criticising the local police who handled the case in any way. They would probably have made a few enquiries in that direction if Merle had not been taken almost red-handed. There seemed no need to look further. I should have felt the same. The trial was over and the verdict had gone against the prisoner, but Merle's sister would not abandon hope. She had learned the terms of Joshua Fallowes' will. He left everything to his great nephew, Oliver Ramblett, of Sard Manor, near Bedesford, in Somerset, but in the event of Oliver dying before he was twenty-one the estate was to be equally divided between his three half-sisters. She went down there and got taken on at the Manor as house-parlourmaid—" he broke off. "Is this what you want, sir? I have not had time to draw up a full report. I made some notes in the train coming up."

Mr. Maclean was leaning forward in his chair, with his hands on his knees, and his shrewd, grey eyes, deep set under beetling brows, fixed on Collier's face!

"Go on," he said.

Collier went on. The three older men listened with close attention.

"Judith Merle was there for over a week and she made some interesting discoveries. The second Mrs. Ramblett, Oliver's stepmother, was a drug addict and apparently completely under the doctor's influence. The doctor, who called almost daily, a married man, was carrying on an intrigue with her daughter, Helen Ramblett. Oliver himself was described as an invalid, and was only seen by his stepmother and his medical attendant. This information came into my possession and I submitted it to Superintendent Cardew. The girl had sent what amounted to an appeal for help. He thought we should be justified in making a few enquiries." Collier went on to give details of the steps he had taken. "I became more and more convinced that all the clues I had picked up would lead in the end to Dr. Farwell. He did not intend that Oliver Ramblett should live to attain his majority. After his death Helen would inherit her share of her great uncle's estate, round about thirty thousand pounds. Farwell was married, but when I called at his house yesterday his wife told me that she believed he meant to poison her and begged me to take her away. It was there that I learned from his dispenser that he was away on the 3rd of November and did not come home until the following morning. He said he had gone up to town to meet a friend and go to a theatre. He was driving himself. That means that he has no alibi for the night Mr. Fallowes was murdered. The woman verified the date from the case book and I could see that she had no idea of the trend of my questions, but later she became alarmed and rang him up at Sard Manor. He must have realised that the game was up, for he drove off, taking Helen Ramblett with him and just avoiding a meeting with me. But first he opened the doors of all the cages and cut the telephone wire."

"He seems to be a resourceful person," said Mr. Maclean. "Has he been caught yet, Sir George?"

"Not yet, sir. We've issued an all stations call and a description of them both. All the ports are being watched. He had a good start thanks to that bright idea of his."

"His flight proves that he had a guilty conscience. He may have planned to murder his patient and to follow that up by poisoning his wife, but we can't put him in the dock for the crimes he's merely thought of," said Mr. Maclean with a certain dryness. "What are you going to charge him with when you catch him? That seems to be a point to which you have given insufficient attention."

Sir George looked at Collier.

"He was a member of the local dramatic society two years ago, though he has since resigned. There is a photographic group of the cast of a play in which he took part. He was made up with a grey wig and a beard. When his dispenser learned that he had bolted with Miss Ramblett she was quite ready to speak. She's prepared to swear that she saw the wig and the beard and a theatrical make-up box at the back of a drawer in the surgery last September when she was having a turn out. They have since disappeared. She remembers noticing an unpleasant smell of burning hair, but she did not pay much attention to it as it was on the 5th of November and the neighbour's children were having a bonfire."

There was a pause that seemed longer than it was to Collier before the Home Secretary spoke.

"I don't know if you've got enough to convict him, but I shall certainly reprieve Merle on the strength of this."

"Oh, thank you, sir," cried Collier, and turned very red, realising that he had made a gaffe.

But Mr. Maclean smiled not unkindly. "You take a warm personal interest in this case, it seems?"

Collier was still too disconcerted by his own unpremeditated outburst to answer, and Cardew replied for him. "He always does, sir. He takes things too hard."

Mr. Maclean got up. "No. Stay where you are, gentlemen, please. I am going to ring up the Governor of the prison. It would be inhuman to keep the prisoner in ignorance a minute longer than is necessary." He went into the adjoining room. Collier looked about him at the towering bookcases. His eyes were smarting with lack of sleep. He had only dozed fitfully in the train coming up. They could hear Mr. Maclean's voice speaking over the telephone.

He came back presently. "Good," he said "good. This would have been the seventh execution since I've been Home Secretary, One was a woman. In two cases there were petitions. I felt it my duty to disregard them."

They were all silent for a moment. Then Sir George said tentatively. "We're taking up your valuable time."

Mr. Maclean smiled. "I'll tell you when to go, Trant. I wanted to ask the Inspector about this zoo business. I've often wondered what would happen if the inmates were set free. One of my nightmares, in fact."

"I wasn't there all the time," Collier said. "Major Benson spent a good many years in India and is an experienced big game hunter. The tiger came into the path from the back of a row of cages. He was only a couple of yards away and had crouched to spring. The Major had to shoot him. It was a pity. He was a magnificent beast, and none of this was his fault. After that some of the police and the two keepers tried to get the rest of the animals back to their cages. They found the surviving deer all huddled together against the wire fence at the bottom of the hill. Three of them had injured themselves trying to jump the fence and had to be destroyed. The wolves had hunted and killed four of the antelopes, and then, having gorged themselves, had slunk back to their enclosure. I expect they were afraid of the tiger. The hyena was still gobbling what the wolves had left, but they drove him back to his cage easily enough. One of the bears, a harmless old fellow according to the keepers, was hiding in the straw at the back of his den. The other bear, a savage, ill-tempered brute, had strayed into the field where the buffaloes are kept. There wasn't much left of him when the bull had done with him. They told me that Jerry, the under keeper, was in a terrible state about his monkeys. He was running about under the trees, calling them by name, tears running down his cheeks."

Mr. Maclean beamed. "Most interesting. I think, Trant, that Inspector Collier is to be congratulated on the way he has handled this enquiry. He has prevented a miscarriage of justice. He has saved a life. That is a great thing." He shook hands with them all. "And now I am afraid I have an engagement."

Superintendent Cardew's room at the Yard seemed agreeably home-like to him and to Collier after the unfamiliar grandeur of Mr. Maclean's library. Cardew, grunting as he stooped, put a match to the gas fire. He had still some hours of work before him.

"All very well," he said as he stuffed his pipe, "but don't you go getting a swollen head. Most of the work in this case, the head work, I mean, not the running about, was done by Merle's sister and young Toby, and that should be a humbling thought."

"It is," said Collier, grinning.

"I haven't seen that kid since I came to your wedding, but he seems to be shaping well."

"We'll be throwing a party one of these days. We'd be honoured if you'd come to it."

"Maybe I will. Meanwhile"—he glanced round at his subordinate and caught him in the act of smothering a yawn—"what you need is a night's rest. See you in the morning. We may have got those two by then."

When Collier came out on to the Embankment the fog that had been thickening from hour to hour was lying like a damp black pall over London. Useless to think of going home by bus. He joined the crowds pouring into the Underground Station.

The fog, he thought, would help the fugitives. The police could not be expected to read number plates in such weather. Farwell would give them a run for their money.

He found Sandra and Toby playing Lexicon. The warm lamplit sitting-room looked very cosy, but Toby's eyes were suspiciously red and his mother seemed worried.

Toby jumped up, spilling his cards. "Oh, Hugh, is it—have you—" He could not go on.

"Merle is being reprieved. Sir George and Cardew went over to see the Home Secretary and took me with them. There's evidence enough against Farwell to throw fresh light on the whole case."

"Fine," said Toby, beaming. "Will they let him out at once?"

"A reprieve might only mean that he works out a life sentence instead. But I hope and believe Merle will get a free pardon."

"Pardon my foot," said Toby indignantly. "It's he who has to pardon them. But I'm jolly glad. Jolly glad. How's Judy?"

"I told you she has measles."

"Rotten for her. I've had them though, so it will be all right asking her to come to stay."

"Is that your mother's idea?"

"Well, she thought it might be a good wheeze if you didn't object."

"We'll see." Collier looked pointedly at the clock. "Past your bedtime."

"All right," said Toby handsomely. "I don't mind going up now."

When he had left them Sandra said, "I'm so thankful, and not only on that poor young man's account. Toby knew that he—that it was to be to-morrow morning. I've been really worried about him. I sometimes think he's too soft hearted to be a policeman."

"Thank you," said her husband.

CHAPTER XXV
THE END OF THE CHASE

THE fog was still very thick when Collier arrived at the Yard the following morning. The river was invisible and the wailing of fog horns and the melancholy crying of gulls sounded eerily across the water.

Cardew had just come and was divesting himself of his disgracefully shabby overcoat.

"I had a report from Bedesford last night after you left. Oliver Ramblett has been examined by a specialist on diseases of the brain. He says definitely that there's no tumour and never has been. He can't find anything wrong organically. He's in a weak state and generally run down, but he has no symptoms that would not be accounted for by persistent drugging over a period of several weeks, combined with lack of air and exercise and underfeeding. The specialist asked who had been treating him, and when he was told he said the Medical Council should be informed."

"He'll recover?"

"Oh yes. Would you say his stepmother and sister knew what Farwell was doing?"

"No. The older woman was in a stupor most of the time. She depended on Farwell for her dope. She's got to the stage when she can't be held responsible for her actions. And the girl was infatuated. They haven't been found, I suppose?"

"Farwell and the girl? No." The telephone on his desk rang sharply. He picked up the receiver. "Yes. Superintendent Cardew speaking. Yes."

He listened for some time and Collier, watching his face, knew that there was news at last.

He hung up the receiver thoughtfully. "His car has been found. A ploughman leading his horses into a field this morning found it parked behind the hedge where it might easily not have been noticed for a day or two."

"Where was this?"

"Off the London road about two miles this side of Horsham. The ploughman thought it odd. Moreover, he has a wireless and a description of the car was broadcast before the nine o'clock news last night. He had forgotten the number, but remembered it was a blue saloon, so when a policeman on a bicycle rode along half an hour later he hailed him. The Horsham people got busy, and discovered that the garage of one of the big houses on the London Road just outside the town had been left open last night. It holds two cars, and one of them had taken some of the family to a dance. They were persuaded to spend the night at a friend's house, and so did not discover until this morning that the second car had been stolen. A full description has been sent to all stations from Horsham. Here it is"—he had been writing on a pad while he listened to the voice sounding faint but clear along the wires, and he passed it over to Collier. "We can't leave all the work to Horsham. Get that out to all the metropolitan stations. Put Lowell and Radnor on to it."

Collier hurried out to set the innumerable wheels in motion. When he came back to the Superintendent's room Cardew said, "That stolen car was found in a road at the back of Brighton, a turning off Preston Park, a quarter of an hour ago. It's a cul de sac and cars are often left there for hours, it seems. There are several there now, and no way of finding out if there's one missing until the owners come back."

"Do you want me to go down?"

"It might be as well. I've a feeling they may have gone to ground in Brighton."

Collier had expected to find the fog lifting after the train had passed through Croydon, but the Weald lay hidden under a thick white curtain of mist. A fellow passenger assured him that they would come into sunshine on the other side of the Downs, but for once he was wrong. In the Brighton streets the fog was not so dense as it had been in London, but it was bad enough. Collier went directly to the police station, where his arrival was expected.

"They can't get away," he was told confidently, "but it may take some time. There are thousands of lodging-houses kept by women who never look at a newspaper and don't own a wireless. In fact they can lie doggo as long as their money lasts. We'll do all we can."

"I'd like to see the car."

"We left it where it was found, with a constable to watch it from a discreet distance in case they came back to it."

He was about to start with the plain clothes detective who had been told off to accompany him when they were both recalled to the Superintendent's room.

"There's a call just received from an A.A. scout. He was riding along the coast road towards Newhaven when he noticed that some of the fencing at the edge of the cliff has been broken away. There are skid marks on the road, and it looks as if a car had swerved there and gone over. It must have happened quite recently. He says the fence was there when he rode by the same spot an hour ago. No one in his senses would drive fast along that road in this fog. We've got to send some of our people along to see if there's anything at the foot of the cliff before the tide comes up."

Collier thought a moment. All the ports were being watched. Farwell would be stopped on the quay if he tried to board one of the cross-Channel steamers at Newhaven. He must have been prepared for that. But there was another possibility. It is easier for a doctor than for a layman to obtain drugs, but there is some check on his legitimate supply. It seemed not unlikely that Farwell had some connection with smugglers of cocaine and heroin. In that case he might know of bolt holes along the coast.

"I'll come with you, I think," he said, "the car they left can wait."

The sea was still invisible, as they clambered down the cliff path, and from near and far ships' syrens blared incessantly.

"The worst fog of the year," said the A.A. man who had met them on the road and showed them the long, slimy skid marks on the sodden grass, the crumbled chalk edge broken away and one remaining post with dangling wires hanging in the void.

"How far down is it?"

"Between two and three hundred feet, and rocks below."

The rocks were round and black and shiny like dolphins' backs. Curdled brown foam crept about them as the tide seeped into the pools. The shattered fragments of the car lay where they had expected to find them. There were two bodies. They were lifted out of the wreckage."

"It'll be a job carrying stretchers up that path."

"Do you recognise them, Inspector?"

"Yes."

He returned to Town by an afternoon train.

"It's all for the best," said Cardew. "Sir George sent for me again this morning. He said, 'I agree with you that we're after the right man, but if we've got to charge him with the murder of Mr. Fallowes, God help us. Put the evidence you've collected that implicates him against that which the prosecution put forward at Merle's trial, and the case against Merle still looks the blacker of the two. I don't know what the Public Prosecutor will say. There'll be questions in the House,' and I believe he was right. I doubt if we could have had Farwell convicted."

Collier nodded. "He's gone, and the girl with him. Queer how women fall for a man like that. Utterly ruthless. He meant to get rid of Oliver Kamblett, and then his wife. I fancy he was responsible for Bateman's death. I know the keepers think so."

A week later Collier, who was by then engaged on another case, had occasion to go to his Superintendent's room.

When the business in hand had been settled Cardew said, "About that man Farwell, you said it was queer the way women fall for that type. One of the men who was on duty at the cemetery where he was buried told me there was a wreath of white lilies with a card inscribed 'To my darling Ambrose, from his loving wife, Myra.' And then ('Mousie') in brackets. Can you beat it?"

"Women——" said Collier profoundly.

The Superintendent grinned. "Exactly."

A few days before Easter Collier asked for a few days' leave.

Cardew, who seldom took holidays himself and was rather reluctant to grant them even to his most favoured subordinates, grunted disapprovingly.

"What for?"

"To attend a wedding. It's young Ramblett. He's marrying Judith Merle. She stayed with us for a bit while her aunt was in hospital. Ramblett was always keen on the animals. He's reorganising the zoo on the most modern lines. A sort of miniature Whipsnade. He's taken David Merle on as his second in command. The three of them seem to hit it off remarkably well. Poor Merle is very quiet and subdued, but I think he's as happy as one can expect after all he went through. As for Judy, Ramblett says he fell in love when he first saw her peeping down at him through a skylight. Toby's a great favourite down there. He's to spend part of his Easter holidays with David while they're on their honeymoon."

"Trust Toby," said Cardew, "to fall on his feet. What's become of Mrs. Ramblett?"

"In a home for addicts, and likely to remain there."

"Well," said Cardew grudgingly, "you can have two days. Shut the door after you."

THE END